No Good Deed

Anne Cleasby

Acknowledgements

I would like to thank my Kendal writing group, *Writer's Rump*, for reading multiple copies of this manuscript, and sharing their comments and feedback. Caroline Moir, Anne Banks, Jill Clough and Adrian Horn - thank you. My sister, talented artist, Helen Dunning, designed the cover, and read through the final draft. Thanks, Helen. Thanks too, to my Lancaster MA writing group, for their support and comments on examples of my writing.

No Good Deed

Book 1 in Leaving Earth series

By

Anne Cleasby

Anne Cleasby

No good Deed

Copyright © 2021 by Anne Cleasby

Prologue

Her body sprawled on the bunk with an annoying lack of grace, a lifeless lump of flesh and bone now. One thin arm hung over the edge, gold-tipped fingers trailing on the rough floor.

He stared at her, vision blurring, shoulders twitching as satisfaction drained out of him. Euphoria had flooded his mind and warmed his body while he'd played, just like it had the first time. The sensation hadn't lasted as long, though. This was the fifth one he'd killed, and each time the thrill was less. He tapped the points of his nails against his teeth. Why? The empty flesh belonged to the right sort of femme physically. Tall, slim (sharply defined ribs pressed against her pale skin, so maybe she was too thin for him), and blond, but she hadn't felt right. She was so young, so willing to take his money and accommodate him, at least until she realised what was happening. He'd paid for her company and he didn't want that sort of femme; he wanted the sort who would choose him voluntarily. The sort of femme who would think she was in charge, until she discovered she wasn't; he wanted a wealthy, entitled, matriarchal figure. Someone he could undo. Someone like...

He rubbed his chin and pulled the girl off the bunk, letting her drop to the dirt floor with a dull thud. Crouching at her side, he worked the leather gag from between her teeth, tossing it to one side, and studying her face. Blood leaked from her open lips. Nothing of her humanity remained. It was over. He rose to his feet, extinguished his lamp, and shoved the door open. Four of his bodyguards waited outside.

"Deal with that." He pointed into the darkened room.

Two of the guards edged past him, avoiding his eyes. Grabbing the girl's wrists and ankles, they dragged her through the door.

He strolled towards his transport, followed by the remaining guards. Maybe it wasn't the femme's fault, maybe the last batch of Wildwolf wasn't up to scratch. Perhaps he should find a new dealer. The thought disappeared as he piloted his aircar above the treetops and towards the city walls, his mind already moving on to the next thrill.

Chapter 1

Maeve crouched on her knees at the bottom of the double bed. Her heart thudded against her ribs. "Time to go? What do you mean? Go where?"

"You're eighteen now." Instructor Holbeck stood in the narrow space between the bed and the wall. He was already dressed, his fingers tapping impatiently on his thigh. "You can't stay here any longer. You know the rules as well as I do. Get your clothes on."

"You said you'd look after me." She squinted up at him, trying to read his expression. This had been coming for a while, but she'd tried hard to pretend otherwise. "You can't just throw me out. I haven't found any work. They'll take me and..." She shuddered as she thought of the fate that awaited non-citizens. She'd be sterilised and if she was lucky, tossed outside the city wall. "You know what they'll do."

Instructor Holbeck's lips curved in an appeasing smile. He looked like the weasel he was. "Now Maeve, you know I wouldn't just abandon you. I keep my promises. I've found you a job."

"A job? What sort of a job?" She'd been trying to find a job since she turned seventeen. All that was on offer, for her, was the sleazier end of the sexscorting trade, or entry level military. So far, she hadn't been that desperate, but her eighteenth birthday changed everything. "Can't you let me stay here? I'd do anything you wanted."

"No." His face hardened. "What sort of work do you think you could do? You've minimum qualifications and zero citizenship. You're an illegal. If I keep you here, I'll be in trouble as well. You need to move on to your own life."

Her own life? The Institute for Displaced Minors had been her home since she was born and abandoned, all on the first day of her existence. What sort of life would she have outside it? Without work? Unlicensed? Maeve squeezed her eyes closed, blocking him out. He was a slimy worm of a man, but his protection was better than nothing. Life was hard for people like her in this sort of institution, where children of all ages, sexes and sizes were mixed in together. She was slight, small, and looked younger than her age. She'd struggled to increase her strength and fighting ability, but there was only so much she could do with her raw material. Cunning and strategy helped. So did luck, and she'd viewed Holbeck as her share of luck. He wasn't very nice, his expression was permanently sour, and his breath stank, but he'd promised to help her find a job with citizenship. She'd had her doubts, but maybe he'd meant it.

Swallowing her anxiety, she forced gratitude into her voice. "Thank you, Sir. You've done a lot for me. I appreciate it."

She'd done a lot for him, too. *Filthy, pervy bastard.*

One day, when she had power, she'd come back for him. It was a pity she couldn't tell him now, what she really thought, but she already knew it was a bad idea to burn bridges behind her.

"Hurry up, will you? I haven't got all day." He tossed her uniform coverall at her.

Shaking the garment out, she sat on the bed and pulled it over her feet. It was pale blue, shapeless, and made from a cheap fabric that clung uncomfortably in all the wrong places. "What sort of job?" she asked again, as she slid off the bed and dragged the top of the coverall up to her throat.

"Get some shoes on and I'll take you to meet Elise," he said. "She'll be your new boss."

"Elise?"

"You'll be working for her sexscort agency."

Maeve hid her trepidation. Why would this Elise employ an unregistered non-citizen? It sounded like she ran an illegal pleasar house, and that would be worse than the places Maeve had found by herself. She would never earn her citizenship if the job wasn't lawful. "Why—"

"Don't you worry." Instructor Holbeck patted her head, running his fingers through her tangled curls.

Maeve fought her longing to bite him. It might give her a short-lived satisfaction but wouldn't end well.

"Come on, now," he said. "Tidy yourself up. Comb your hair. You don't want to lose this opportunity."

Maeve slipped on her cheap boots, while Holbeck waited, arms folded, barely concealing his impatience. She edged round the bed and followed him out of his room and through the main gates of the institution. Only the site security staff watched her departure. Her friends had already left for a variety of dead-end jobs. None of them had much hope of working their way to citizenship.

Instructor Holbeck led her away from the city. He turned onto the highway that ran parallel to the protective plascrete wall surrounding London.

"Where are we going?" The wall loomed. Twelve feet high and topped with razor steel, it cast a dark shadow over the cleared land between its base and the road.

"To the Woodgreen gates." He took her arm and hurried her along.

"Outside the wall?" Maeve dragged her feet. "No. No way. I'm not going there."

His grip tightened. "Come on, for fuck's sake."

"Ow." His fingers squeezed enough to leave bruises. She wriggled, trying to free herself, but he hung on, forcing her after him. Panic swamped her. He was six feet tall, and while he was lanky, ageing and unmuscular, he still had more than twice her mass.

"Sir, I don't want to go outside. I'll take my chances." Maeve dug her heels into the dirt of the road, tried to slow him down. "I'll register at one of the employment agencies."

He paused. "Don't be stupid. What's the best you could hope for?"

"Better than—"

"Compulsive sterilisation and enrolment into the military." He gave her a contemptuous look. "A little thing like you? How long do you think you'd survive?"

Maeve's heart picked up pace. She thought she might prefer that to an outer pleasar den. She'd heard that there was an increase in military action and an increased uptake of conscripts. Of course, the conscripts got the worst jobs, on nuclear or chemical clean-up teams, or as search and report troops in the abandoned regions. Holbeck was completely right; she wouldn't last long, but she didn't imagine she'd last long in some unlicensed flesh peddling dump either. On the wrong side of the wall. They didn't have escort agencies there; they had flesh dens. She tugged on her arm again.

Holbeck's grip tightened.

"You're hurting me."

"Hurry up, then." His fingers loosened, but he kept a firm hold of her.

At the city gate, a guard rose to his feet as they approached. He checked Instructor Holbeck's registration, and held out his scanner for Maeve's wrist.

Holbeck shook his head. "She's not licensed. She's eighteen today."

The guard raised his eyebrows. "Cute. You selling her?"

Holbeck avoided her furious gaze. "No. Not selling. I'll take a finder's fee of course."

Maeve clenched her jaw. He *was* going to sell her. She turned a pleading look on the guard. "Don't let him take me out there. I want to register for the army."

The guard grinned as though she was joking. "You? Get on with you." He watched as Instructor Holbeck dragged her out to the wrong side of the city wall.

The gate closed. Black plastone rose behind her, blocking out the city, cutting off all her hope. She struggled in earnest. It was easy to leave London, but almost impossible to return. The outside was uncharted country, full of illegals and criminals. People starved.

Cannibals lived out there. She'd heard that rich citizens hunted the illegals for sport. She kicked hard, her boot connecting with the back of Instructor Holbeck's knee.

He stumbled. "Stop that, you little bitch." Righting himself, he turned and smacked her hard across the face.

Maeve staggered and slipped sideways, landing hard on one knee. Her vision blurred. Her cheek burned. He'd never hit her before.

Holbeck's hand still clasped her wrist. "Behave yourself." He yanked her upright again and shook her.

Maeve bared her teeth. Fear and rage brought tears to her eyes, but she blinked them away. She wouldn't give him the satisfaction. She'd never hated anyone so much, ever.

He grabbed a handful of her hair and pulled her forward, fist clenched.

"Hey."

Holbeck paused at the stranger's yell.

"Don't damage the merchandise. Elise pays top price for perfect condition."

Maeve took a deep breath. Her cheek stung and her head hurt. She blinked again to clear her vision.

A thickset man of medium height approached from the junction, where the road joined a poorly maintained track. He wore a set of cobbled-together body armour and a protective facemask. Behind the visor, magnified eyes focused on her. "Is this the fem?"

"Maeve." Holbeck released his grip on her hair and pushed her towards the stranger. "Where's my fee?"

The man pulled a small scanner from his belt. "Give me your wrist."

Holbeck held out his arm.

Maeve's face heated as she watched the credit transfer. Holbeck was supposed to look after the minors he was entrusted with. He was supposed to help them find proper employment, a job that would give them the chance to become registered citizens. Of course, everyone, including Maeve, knew the odds were against them, but even so, he wasn't supposed to use them for his personal

11

satisfaction. He wasn't supposed to *sell* them. Rage fought with fear for possession of her body, and rage temporarily won. She spun round and launched herself at Holbeck, hands curled into claws. Her nails missed his eyes on her first attempt, but she raked them across his cheek. *Traitorous bastard. Exploiter. Lying pond scum.*

Blood ran down the side of his face. He squealed and pushed her away.

Maeve launched a ferocious kick at his kneecap. When his leg collapsed under him, she booted him in the face, flung herself on top of him and sank her teeth into his arm, ramming her knee into his crotch at the same time. He yowled and curled into a protective ball. *Coward. Slimy piece of shit.* She closed her eyes and clung, nails again reaching for his eyes. She'd wanted to do this for a long time.

"Get her off me." Holbeck screamed at the other man.

Hands grasped Maeve round her waist and dragged her away.

She spat something disgusting onto the ground and grimaced at the metallic taste of blood. "Let me go. I'm going to rip his eyes out."

"No, you're not."

A pulse pounded at her forehead, and her breath came in gasps. As she continued to writhe and to kick at her new captor, he dropped her on the ground. She stumbled, found her balance, and flew at Holbeck again, almost blinded by a killing rage.

A savage blow across the back of her head brought her to her knees and darkened her vision further. She flattened her palms on the ground, bracing herself as the rage drained away, leaving weakness and nausea behind.

"You behave like that with Elise, and she'll have you skinned," her new captor said. "Literally." He grabbed a handful of her hair and dragged her to her feet.

"Ow." She wailed a protest.

When he let go of her hair, her head throbbed and the sky spun.

"Come on." His other hand cuffed her wrist. "Are you going to behave?"

Maeve's legs shook. "Yes." She shouldn't have lost control so completely, but she wasn't sorry. Holbeck deserved what she'd done. He deserved a lot worse. Giving up the fight, she followed the man along a path that cut through the encroaching woodland, head throbbing, body aching and mind racing. A last glance over her shoulder showed her Holbeck, still sitting on the ground, face running with blood and his nose crooked. She must have broken it. *Good, perhaps he'd choke on his own blood.* Fury and betrayal flooded through her. She stumbled, tripping over a thin, low creeper that obscured the path.

"Watch where you're going." Her captor tightened his grip on her wrist, jerking her after him. "And hurry up."

Chapter 2

The murmur of hushed voices pulled Scarlet out of the light sleep he'd finally fallen into. He took a deep breath of the muggy air, before pushing the thin cover off his body and turning on his side, away from the damp warmth of Koo-Suki. She didn't seem to have any problem sleeping in the heat.

"Scarlet?" A voice merged with the sound of running feet, the volume loud enough to be heard in the first-floor bedroom. "Scarlet?"

The muffled conversation that followed the shout made him strain his ears. Who was it and why had the lookouts allowed someone to come so close to the house? Who was on duty tonight?

Next to him, Koo-Suki stirred.

He sat up, glancing towards the shuttered windows. No light leaked through the gaps, so it must still be dark outside. He swung his legs to the floor, slipped off the sleeping platform and felt his way to the window, banging his toe against someone's discarded boot. Mink's, from the size and solidity of it.

"Fuck." He kicked it out of the way with the side of his bare foot. His mouth stretched wide in a yawn.

Opening the shutters, he peered through the security bars. The faint light rising above the trees helped him pick out a small shadowy figure, arguing with one of the lookouts. The other watched, arms folded.

Scarlet leaned his elbows on the sill. "This had better be good." He'd had about a quarter of the amount of sleep he needed.

Both lookout and boy turned towards him. The lookout raised his shoulder in an exaggerated shrug as the boy dodged past him.

"There's another dead one." The boy yelled up at Scarlet's window.

Scarlet rubbed his forehead as he recognised the visitor. Temmy was one of the street pedlars; an undersized juvie from God knows where. "Another dead what?" Dog? Substance abuser? Scarlet's mind hadn't woken completely yet. "*You'll* be dead if you've woken me for nothing."

Temmy's teeth flashed as the beam from the guard's head lamp caught his grin. "A fem. Like the last one. We found her an hour ago. You said—"

"I'll be right down. You wait there." Scarlet closed the shutters and turned away from the window, colliding with Koo-Suki, who flattened her hands against his bare chest.

"You woke me up. What's going on?"

"Some of the juvies found a body," he said. "They think it's another of the Silencer's victims."

Koo-Suki's hands curled into fists. "I'm coming with you. That's the fourth one this year." She groped around for her clothes. "And that's just round here."

"Fine." Scarlet bent to sift through the pile of clothes next to the bed. His mind cleared. "Where's Mink?"

"I don't think he came home last night. That monster of his isn't around." Koo-Suki dressed quickly and fastened a weapon belt round her waist. "Didn't he leave a message?"

Scarlet shook his head as he pulled on his skinsuit. "No one's said anything." He added an armoured jacket and boots, and slipped a knife into his thigh holster. "Bring a weapon."

"Do I look like a noobie?" Koo-Suki picked her precious sabre-pistol off the table by the bed, checking it as she shrugged into her own body armour. Like him, she wore a close-fitting skinsuit under her jacket. She inserted the pistol into the holder on her belt, while Scarlet waited in the doorway.

"Come on." He grabbed her arm, hurrying her downstairs and outside to where Temmy waited.

15

"She's dead," Koo-Suki grumbled. "She's not going anywhere."

Scarlet, fully awake now, released her and strode over to where the guard held the boy by one shoulder. The sky was beginning to lighten, and a small shooting star rose above the horizon. The early morning moon shuttle, he thought. He was rarely up early enough to see it. It might be taking potential miners to the asteroid transfer station, or it could be delivering supplies for the moon base. He watched it disappear before dragging his eyes away and turning his attention to Temmy. "Where did you find this body?"

"In that old park," Temmy said. "Springfield's Bog. Me and Cara, we'd finished for the night and wanted somewhere to smoke and no one goes there. She was just inside the railings."

"Where's Cara now?" Koo-Suki peered into the darkness.

"She went back to the flop," Temmy said. "She felt sick."

"How do you know this dead fem was done by the Silencer?" Koo-Suki asked.

"She was. It had to be him. Her tongue—"

"Dreamer?" Scarlet glared at the boy. "You were smoking Dreamer? You know—"

"I paid for it." Temmy scuffed at the dirt under his feet with one fraying boot. "I wouldn't steal from you, Scarlet. Honest."

"You shouldn't be smoking it at all. You sell it, right? That's your job. You don't use it. Stick to R'lax. The other stuff'll kill you."

"But—"

"Scarlet?" Koo-Suki interrupted. "Let him tell his story."

Scarlet took a breath. He didn't want his workers turning into addicts. Temmy was only fourteen; too young to destroy himself with street chem. He should still be in one of the institutes, hoping that one day he'd become a full citizen. Just like Scarlet had been. And Koo-Suki and Mink, and look where they'd ended up. They'd still had more chances than Temmy or Cara. Chem was the biggest killer amongst the child crews.

"She was cut like the others. I saw the pictures." Temmy's voice dropped to a mumble. His bravado faded away as he looked sideways at Scarlet. "She was all slashed up and they'd tried to burn her. I felt sick as well, but I came to find you."

"Show me." Scarlet turned to Koo-Suki. "Are you sure you want to come? We don't both need to see it. It's going to be pretty nasty."

She punched him lightly in the arm. "I've a stronger stomach than you, remember? Maybe you should wait here?"

"Yeah. Right." Scarlet beckoned to one of the lookouts to come with them. They had pistols, knives and personal lasers. Few people would be around at this time of the day, but it didn't do to take chances. Not round here. The presence of an armed lookout would discourage most opportunists.

Temmy followed Scarlet and Koo-Suki, skipping and jogging in an effort to keep up with their longer strides. The perimeter of what had once been an outer London park, but now was more reminiscent of ancient semi-tropical forest, lay about ten minutes from the den. Rust-eroded iron railings marked one corner, pushing back against a dense jungle of trees and rampant undergrowth. They wouldn't last much longer.

Scarlet stopped. "How did you get in there?"

Temmy pointed at the ground, where a gap in the bushes led to a dark tunnel. "It's private. No one can see you from the path."

Scarlet studied it, thinking about Temmy's assertion that no one ever went to the park. The tunnel appeared to be regularly used. Did more of the young chem-pedlars use the park to experiment with the drugs they sold? He wrenched his mind back to the present issue. "So, whoever brought her there must have been local?" No one else would have known about this. "How many people use this tunnel?"

"They didn't come this way." Temmy avoided the question. "The bushes are all blasted on the other side. Someone burned their way in. Anyone with a pencil laser could have done it. I'll show you."

"Wait." Scarlet's armed escort stepped to the front of the group and waved Temmy forward. "We'll go first."

A barely discernible path had been forced along the edge of the railings, just a narrow line of crushed grass and sedges where the plant growth was sparser. The scent of charred vegetation grew stronger, mixing with the aroma of damp decay. Koo-Suki sneezed.

Temmy pointed to where blackened bushes lined a newly carved path into the woodland. Something had burned away the greenery, leaving wide gaps between the trunks of mature trees. Scarlet pushed past the guard and walked over the black residue into the new clearing, squinting in the dim light.

Temmy hesitated.

"You. Wait here," Scarlet said. He and Koo-Suki stepped into the darker shade of the trees. The metallic odour of blood and something else drifted on the air, forcing its way past the stench of burning. Scarlet sniffed cautiously. Shit and vomit. That might have been from Temmy though. Or Cara.

The fem's body was spread on its back at the centre of the clearing, limbs splayed wide.

This was the first time Scarlet had seen the Silencer's work for himself. He clapped his hand over his mouth, swallowing the nausea along with the stench.

"Fuck." Koo-Suki grabbed his arm. "I know her."

Scarlet crouched next to the body, focussing on the fem's face, so he didn't have to look at her torso. Pale hair was brushed away from her forehead, revealing wide eyes and a slack mouth in a mostly undamaged face. Blood had leaked from between her lips, drying to a brown crust over her chin. He'd never seen her before in his life. "Who is she?"

"She works down by the wall," Koo-Suki said. "Sells – sold her body as well as any chem she could source. She was an independent."

Scarlet tore his eyes away, not wanting to dwell on the ruin that had once been a fem. At least two sets of footprints churned up the wet ground, mixing the blackened grass into mud. Large footprints, big men. He glanced at the fem again, hoping she'd been dead before they tried to burn her body. It looked like she'd bled plenty.

Whoever set her on fire hadn't been very thorough, and he wondered why they'd even bothered. Poor baby fem. Had anyone missed her yet? Why would *anyone* go independent? Everyone needed protection; someone to guard their back. A momentary gratitude for Koo-Suki and Mink flooded him. He stood up. "Let's go. We can't do anything here."

"We aren't going to leave her there, are we?"

Scarlet shook his head. "I'll send a message to the City Guard. But you know—"

"The Guard won't do anything," Koo-Suki said. "They won't even collect the body."

Sadly, she was right. The murder had taken place outside the walls, so outside the jurisdiction of the law, and no one cared about this sort of victim. Scarlet kicked at the charred grass, watching burned blades crumble into black dust.

"I'll let her friends know." Koo-Suki nudged him. "They'll take the body. Her name was Kita. I don't think she was even eighteen yet."

"Unregistered?"

"Yeah."

All of them were unregistered. No one who had a right to life within the protected zones would live outside the walls, where the limited law that existed was created and administered by the dominant criminal crews. "We need to do something," Scarlet said. "This is our territory. It's an insult."

Koo-Suki shrugged. "Yeah, but what? We can't be everywhere."

"Something," Scarlet said.

"I'll get the workers together, later," Koo-Suki said. "Warn them at least. We should find Mink. He might have some ideas."

It was just after seven, and already the temperature was rising, the warm air carrying the essence of death and fire with it. Scarlet wiped moisture from his forehead. "I want it stopped."

"Me too."

They returned to Temmy, still waiting at the edge of the clearing. "It was, wasn't it? The Silencer?"

"I think so," Scarlet said. "I wonder how long she'd been there."

Temmy shook his head. "We hadn't gone in for a few days. Dreamer's expensive."

"I meant what time was it dumped. You'd have smelled it a lot sooner if it had been left for longer than a few hours. You might have just missed them." Scarlet took Temmy's wrist, turning it to access his datachip. Touching it with his own, he transferred a credit. "Don't spend it on chem. Get something to eat. You did well, letting us know."

Temmy gave him a wide smile, marred by the loss of two upper teeth at one side of his mouth. "Thanks. When I've got enough credits, I'm going to get eyes like yours."

Next to him Koo-Suki gave a huge sigh, but Scarlet grinned. "I think blue would go better with your skin colour. Red would be too much."

Temmy glanced up at him. "Then I can change my name to Blue."

"So you can. Or Azure. Or Sapphire."

Koo-Suki shook her head. "Buzz off, Temmy."

"Or Cobalt." Scarlet forced a smile. "And remember what I said about the chem. Stay off it, or you won't be working for us much longer."

Temmy jogged off. Scarlet linked his arm with Koo-Suki's. "If you get our people together, and let them know to be careful, I'll talk to as many of the independents as I can reach," he said. "And we should set up a meeting with some of the other crew leaders. We need to know who's doing this on our territory."

"Some psycho fuck." Koo-Suki kicked at the muddy track. "I've seen some nasties in my time, but that's just sick."

Scarlet shook his head, not wanting to think about the mutilations. "He must have used a laser knife. I really hope he's not one of ours." Some of their team were a long way from normal, but off-hand he couldn't think of anyone who'd do this. Kill a lover in anger maybe, kill a rival, but not planned, premeditated torture and murder. "Did you notice there was more than one set of footprints?"

"Yeah, but that doesn't mean anything. Someone might have stumbled on the body like Temmy did. Who knows? Is it too early for breakfast?"

He shook his head, not sure whether he could eat.

They walked towards the rough caff, set up not far from the sleeping dens and kept open for their crew workers. The flophouse was a hundred metres away, well hidden in the mixture of ruined houses and woodland. Mink already sat at a bench, nursing a beaker of coffo, one of the common coffee imitations. Scarlet knew what real coffee tasted like. He'd drunk it at a meeting with some rich citizens who wanted to buy product for one of their lame parties. Mink looked up, and waved a hand.

Mink, Scarlet, and Koo-Suki had grown up in an institution for displaced minors, just inside the city walls. Six years ago, a few weeks before they reached their eighteenth birthdays, they escaped over the wall. None of them had much chance of a decent job, with citizenship rights, and the alternative was conscript military, or low-level indentured work. And, as Mink had said, 'Ain't nobody coming near me with a pair of shears.' He'd watched too many 3dvids, but neither Scarlet nor Koo-Suki argued with him. No one liked the idea of compulsory sterilization.

Scarlet hooked one arm round Koo-Suki's shoulders, affection washing over him. Her five-foot frame and baby-face made people think they could take advantage of her, but anyone who tried, quickly found out how wrong they were. Not many people messed with her nowadays, even if her facial tattoo and the spiky hairstyle made her look like a wonky kitten.

Mink looked up from his coffee as they approached, pushing a mass of plaited fair hair away from his face. "Heard you got called out. Almost before first light?"

"Well before first light," Scarlet grumbled. He followed Koo-Suki as she slid onto the bench opposite. "The morning moon transport was just going up. Haven't seen that for years. One of the juvies found a body."

21

Mink raised his eyebrows, managing to convey that *he* wouldn't get out of bed for any random body. Bodies weren't that uncommon. He leaned back in his chair as a shaggy black head appeared from underneath the table. It rubbed against Mink's thigh and disappeared again. Scarlet pulled his legs back. That thing would probably eat him if Mink hadn't fed it.

Mink smirked and reached down to stroke the animal.

"Where've you been?" Koo-Suki asked.

"Visiting." Mink had a lover who lived in the city, a woman with citizenship. Liddya liked to imagine she had revolutionary tendencies, she liked to think she lived life on the wild side. "Never mind that. Tell me about this body."

"We think it was that killer again," Scarlet said "The one they call the Silencer. The body was a baby fem. Kuzu knew her."

"She was harmless," Koo-Suki said. "And the way she was killed? It didn't look like a warning or someone getting rid of the competition. It looked like someone had been playing with her. Her tongue was missing, just like they said about the last one."

"Sick." Mink pulled a face. The media hadn't held back when describing the murders. Everyone knew about them, and normally a serial killer operating outside the legal zones wouldn't have registered in the newsfeeds.

"We sent a message to the City Guard," Scarlet said. "Told them where to find the body." He beckoned to the juvie behind the caff counter and ordered a beaker of coffo.

"Was that a good idea?"

Scarlet shrugged.

"They'll try and pin it on one of us," Mink said. "It could mean the City Guards swarming out here like ants. We should be ready to move out."

"They won't care," Koo-Suki said. "She was only a non-citizen. Unregistered. They'd never bother for someone like her."

"We're always ready to move, anyway," Scarlet said. "The next safe house is there if we need it."

"The thing is," Mink said, "I've heard there've been murders in the city as well. One at least."

Scarlet froze. That put an entirely different complexion on things. Murders rarely happened inside the walls, or if they did, they were quietly hushed up and the perpetrators disappeared. "How do you know that? It's not been on the holos."

Mink leaned his elbows on the table. "I was dropping off a batch of Dreamer and the last of that Muzak down by the river. Right in the centre of the city. I picked up the credits and stopped off for a drink with Liddya. You know she's got a cousin in one of the security services? Well, he told her, but she said everyone's talking about it."

"You were drinking down by the river?" Koo-Suki frowned. "I wish you wouldn't do that. You should go in and get out quickly. If you were caught—"

"Yeah, yeah." Mink slipped in and out of London regularly. He claimed he had ways. Scarlet had no idea what they were, as Mink wasn't likely to fade into a crowd. He was six and a half feet tall, for a start. "What I was saying, was that a body was found in one of the riverside apartments, one where the second-tier citizens live. Over a week ago, and they tried to hush it up. No one's reporting it officially, but you can't stop gossip, Liddya said. Her cousin told her it wasn't mutilated like the ones round here, but they have such a low crime rate, they're bound to try and tie it to those. It means the City Guards are going to be more thorough than usual."

Scarlet chewed at the edge of one of his red-painted nails. The Guards were a major threat if they were serious. None of the people outside the walls had a legal existence. Anyone could kill them without repercussions, and some of the guards were the sort who'd use unlicensed children for target practice. "Fem or hom?"

"What?" Mink said.

"Who was the victim?"

"Hom. Young, still a student, Liddya heard. They say he took the killer back to his family unit."

"So, it must be a citizen?" Koo-Suki said, hopefully. "The killer?"

"Nah." Mink smoothed his plaits back over his shoulders. "You know that non-citizens trawl for credits down there, and as long as they don't look too unsavoury, a lot of the gatekeepers turn a blind eye. If I can get in and out, other people can as well. The theory is that the victim was looking for ruffstuff and picked the wrong partner."

"It must be a different killer," Scarlet said. "The others've all been fems, light-haired ones."

"Only one in the city?" Koo-Suki asked.

"So far," Mink said. "As far as I heard."

"Shit." Scarlet gave up on his nail — it was reinforced with plasgel and wouldn't break for anything less than a laser-cutter. "I hope we don't get the Guard sniffing round here." They'd been in their present location for over a year. Everything was set up as he liked it; the den he shared with Mink and Koo-Suki, the caff which provided food and drink for everyone, the mini-manufacturing plant, and the flophouse for the young workers. It would be a real pain if they had to move again.

"Yeah," Mink said. "There's already been a crackdown. Just as well I know the staff at the Wood Green Gate. I might not have got out, otherwise. The gatekeepers everywhere are twitchy as hell. You won't find a non-citizen inside the walls now. Unless you look in the dungeons of Security Central."

"I told you," Koo-Suki said. "Be careful. It's not like you're nondescript or anything."

Mink was tall, broad, muscular and looked like a thug. A handsome thug from one of the 3dvids. He shouldn't be taking such risks. Scarlet picked up his coffo beaker, frowning at Mink over the rim. It wasn't just the security of their home that worried him. Business would be affected as well. A benefit of Mink's arrangement with Liddya meant they got occasional requests to supply chem party aids for the young, privileged crowd. Users in the city would pay a lot more than the dispossessed. It would be annoying if the patrols were on high alert.

No Good Deed

Chapter 3

Scarlet steadied his hoverboard as he glided down to the front of the low building that served as Claw's present headquarters. Claw's base was a couple of miles further from the city walls than his own, and not as well-maintained, or as well-hidden. The forest had been hacked back to leave a rough oval of short grass and decimated shrubs, easily visible from the air. He brought the hoverboard to a halt just above the top of the stunted growth, balancing easily as he turned in a tight circle. Mink pulled up beside him, swerving to avoid a pile of rubble. The two of them waited while their armed escorts landed.

"What a mess." Scarlet surveyed the area, while ignoring the heavily armoured cluster of men blocking his path. "You'd think they'd either clear the ground completely or leave it as it was. It's fooling nobody."

"No. Any idiot can see there's people here." Mink's full lips twisted in contempt. "Lots of them."

"Great ride though." Scarlet patted the console of his board. "Don't you think?"

Mink grunted.

"Go on. It was a brilliant idea to buy these," Scarlet said. "*My* brilliant idea. They get us around real quick."

Mink grunted again. It sounded like he was in a sour sort of mood. Behind him the escorts jumped down from their own hoverboards. Scarlet had bought a whole batch of the things in an excess of enthusiasm and handed them out to anyone who asked. He hated to think Mink was right about them.

"They're ostentatious, Scarlet." Mink shook his head, pale beaded braids whipping across his face. "There's no way anyone could miss

26

us on these. We're the only things in the sky, a clear target for anyone who's looking. No one outside the inner wall uses them."

"Yeah." Scarlet agreed, but he'd wanted to try riding on the hoverboards. What was the point in raking in shedloads of credit if he couldn't indulge himself occasionally? "I suppose so." He pulled his crest of stiffened hair straight and checked his body armour. The two escorts moved closer to him and it occurred to him that if anyone wanted to get rid of him, his own employees had the best chance. He pushed the thought aside. They were absolutely trustworthy. "We'll keep the boards for special occasions after this. You've got to admit they're wild though."

His partner grunted again.

"You're such a killjoy."

"And you're a showboat." Mink's mouth widened into a smile. He slapped Scarlet's shoulder making him stagger. "Boards are awesome, brother."

Scarlet rubbed his shoulder. "Don't mess my look, okay?"

Mink gave him a sideways glance and pulled a single cobalt-tipped spike of black hair away from the arrangement on Scarlet's head. "Oops."

"Get off me."

Mink laughed.

"Let's get this over with." Scarlet walked past Claws's men, towards a single storey building at the opposite side of the clearing. Earlier rain had soaked the ground and drenched the thick, long grass. Only his high-spec skinsuit stopped it drenching him, too.

Two men who rivalled his own escorts, in size and in the ferocity of their facial expressions, pushed themselves away from its wall. They showed no visible weapons other than the nail gloves (and Scarlet bet they were loaded with poisons) but he was sure that someone, somewhere, had killing devices pointed at him. He raised one hand to check his face protector and nodded at the two guards. "We're here to see Claws."

The two hulks stepped aside as a smaller man emerged from the shadows of the building, smiling through the plasglas around his head. Needle-sharp metallic teeth flashed briefly, before his mouth closed again.

Mink shuddered and bent his head towards Scarlet, muttering close to his ear. "I'd love to know what he wants with those."

Scarlet bumped his shoulder against Mink's. "No, you wouldn't. It would turn your stomach."

"What do you—"

Scarlet laughed.

"Welcome." Claws stopped several feet away and made a small bow. Straightening up, he gestured towards the open doorway. "Come in."

Scarlet nodded to the escorts, and one of them marched to the dark entrance. He paused to exchange a few words with Claw's men before disappearing inside.

The small group waited in silence until he emerged. "It's safe. Clear."

Scarlet removed his dark glasses and slotted them into a belt loop, before following Claws through the doorway, into what must have once been a big storage facility. Rubble, rotten wood and broken glass covered most of the floor, and daylight slipped through holes in the roof. The cavernous room contained a small plasscreen table, far too tiny for the vast space. Four chairs had been placed around it, two on each side. A woman in full body armour sat facing the door. She tapped the surface of the table and it flashed into illuminated life.

Claws took the seat next to her, waving Scarlet and Mink to the opposite side, backs to the door; Scarlet's most unfavourite position in any room and a reason to get the business done and over with as fast as possible.

"You know Lucil?" Claws indicated the woman.

She was bulky in her old-fashioned body armour, and her dark hair formed a helmet around her head. Scarlet studied her. Maybe it really was a helmet. That would be cool. "We've met."

"Lucil?" Claws gestured at the table and she touched it again, bringing a map to life. Everyone leaned forward as the edges of the map shrivelled away, until an expanse of outer north London remained.

"We sell all round here, now." Claws pointed at the map. "From old Enfield right up to the edge of your territory. I've a team of distributors, as well as armed bodies, all over the area. No one else would try to deal on my turf. I'm expanding fast."

Scarlet nodded, although he wasn't certain fast expansion was the right way to do things, and, anyway, the further you got from the London walls, the thinner the population (and the market) became. He had a strong notion that Claws would be displaced, probably dead, within a couple of years. "What products are you moving?"

"We've got a growing market for DeathDreamer. Mostly older users."

Scarlet grimaced. He would have thought the name was a good reason to give the chem a wide berth; he might manufacture the stuff, but he certainly wouldn't touch it.

After a moment, Claws added, "Frenzi's picking up as well."

Frenzi was a party favour – great high, but one hell of a comedown afterwards. They sold small quantities to a dealer in the first circle of the city, one who supplied the young, rich and decadent; the party people. It would be a bonus if he could sell to the outsiders as well, the non-citizens and illegals. Of course, they wouldn't be able to pay as much, but there was a pretty big profit margin on the stuff.

"Okay," he said. "We'll let you have the next batch of DeathDreamer, and we've a stockpile of Frenzi." He thought about what they had in store. Enough for everyone at the moment. "It'll cost you though. We're giving you preferential customer status."

Next to him, Mink nodded approvingly, and after a little back and forth discussion, a price was agreed.

"One other thing." Claws glanced at Lucil. "We've heard there's a growing market for Wildwolf. What do you think?"

"We're not making it at the moment," Scarlet said. "It's difficult and expensive to prepare. So far, the only market is in the city. Why?"

"Just that I don't want to be behind in my stock."

"Leave it alone. You won't make a profit," Mink said.

"Mmm." Claws didn't look convinced.

"I mean it," Mink said. "It's just taking off in the city, and rumours about bad reactions are already going the rounds. Expensive, instantly addictive, and nasty. Not many outside the walls would be able to afford it, and you'll bring the Guards down on us all, if you start stocking that. Come on Scarlet, let's go."

Scarlet and Mink got to their feet, bowed to Claws, nodded to Lucil, and backed out of the dark room. The light faded from the table top and the map disappeared with it. Claws and Lucil remained at the table, talking in murmurs.

"Wildwolf," Mink muttered to Scarlet as they left. "It's worse than double D. It fries the brain."

"Not a problem for Claws," Scarlet replied. "There isn't a brain cell in that tiny skull."

Raised voices filled the air outside the building.

"What's happening?" Mink paused in the doorway, between Claw's two heavies. Scarlet nudged him out of the way so he could get a better view of the two people grappling on the mud-smeared greenery. One of them slipped and fell sideways. Heavy rain had turned the ground into a quagmire.

"Romero," the taller guard said. "He's beating one of his pleasars. That's her squealing." He didn't sound interested.

"He's in a rare mood this morning," the other man said. "He'll kill her if he's not careful."

The man pulled back one foot and kicked the figure on the ground. Romero was the manager of Claws's pleasar rooms. Scarlet had seen him around, but hadn't much to do with him. He'd never bothered paying for his lovers, never had to, not with Koo-Suki and Mink permanently around.

Claws joined Scarlet. "It's the new fem. The one he bought for the pleasar house. I told him she'd be trouble."

The fem wriggled away, her hands protecting her head.

"He's not going to kill her," the tall thug said. "Look. He hasn't touched her face. He must mean to preserve her value."

Scarlet shook his head and strode forward. Enough was enough. Employees had to be disciplined, but the fem was tiny; her assailant could easily kill her or cause serious damage. He tapped Romero on the shoulder. "Stop. Now."

Romero clenched his fists. As the fem tried to crawl away, he kicked her again. "Take that, you useless, overpriced bitch. I should have let Elise skin you."

She collapsed onto her belly.

Romero swung round to face Scarlet, his face flushed and furious. "What do you want?" He spat into the mud, just missing the fem's body.

"I think she's had enough."

"What do *you* know? Do you *know* how much I paid for that vicious, intransigent piece of tail?"

Intransigent? Scarlet was impressed. "You've wasted your money if you kill her."

"I've wasted my money anyway. She's a liability." He turned back to the fem.

"Leave her." Scarlet grabbed his arm.

He spun round, punching with his free arm, his fist missing Scarlet's jaw by a millimetre. Scarlet's temper frayed. He pushed Romero away from the fem. Her face was hidden by her arm, but as he looked, she moved and one bright blue eye peered at him, before disappearing under her forearm.

Romero's face twisted with unchained aggression. "Stay out of my business." He pulled a blade from his belt.

Was he insane? He must know that even if he won a fight, Scarlet's escorts would annihilate him and no way would Claws intervene. Not if his staff started killing his business contacts. Scarlet brought the edge of his hand down on Romero's wrist, making him drop the knife. He shuffled backwards before running at Scarlet again. Either he was on some sort of artificial aggressor, or he was naturally too stupid to live. Scarlet stuck out a foot and tripped him, back-handing him in the face as he toppled forwards.

Romero landed on his hands and knees, blood pouring from his nose. He scrambled to his feet and threw himself at Scarlet again. *Definitely on stimulants.*

"If you get blood on my armour, I'll kill you," Scarlet muttered. Bad enough that the rain had started again, soaking his hair and trickling down his face.

"Romero?" Claws yelled from the shadow of the building. "Just leave it."

Romero paid no attention and swung a fist again at Scarlet's head. Scarlet slid sideways, and punched him in the midriff. He sank to his knees, spitting blood. Scarlet stepped back and waited. This time, Romero stayed on the ground.

The fem pushed herself to her knees and then, painfully, to her feet. She was naked, her pale-beige skin covered in streaks of mud, wet hair clinging to her scalp and dripping down her back. Her pretty, elfin face was unmarked, save for a smear of dirt down one cheek. She scowled, limped over to Romero, and kicked him in the stomach with one bare foot. "How do you like it?" She kicked him again, this time connecting with his jaw. He grunted. She yelped, hopping on one foot.

Romero dragged in a loud breath and tried, unsuccessfully, to get up. He grabbed at her ankle. "I'll kill you for sure."

The fem staggered out of his reach, clutched at her ribs, and sat down heavily. "Piss off."

Romero managed to pull himself into a sitting position. He hunched over, hugging his stomach. "You're dead, you mangy, treacherous little whore."

Scarlet took her arm and hauled her upright. She was battered, her muddied body covered with grazes and the beginning of some impressive bruises, but she didn't look as though she had any serious injuries. He walked her over to where Mink leaned against the building wall, flanked by the escorts, shook the water from his stiffened hair, extracted his dark glasses from his belt and put them on.

Claws shook his head. "I told Romero she was trouble. Why would Elise sell her so cheaply, otherwise?"

Scarlet shrugged, and brushed a smear of mud off his sleeve.

"You should have let him kill her. She's completely worthless now. Everyone knows what she's like."

"What did she do?"

"Killed one of Elise's clients, or so they say." Claws looked doubtful. "I doubt it, myself. I mean, look at the size of her. I don't know what she did to rile Romero."

Scarlet doubted it too. She wouldn't be alive if she'd upset Elise. The old witch had a terrible reputation. He let go of the fem's arm and she sagged against the wall. "Come on Mink."

"Take me with you." Her small voice was pitiful. Huge blue eyes peered out from a mass of wet tangled hair.

Scarlet glanced at Mink.

"You can't save everyone," he said.

"You're one to talk," Scarlet muttered. "What about that mutant dog thing you brought home?"

"Mutant cat. And she's got a name."

"Whatever." Scarlet waved a hand, dismissively. Mink's monster pet could have been anything.

"I'll work hard." The fem shook her hair away from her face, sending drops of water everywhere. "Please?"

"Ha," Claws interjected.

Scarlet hesitated. She was obviously no good as a pleasagurl, not if she had notions of escape through violence, but Koo-Suki could probably find her something in the organisation. Production maybe? He had a brief flashback to the fem they'd found dead and mutilated. He couldn't leave this one to Romero's mercy. "I'll pay her meat value," he said to Claws. "You said yourself she's useless."

Chapter 4

Maeve wasn't sure she would be able to stand if she moved away from the wall. That bastard, Romero, he was another one she would deal with, once she had some power. He still lay on the ground, groaning. *Fat cowardly piece of shit.* She took a deep breath, wincing as her lungs expanded against her bruised ribs. She'd felt like a walking ball of fury for the last few days, too angry to be scared.

The hom, who'd stopped the beating, was talking to Claws about paying for her. If he thought he could abuse her as well, she'd soon show him different. Her heart thudded, but she decided he couldn't be worse than Romero. As the adrenaline drained from her system, she started to shake. "Please? Don't leave me here." From the way Claws was eyeing her, he didn't care about her price, he'd just slit her throat.

The hom took Claws wrist and did a credit transfer. "What's your name?" he asked her.

"Maeve." She forced herself to smile at him. "Do you own me now?"

"No. We don't employ slaves or indentured servants." The hom removed his dark glasses.

Maeve covered her mouth with the back of one hand. She hadn't noticed before, but the whole expanse of both his eyes was red. Bright crimson filled them from corner to corner, a vivid contrast with his light brown skin. How could he see through them? They were awful, and the colour made it impossible to read him. Was he planning on leaving her behind? She couldn't tell. Claws or Romero would kill her, if she didn't get away. "I'll work hard," she repeated.

"What do you think?" The red-eyed hom glanced at his companion, a tall, muscular man, with fair skin, and eyes as blue as her own. He was huge, with long, dirty blond hair, bound in a bunch of beaded plaits, and a forbidding expression.

"Up to you," the big man said. "Koo could probably find work for her."

The red-eyed hom turned to Claws. "Get her something to wear."

Claws narrowed his eyes and pursed his lips. "I suppose I could throw something into the price." Lucil, who had been leaning against the doorpost, disappeared, returning with a skinsuit. It was threadbare and stank of its last owner, but she pulled it on. The arms and legs had been designed for a spider monkey, the body for a hippopotamus, and she really needed boots. A movement from Romero caught her eye and she decided to keep quiet. The muddy ground was soft enough, anyway.

"I see why Romero thought she was worth taking a chance on," Big-man said to Red-eyes. "Not in that thing though. You could get three of her in it."

"Teach him not to judge by appearance." Red-eyes turned to Maeve. "Come on. You'll have to share my hoverboard." He glanced at Mink. "Or could she—"

"No way. She's your problem."

Red-eyes sighed. "Just try not to get mud all over my new armour."

She stepped warily onto the flat board, flinching when the surface wobbled under her bare feet. She'd never seen one before. How did it work? She couldn't stop a small squeak escaping from her lips when it rose a foot into the air.

"Hang onto me." Red-eyes removed his dark glasses. One of the escorts handed him a face protector. "Hold onto my waist, and for fuck's sake don't let go."

The big man activated his own board and jumped onto it, hovering six feet above the top of the grass. Red-eye's guards did the same.

Maeve wrapped her arms round Red-eye's waist, pressing herself against his back and turning her head to one side as the board rose. Big-man guided his board upwards, above the tree-tops and Red-eyes followed him. Maeve squeaked again, briefly squeezing her eyes closed. How did Red-eyes stay on the board? What happened to her, if he fell off? She tightened her grip on him and peered around. They were above the trees; Claws's compound a cleared space underneath them. She'd been there a day and a half. It was only three days since she'd been sold to Elise. At least she was still alive, and not chained to a bed in a flesh palace. A gust of wind found its way past Red-eyes and dashed a flurry of rain into her eyes. Her hair flopped across her face. She shook it away, wincing as a bruise on her shoulder made itself felt. The board changed direction, swooping round one of the others. Maeve grabbed onto Red-eyes and yelped as her ribs protested. She loosened her grip when the hom swore under his breath. The board descended to a small clearing in the trees, followed by two of the escorts. Maeve let go and stepped off the board, bending forward to ease the ache.

"What's wrong?" Red-eye's voice was rough with impatience.

"My ribs hurt. My back hurts."

"And you don't smell too good, either," he said. "Can you hang on if I go smoothly?"

"I'll try." She stared up at him, widening her eyes in a way that had always worked on that pervy guardian, at least until the last time.

Red-eyes turned away. "Okay. Let's try again. It's only about five minutes away now."

She pushed herself to her feet and climbed back onto the board, assessing her injuries. She didn't think anything was broken, but every bit of her body ached and throbbed and stabbed when she moved. When the board finally landed in a circle of long grass, Maeve let go of Red-eyes and stepped off, taking a deep and painful breath. The rain had stopped but the trees and shrubs, surrounding the small patch of grass, drizzled streams of water down the back of her neck. The stinky skinsuit wasn't even waterproof. Steam rose from the ground and her bare feet sank into the grass and mud. At least the water was warm. She pushed strands of wet hair out of her eyes and looked around, catching a glimpse of buildings through the gaps in the trees, as well as rubble supporting a thicket of scrambling briers.

Red-eyes joined the rest of the group and removed his face protector before following Big-man along a narrow pathway through thick bushes to a wooden door, partially hidden by the trunk of a fallen tree. It looked as though it hadn't been opened for years. Big-man ignored it and turned round the corner of another partially collapsed building. Red-eyes looked over his shoulder at Maeve, gesturing for her to come with them. She limped towards him, arm pressed against her ribs, hoping she was doing the right thing.

He frowned. "We'll get someone to look at you."

"I'm just bruised." She could handle bruises.

At the back of the building, a few rough wooden tables clustered under the tree canopy, several yards from a rickety stone outhouse. A woman sat alone at one of them, a tall drink container in front of her, an infounit in one hand. She looked up as Big-man and Red-eyes approached. Her eyes moved past them, focussing on Maeve, who added a tiny exaggeration to her limp. The woman's eyes narrowed. Maeve sank onto the end of the bench farthest from her.

"How did it go?" The woman stared at Maeve. She wasn't giving out any friendly vibes.

"Just like we expected," Red-eyes said. He sat down opposite the woman. "We can offload a lot of that surplus Frenzi. Claws says he can move it. And he wants some DeathDreamer."

"Good. And who's this?"

Maeve lifted her lashes and surreptitiously inspected the woman.

"We picked her up at Claws's place," Red-eyes said.

"Why?"

"Romero was about to beat her to death."

"What did she do?"

"I—"

"I'm not talking to you." The woman cut her off.

"She failed as a pleasagurl," Red-eyes said. "I think Romero was pissed off at losing his financial outlay."

The woman studied her. "She's got what it takes to pull in the customers. Young and female's enough for Romero. Difficult to tell what's under all that material."

"It reeks." Red-eyes rubbed his nose. "She clung to me all the way back, so I bet I stink too."

Maeve grimaced.

"And she's got a bad attitude, according to Claws," Red-eyes explained. "I offered to find her a job with us."

The woman turned her attention to him. "How much did you pay?"

"Rock bottom, honest. If he'd killed her, he'd have got no return at all."

"I suppose she can pay it back once she starts earning. What did you have in mind? We're not going into the pleasar business, are we? Because if you think—"

"No." Red-eyes scowled. "Anyway, I told you she'd failed as a pleasagurl and if someone's going to beat her to death, I'd rather it was Romero than me. I thought she could work in one of the production plants."

The woman pursed her lips. "Shame to waste her. She's quite pretty. We'll have to see. It'll do for now, I suppose. Is that satisfactory, girl?"

Maeve nodded. A wave of relief left her weak. "Thank you."

"We've got a flophouse you can stay in for a small fee."

"I've no credit," she said. "I was indentured."

"When you're earning and you've paid Scarlet back, you can pay that as well." The woman stood up. "I'll take you there now."

"Get someone to have a look at her ribs," Red-eyes said. "I don't think they're broken but—"

"I'll check them." The woman took Maeve by the wrist and led her out.

Maeve winced as she moved. Why did everyone feel they had to drag her after them?

The woman slowed her pace. "What's your name?"

"Maeve." She glanced sideways at the woman, who was the same height as her, but lean and athletic, where Maeve was merely slight. Her black hair was short and spiky, exposing multi-pierced ears. She had a tattooed dagger on her cheekbone, a red slash across her golden-brown skin. She wore a weapons belt round her waist.

"I'm Koo-Suki."

"Do you work here?"

"I suppose so. I'm part of the management team." Koo-Suki turned towards a stone wall that looked like the remnant of some old settlement. Parts of both ends crumbled, and spikes of green grew from the roof and from gaps in the walls. The door at the front was blocked. Koo-Suki led her to the back, over a pile of rubble, through a gap in the wall, and into a dark room. As Maeve's eyes adjusted, she realised it was unfurnished and a complete ruin. The back wall was intact and had another door in it, a sturdy door. Koo-Suki placed her hand on it, pushing it open. "It's plasteel, opened by a thumbprint. You'll need to come and go with someone else, until we get you registered."

The room had two rows of narrow beds with thin covers on them, basic, but it smelled dry and clean. Two windows were heavily barred.

"Am I a prisoner?"

Koo-Suki gave a brief snort of laughter. "The bars are to keep people out, not in. You'll be able to get out through the door without id, but not in."

"Oh."

"Should I look at your ribs?" Koo-Suki asked. "Is anything broken?"

"Just bruised. Romero had barely started when Red-eyes stopped him."

"Red-eyes? Oh, you mean Scarlet."

Maeve nodded. The name would be easy to remember. "Who was the other one? The big one?"

"Mink."

"Are they management, too?"

"Yeah." Koo-Suki hesitated. "Do you want to stay here for the rest of the day?"

Maeve breathed a long sigh of relief. Everything ached and she hadn't slept properly since the perv dumped her on Elise. "Please."

"What did you do, to make Romero want to beat you to death?"

Maeve glanced at her, wondering if she should tell the truth. The considering look on Koo-Suki's face made her think it might be a good idea not to lie to her. Not yet, anyway. "I attacked my first customer."

Koo-Suki frowned. "Why didn't they just beat you and tie you to the bed?"

An echo of the fury she'd felt when they'd secured her on the bunk, brought heat to her face. "I was already tied down. I still managed to kick him. While he was howling and clutching his dick, I told him I'd killed the last person who tried to have sex with me."

"He believed you?"

"Because it's true," Maeve said. A shaft of pride made her mouth turn up in a smile. "I stuck him with his own knife. That's why Elise sold me. She was going to kill me, but Romero was there and offered her money." She shivered as she thought about her narrow escape. Elise was a sadist. Everyone who met her was afraid of her, and Maeve was no exception, especially as Elise had explained how she planned to make Maeve an example. "Elise likes money."

Koo-Suki shook her head. "You were lucky. Elise is a nasty piece." A note of admiration warmed her voice.

"I suppose. I've had enough of being pushed around. Just because I look helpless."

"Someone needs to close Elise down," Koo-Suki said.

"Yeah," Maeve agreed. "One day, I'll get her. She's on my list."

"Nice." Koo-Suki stalked Maeve, backing her up against the wall. She placed the palm of one hand on Maeve's throat and the point of a knife against her stomach.

Maeve froze.

Koo-Suki's dark brown eyes stared into her own. "A warning. If you kill any of our people, or even try, we won't sell you. I'll gut you. Do you understand?"

Maeve swallowed. "Yes." They'd better not give her a reason.

"And if you cheat us, you're out. If I'm feeling mean, I'll let Romero know."

"I wouldn't do that." Maeve filled her voice with injured innocence.

Koo-Suki released her and pushed her onto one of the beds.

"Ow, ow, ow." Maeve pressed both hands to her stomach.

Koo-Suki ignored her. "Don't try and fool me. I can see right through you. I mean it. Cause any trouble for us and you'll be a corpse in the mud." She walked to the door. "The latrines are on the other side of the building. You might want to throw that skinsuit in them. You stink. I'll send someone with a spare."

Maeve waited until her heartrate returned to normal, before assessing the room. She told herself that Koo- Suki hadn't really scared her. It was just the suddenness of her mood change, and the menace in her voice. She was just a small woman with a big knife.

The door was closed, the windows barred. She tried the door. Like Koo-Suki had said, it opened. She let it swing closed again and investigated the windows. The bars were close together, but looked like they were a shutter system. She pushed on one and it opened. The bars moved back again when she took her hand away, sealing with a click. *Secure.* There was nothing in the room but the rows of empty beds. It really was a flophouse, but it seemed clean, and relatively safe. The anger of the last few days drained away. Maeve chose the bed under the window, pulled the thin cover over her head and closed her eyes. Continuous tremors shook her body, but eventually she fell into sleep.

Chapter 5

"Should we be doing this?" Koo-Suki leaned her elbows on the rough wood of the table. Rain battered down on the overhead canopy, a constant drip-drop of water as the clouds emptied themselves, like they did most mornings. "Just now, I mean. With the Guards on high alert?"

Mink tugged on one of his plaits. "It's the sort of deal we might not be able to get again. Rich party people in the city. It's a risk, I know, but a small one. The alert was a week ago. They've calmed down now. At least that's what Liddya says."

"Scarlet?"

The discordant music of the storm had sent him into a trance, but Koo-Suki's voice pulled him back into the discussion. Going into the city just now wouldn't be his first choice, but Mink was right. It was a good deal, with potential new contacts and a profit margin bigger than any of their present markets.

"You'll be the one taking the risk. What do you think?" she asked.

"I don't like it." He picked up his beaker and sniffed at the cooling coffo, wondering why Mink spent so much time on the other side of the wall. The city made the back of his neck itch with nerves. "We've got to take the chance, though, and I'll be careful. The credits are too good to miss." Mink had checked the client carefully, and decided he wasn't a trap. An army officer, he had connections, and a reputation as a determined socialite.

"I'd do it," Mink said, "but I'm already visible enough. I'm too often in the river district and I've been thinking it's time I dropped Liddya. She's getting demanding. Clingy. I don't want to get too fond of her. I've already got the fluffball, here." He stroked the dark, silky head of his oversized monster mutant.

"It's okay," Scarlet said. "I've been down there a few times. I just don't like it much. Not like you do, anyway."

Koo-Suki frowned. "I could—"

"No," Mink said. "You know negotiation isn't your strong point. Scarlet's good at it."

Koo-Suki glanced at Scarlet. "Sorry. He's right."

~~~

Two days later, Scarlet made his way to the Primrose Hill gate and presented his wrist chip to the gatekeeper, who downloaded the info-pack of permissions. He leaned against the side of the wall and folded his arms, while a pair of armed guards glowered at him. His escorts waited in the shadows, loaded with a selection of illegal weaponry. They both wore armoured camouflage skinsuits, and even though Scarlet knew they were there, he couldn't pick them out against the trees. They'd appear soon enough if they thought he was in danger. Unfortunately, his city-permit only applied to himself, so they couldn't come through the gate with him.

The gatekeeper eyed him with disapproval after checking his info. "They shouldn't be letting your sort through. Not now." His voice was loud enough to reach the armed guards on duty. "Nothing personal, but we've had a bit of trouble in the city. It makes more work for everyone." He waved Scarlet through. The gate closed behind him.

"Not my fault," Scarlet said. The gatekeeper had no reason to be so superior, he would only be the lowest level of citizen, one step above Scarlet. It was a giant step, though.

"So, where are you going now?"

"It says on there." Scarlet held up his hard-copy invitation, a simple black rectangle with silver script, and a coded chip embedded in the card.

"I want to hear it from you."

"I'm visiting an apartment in the river complex," Scarlet said. "At the invitation of Major Amarre. Number 732. It's a private party."

The gatekeeper looked him up and down and frowned at the invitation. "You're unlicensed?"

"Yes."

"You understand you have no legal rights? You don't exist as far as the law's concerned."

"Yes. I know." Of course, he knew. The officials told him the same thing, in the same words, every time he entered the city.

"We'll want a DNA scan."

"I don't think so." Scarlet folded his arms. They'd never asked for that before. He'd walk away if they insisted.

The gatekeeper shrugged. "I can't be bothered anyway. You'll have to take the armour off though. And the face protector. You can collect it on your way back. And we'll do a search."

Scarlet stifled his irritation. If they got the deal, he might have to come this way again. It wouldn't be a good idea to antagonise the gatekeeper. He undid his face protector.

The gatekeeper pursed his lips. "What the fuck have you done to your eyes?"

Scarlet removed his chest shield.

"What made you think that was a good idea?"

"I was eighteen." He handed his armour to the man. "I might have it reversed one day. It's a lot of money though. To pay twice. And I still like them. They freak people."

The gatekeeper shook his head and piled Scarlet's gear into a storage locker before beckoning one of the guards to search him. Once he'd finished, the gatekeeper activated the exit and escorted him along a corridor to the outside world. "The skytran leaves from over there. Your permit will work on that. Go straight to your destination and don't go anywhere else."

"Yes Sir," Scarlet muttered under his breath. He bet they didn't treat legitimate citizens in such a high-handed way.

The skytran arrived within five minutes, its final destination flashing up on the wall; the river walkway at Westminster. That would do for him. Doors slid open and he jumped into the bubble compartment, feeling exposed without his armour, his weapons, and his usual entourage of armed escorts. He grabbed at a strap on the side of the transport and braced himself as it lifted at an angle of almost 45 degrees. Riding on the tran gave him a small thrill, he didn't do it often enough to be bored with it. Even before he went illegal, Scarlet had only been on a public skytran a couple of times. His home institution ran educational trips to the city, to restored London landmarks, and to the river, with its carefully impregnable walls. The state education board claimed to prepare all the children in its care for life as good citizens, ignoring the fact that at least three-quarters of them would never attain citizenship. Scarlet kicked at the plasglas wall of the transport. Riding the skytran couldn't compare to riding his new hoverboard.

Flickers of light appeared beneath the tran. Even with the energy rationing, they became more frequent as the transport approached the river and the heart of civilised London. Light spilled out of bars and cafés, illuminating the route of the boats working the river. Pleasure craft, haulage transports and commuter ferries, for the people who worked on the south bank, zipped through the water like fireflies on the black ribbon of the Thames. Beyond it, a mass of angular black plascrete blocked the sky. Security Central. Scarlet shivered and averted his eyes. The place fuelled nightmares. Rumour said that few people, who were taken inside, ever got out alive.

The alarm bell rang in the skytran and it tilted to make its descent to the river hub. Scarlet braced himself. Across from him, a couple of female partygoers swung on their straps. One of them met Scarlet's eyes and did a double take. As the door opened, she increased her pace to catch up with him. "Love your eyes," she said. "Where did you get them done?"

"Thanks." Scarlet gave her his most charming smile. "A little place near the wall. It doesn't exist any longer." No point telling her it was the wrong side of the wall or that the practitioner was unlicensed.

Her friend caught up to them. "Where are you going? We're thinking of trying Club Hex. Why don't you come with us?" She looked him up and down. "Great skinsuit, and your hair's wild. I bet they'd let you in free."

"Wish I could." Scarlet was amazed by how unwary these fems were. Life in the city must be pretty safe if you were a citizen. Casting his gaze over the skytran area, he spotted two pairs of Civilian guards patrolling the terminal. "I'm going to a private party. Can't miss it, I'm afraid."

The first fem pursed her glossy lips into a disappointed pout. "If you get bored, come and find us." She tossed a curtain of silky-smooth golden hair over her shoulder, where it swirled like a cape.

The other fem gave him a smouldering glance. "Maybe we should come to your party?" She was dark; dark-haired, dark-skinned and dark-eyed.

Scarlet might have been tempted to go with them if he hadn't been here on business. "Invitation only, I'm afraid. The host's high-level military."

The dark fem shuddered. "Boring, I bet."

Scarlet hoped so.

"Seriously, you'd have a better time with us."

"Maybe I'll catch you later."

The two fems turned down a small street which ran perpendicular to the river walkway. He watched them disappear into a dimly lit doorway with a faint feeling of regret. On his left, the river swirled against the smooth plascrete walls. He paused, resting his elbows on the top of the barrier and peered down into the depths. He'd heard that river dolphins came this far up into the city, as well as killer sharks. He'd never seen either, and he didn't this time. A brightly lit party boat cruised slowly downstream. Music drifted across the water.

He walked on, reaching the apartment complex a few minutes later. He presented his invitation to the armed security guard, who inspected it carefully before allowing him through the gate.

Another guard escorted him to the block he asked for. "Just hold your invitation to the lock," the guard told him. "It'll let you in."

As soon as Scarlet stepped through the door, it closed behind him, leaving him in a wide hallway, with reception areas on either side. The floor underfoot was marble or a very realistic imitation and the walls shimmered with silver. The hallway itself was lit with dim ceiling lights, but the rooms through the arches were darker. Scarlet peered into the first one, which was large and filled with groups of low sofas and cushions, some of them occupied. Blinds covered the windows completely, and the only light came from a barely glowing central chandelier. On one side of the room, a keyboard instrument stood, not one that Scarlet recognised. A group of people clustered round it.

He stepped through the arch leading into the opposite room. Pulsing music immediately assaulted his ears. The room had narrow benches round the edge, but the floor was filled with a mass of gyrating bodies. Lights faded in and out, cycling through all the colours of the rainbow and a few extra.

Scarlet looked around for the host, a man he'd never met before. He'd seen a holo-image of him though and thought he would recognise him. He couldn't spot him in the crowd of dancers, so maybe he was in the other room. A hand landed on his shoulder as he walked back into the relative silence of the hallway. Instinct spun him round, before he had time to think.

The man backed away, holding his hands up. "Sorry. I just wanted to get your attention." It was the host.

"No problem," Scarlet said. "You surprised me."

"You must lead a stressful life." The man held out one hand. "Rico Amarre. You're Scarlet?"

"Major Amarre?" Scarlet wanted to be sure. The man looked like the holo-image but you couldn't be too careful. He might be a close family member.

"That's right, but call me Rico. Is it just Scarlet, or do you have another name?"

"Just Scarlet." He'd chosen the name himself, on his eighteenth birthday. His previous one had been given to him by the institute and he hated it.

"Just Scarlet." Amarre's mouth twitched in amusement. "Come with me. We can talk in private. Get the business over, so we can relax and enjoy ourselves. I've been told I throw a good party." He led Scarlet to the end of the hallway and placed his palm against the control panel by the last door. It opened into a short corridor. Amarre pushed open a door on his right and led the way into a study-lounge. "Have a seat."

Four comfortable chairs clustered at one side of the room. A console desk stood at the far end. Scarlet sat in one of the chairs.

"Drink?" Amarre picked up a bottle of a pale orange liquid and poured a generous amount into a glass before raising it to his lips and sipping it. "This is good stuff."

Scarlet nodded and leaned back in the chair, stretching his legs out, admiring the elegance of his new synth-leather boots, with their swirls of blue and red. "Thank you."

Amarre poured another drink and carried it over to him. He sat in the opposite chair, a tall man, solid without being fat, and well into middle-age. His features were heavy and his skin tinged with pink. Hair, so blonde it was almost white, swept back from his forehead, and the blue of his eyes was a narrow ring around huge pupils. It looked to Scarlet like Amarre had no problem sourcing chem already. He held his glass up to the light, watching sparkles form in the liquid, before he took a cautious sip, His body warmed as the drink slid down his throat, small droplets popping against the roof of his mouth. His host was right. It was definitely good stuff. He took another sip, wondering what it was, and put the glass down on the low table. "It was good of you to invite me. What can I do for you in return?"

Amarre drained his glass. "I was told you could supply various products. Party favours, and more intimate aids."

"Who told you about us?"

"A couple of people. I know one of your team is friendly with Liddya Benz, but even before that, I'd heard you were reliable," Amarre said. "Do you know a woman called Didi Ramonz?"

Scarlet nodded. Everyone knew Didi Ramonz. Or knew of her. "Not personally."

"Did you know she met an unfortunate end?"

"I heard." Didi was one of the bigger producers of illegal substances in the London area. A few weeks earlier, she'd been killed by a rival, who had subsequently been terminated by a group of her people. The crew had fallen apart afterwards, leaving a lot of unsatisfied customers. Her territory was a long way west of Scarlet's, so he hadn't paid much attention.

"It's caused me a few problems," Amarre continued. "She supplied me, and I supplied my friends. I've a wide circle of friends and I don't like letting them down."

"I can see why that wouldn't be good."

"So, I wonder if you have the capacity to replace her."

Scarlet picked up his drink. "What did you have in mind?"

"Dreamer?"

Scarlet nodded.

"Frenzi?"

"Yes. That's no trouble." He thought of the stockpile he'd promised Claws. There was plenty for both.

"Muzak?"

"I shouldn't think that'll be a problem." They weren't manufacturing it at the moment, as there wasn't much demand among the illegals, but they'd made a batch once. He thought they still had some raw materials for it.

"And I suppose you could sell us R'lax in bulk?"

"Yeah." The common smoke was something they already made in large amounts. It was chem that touched on almost lawful. "Just give me a figure for the amounts you want and I'll give you a price." Scarlet didn't want to commit himself on price until he knew approximately what Didi Ramonz had charged. He didn't want to undersell, and he knew Koo-Suki would be keen to examine the potential profit.

Amarre's eyes narrowed. "I have a few other names. You just came highly recommended. If you try to overcharge though—"

"We won't overcharge you. You'll get a fair price."

"Good. And I might be interested in small amounts of DeathDreamer."

Scarlet nodded. There was no shortage of suicidal idiots, even among the privileged and wealthy.

"And Wildwolf?"

Scarlet frowned. This was the second time he'd heard the new chem mentioned in the last week. "We don't make that. Was Didi manufacturing it?"

Amarre shook his head. "I had a recent enquiry from an acquaintance. Not many people have heard of it, yet. Don't worry about it. I'll send a list of quantities for the other stuff to your private comm. I assume you have good security?"

"Very good."

"Tomorrow, then." Amarre swallowed the last of the drink and rose to his feet. "Thank you. I hope we can do business. I don't want to keep you from the party. You are staying, aren't you?"

"Yes. Thank you. I'll get back to you with a price by the end of the week." Scarlet didn't associate much with fully registered Londoners. Sometimes high-level citizens came through the wall, hoping to experience illegal thrills, but most people avoided that sort. They tended to be the worst of the citizenry and only the people in the pleasar industry had much to do with them. Occasionally some psychopath decided they wanted the thrill of hunting other human beings. Fortunately, they didn't appear often, at least not around outer London. It wasn't illegal to kill an unregistered citizen, but it was definitely frowned on.

"Good." Amarre patted his shoulder. "Enjoy." He disappeared into the quieter of the two reception areas.

Scarlet went into the other room, leaned against the wall and watched the action on the dance floor. He wasn't likely to come to this sort of party again, not in the near future anyway. The dancers were a diverse bunch, old and young, male, female and other, but mostly attractive. They wore a rainbow palette of upmarket party style, from the one who was almost naked apart from body paint, to the one who appeared to be dressed from head to toe in feathers. Artificial ones, Scarlet assumed.

"Hello." A man propped himself against the wall next to him. He had a drink in one hand and underneath the face paint he appeared to be young. Cool grey eyes, outlined in black, squinted at Scarlet. "I've not met you before, have I? Not dancing?"

"I've only just arrived." Scarlet held up his own drink. "And finishing this." He swallowed the last of the orange liquid, relishing the way its warmth spread through him, settling in his groin. He wondered what it was.

The man took the glass from him and put it on the floor next to the wall. "Come on, stranger, dance with me."

Scarlet followed him out into the mass of writhing bodies. He liked to dance and didn't often get the opportunity. His partner was an athletic, if not particularly graceful, dancer. As he jerked and gyrated, the flashing lights picked out different parts of his body. He held Scarlet's gaze, some of the lights giving his eyes a red hue, a pale reflection of Scarlet's own. Black dye outlined his lips. When the music changed, he placed both hands on Scarlet's hips and drew him closer to speak into his ear. "Another drink? Or I know someone who'll get us Muzak?"

"A drink." Muzak was a party chem, designed to elevate energy levels. It made the user feel as though he was part of the music, altered his heartrate to match the beat. Scarlet wasn't stupid enough to touch it, especially if it came from someone he didn't know. He didn't know his partner, wouldn't trust a stranger, and wasn't sure whether he could be bothered to follow up the connection. Networking was useful but he liked to be careful. You never knew if new contacts were powerful, influential, weak, useless, likely to become obsessive, or to see you as a route to riches. He'd met all sorts. This one was obviously rich and entitled, but the pulsing light and loud music made it hard to tell anything else about him.

Scarlet followed him back into the hallway and through the other arch. Here, the music was quiet and unobtrusive and the lights low. The guests sat in small groups, talking or lying back, eyes half closed. The air was thick with pink-tinged smoke, drifting towards the ceiling and spreading the scent of R'lax through the room.

Scarlet sank onto a sofa next to his companion. Immediately, a naked, elaborately painted, very young woman arrived and leaned over the back of the sofa. "What can I get you?"

Scarlet glanced up at her; she was small and slender and much more to his taste than the man he was with. He lifted his hand to touch her, to pull her towards him. She smiled but retreated. He took a deep breath and jerked his arm back, curling his fingers into the sofa cushion. What was he thinking of? The fem was probably an indentured servant and not free to make her own decisions. "A beer," he said. No more of that loin-twisting orange stuff for him. It had gone straight to his cock, taking his wits with it, and he was half-erect. What the hell was it? The thought of chemical mood-enhancers depressed him; he was a dealer not a user.

The woman bent to whisper in his companion's ear. She straightened and disappeared.

The man slung one arm round Scarlet's shoulders. "We haven't met before," he said. "I'm Serran Willim."

"Scarlet. It's my first visit here." Serran's fingers twitched on his shoulder, tapping out a rough rhythm.

"Just Scarlet?"

"Nowadays," Scarlet said. He sniffed discretely. Serran's heavy oriental perfume had a faint hint of sour sweat.

"I don't visit that often. Rico usually has the same crowd. A boring lot, mostly."

Why did he come then? Scarlet examined the other occupants of the room, thinking that boring was good. Everyone appeared quiet and relaxed, but that was probably a side-effect of the smoke. In the other room, it was obvious that many of the dancers were using some sort of stimulants. Frenzi, he guessed, from their jerky movements. A quick glance around the quiet room revealed at least one person who looked like he'd sniffed DeathDreamer. Surely the name was a dead giveaway? Although they did try to market it as DoubleD nowadays. DeathDreamer was the intense, mixed form of Dreamer, and Amarre's request for it bothered Scarlet. A string of chem related deaths at the pinnacle of society wouldn't do his business any good. If that happened, he'd be a priority target for Law Enforcement. He shuddered.

"Something wrong?" His companion squeezed his shoulder, hard enough to bruise.

Arousal shot through Scarlet, unexpected and unwelcome. "Just a thought." He shrugged the hand off, and took a deep breath. What *was* wrong with him? Pain had never been his sort of turn-on.

Serran laughed. "I love what you've done with your eyes."

"Thanks." Scarlet shifted away from him and accepted a beer from the returned servant.

She offered him a selection of tubular smokes. "Just R'lax, Sir."

Scarlet accepted one. The woman held a flame to its tip. She passed a small shiny box to Serran.

Pleasant indolence filled Scarlet and he closed his eyes. Perhaps he shouldn't have accepted, but R'lax was pretty harmless. He wondered again what the orange liquid had been. He asked Serran.

"Rico gave you that?" Serran moved closer to him again.

"Yeah."

"It's a mild aphrodisiac," Serran said. "Sort of Wildwolf without the stimulant. Rico dilutes it and mixes it with alcohol."

"Wildwolf?"

"New chem come to town. Makes you feel like a god. You should try it. I can get you some."

Scarlet's brain wasn't working at full speed, but a sample of the chem might be useful. He kept hearing about it. "Thanks. I've heard it has a nasty aftermath."

"Only if you're careless."

That wasn't what Scarlet had heard, but he dropped the subject.

"Shit." Serran pulled his arm away from Scarlet's shoulders and sat up, his body rigid.

Scarlet opened his eyes. Three people were settling onto the companion sofa to theirs. His eyes widened at the sight of the central figure, a tall femme, whose slim athletic build was enhanced by a close-fitting indigo skinsuit, under a translucent crimson robe. A halo of blond corkscrew curls surrounded her head, and a sunray of silver sparkles circled each eye, perfectly painted to enhance their shape. She wasn't beautiful and she wasn't young, but she was the one who held his attention. It had to be her eyes, the iciest of pale grey, and as opaque as a frozen puddle. Her two companions faded into insignificance.

"Scarlet, this is my mother," Serran said. "Fallon Willim."

The woman nodded graciously.

"And this," Serran pointed to a blond femme to the right of his mother, "is my sister, Flora."

The femme was a copy of her mother, without the charisma. Her smile didn't reach her eyes. Scarlet turned his attention to the last member of the trio, a lanky youth, with dark undecorated skin and short curled hair, coloured metallic gold. He wore a simple indigo coverall.

"My baby brother," Serran said.

"Brother?" The youth didn't look anything like the rest of them, and it was odd that there were three siblings anyway. Even the highest levels of society didn't flout the population laws. Two children, if you were lucky, more were almost unheard of.

"Chosen brother." Fallon Willim answered his unspoken question. "Ashkir was a refugee from one of the lost desert states. He made it onto the relocation list when he was ten. His family didn't. We took him in." The youth flinched when she patted his cheek. His smile looked forced. "So, Scarlet, you are a friend of my son?"

"We met an hour ago." Serran's tone was sullen. Any charm he'd displayed had vanished when his family appeared.

"I was asking Scarlet," Fallon said.

Scarlet smiled at her. "We danced together, and came out for a break."

"Tell me about yourself."

"Not much to tell." Scarlet spread his hands. "I was lucky enough to be invited tonight, but it's the first time."

"Your family?"

What was this? An interrogation? "Like your chosen son, I don't have a blood family."

She stared at him. "Level of citizenship?"

"Ma!" Serran's voice raised in protest. "I barely know him."

"I'm unregistered," Scarlet said.

She raised her eyebrows. "Rico is broadminded, isn't he?"

Scarlet hid his amusement. "As I said, I'm honoured to be here."

"Mmm. I wonder..." Her voice trailed off as the painted servant arrived to take the drink orders.

While the group were occupied, Serran whispered in his ear. "I'm sorry. We'll leave soon, but I can't just walk out now. She'd take it badly."

Scarlet had no intention of spending any more time with him. He was a rich chem head, and while Scarlet might sell drugs, he despised those who had fortune and opportunity and squandered them. He'd had enough of the party, which was nowhere as good as some of the ones he'd been to in the outer zone. The aftermath of the orange drink still bothered him. "I need to visit a bathroom."

He got up and looked round the room. It couldn't be that hard to find a bathroom. Afterwards he would leave. As he paused under the brighter lights in the hall, feet shuffled behind him. He turned his head.

Ashkir had followed him. "I can show you the bathroom. We've been here a lot."

"Thanks."

"Your eyes are great," he said as he led Scarlet past the music room. "Scary. I could do with scary."

Scarlet glanced at his dark brown eyes. There was nothing wrong with them. He said so. "And your hair colour's a great contrast with your skin. You look good."

"Yeah. I'd still like to be scary." Ashkir pushed open a door on the far side of the music room and stood back to let Scarlet go through. "I'll wait for you."

After using the luxurious bathroom, Scarlet re-joined Ashkir. "I'm leaving. Make my apologies to your family. Will you tell Serran I had an appointment."

Ashkir walked with him to the entrance. "Wish I could leave too."

"Come on then," Scarlet said. He wanted a coffee. Something to wash away the languid apathy he felt. "Let's get a drink by the river."

"I don't know." Ashkir pursed his full lips. "They won't like it."

"Do what you want," Scarlet said. "You're an adult, aren't you?"

"Yes, but I'm not quite eighteen yet, so I haven't got full citizenship." A brief flash of distaste crossed his face. "It depends on them. Fallon has to complete my registration."

Scarlet shrugged. "They might not even realise you're gone."

"I hate these parties." He hesitated. "Okay."

The two of them walked along the river road towards the skytran hub. After a minute, Ashkir cleared his throat. "So, you don't know Serran that well?"

"No. I told your mother, I just met him tonight."

"You should be careful with him," Ashkir said. "He's hard on his friends."

Scarlet's eyebrow raise was mental. "I shouldn't think I'll see him again. He's a bit of a narco-freak, isn't he? Sorry to say it about your brother, and feel free to tell me if I'm wrong."

"No." Ashkir lapsed back into silence.

Scarlet was content to walk along, watching the river. He wished he hadn't suggested a drink. He wanted to go home.

"What about this?" Ashkir suggested, pointing at a café on the edge of the walkway. It looked out over the river and had a veranda that would offer shelter from the daytime storms. "I've been here before. It's okay."

Scarlet stuck to coffee as he still wasn't sure what had been in the pale orange drink that Rico had given him. Dilute Wildwolf? Serran didn't strike him as a reliable source. Whatever it was, he'd liked it. Too much. If he encountered it again, he'd walk away.

"You said you've been living with the Willims since you were ten?" he asked Ashkir. He needed something to take his mind off the waves of arousal that still washed over him.

"Yes, they volunteered to take a child from the Badlands. They came to the refugee centre and chose me." He avoided Scarlet's eyes. "They did it for the publicity, but I know I was lucky."

"Lucky?" Scarlet shifted position on the bar stool, unable to get comfortable.

"Everyone who made it to the centre was lucky," Ashkir said. "I didn't want to go with them. My mother forced me. I don't know what happened to the rest of my family, but hardly anyone made it out of our part of North Africa. You can't imagine the heat that year. It was enough to fry your whole body. They used to have cooling facilities, but the environmental laws stopped that."

"Is it all Badlands now?"

Ashkir nodded. "It hadn't rained for years. I don't think anyone could survive there, now." He sipped at his coffee and stared out at the water. "I love the Thames. It's so big. You can't imagine it ever drying up."

"Not with the way it rains round here." Scarlet found the river fascinating. It was like a huge snake, wriggling through the city, a constant threat as well as a travelled waterway. "It's more likely to crawl over the walls and swamp everything. I can see the headlines – mass drownings in London."

"Yeah." Ashkir's smile was forced. "I can't see it happening. Not with the flood defences, they've got. And too much water has to be better than none. There's talk about using terraforming technology to make it possible for people to live in the Badlands again, but..."

So much of the Earth was no longer habitable and even if the technology was successful, it wouldn't happen in Scarlet's time. Or even in his grandchildren's time. If he ever had children. He couldn't imagine wanting them, or ever reaching a stage in his life where they would be a good idea. He thought of Koo-Suki's reaction if he suggested it. "Have you ever thought of emigrating to one of the colonies?" Terraforming was creating human compatible environments in several distant planetary systems. Even Earth's moon had settlements nowadays. And Mars, and some of Jupiter's moons.

"That would be magic. It costs a lot though, and I'm dependent on the Willims. I'm waiting for them to confirm my citizenship. What about you?"

"Yeah," Scarlet said. "Sometimes I think about it. There's no way I'd get accepted though. They don't take non-citizens. And there are three of us."

"Three?" Ashkir asked.

"In my family," Scarlet said. "We're not blood, but I wouldn't go without them."

"You're permanent?"

"We've been together since we were children," Scarlet explained. "We looked out for each other. They're my family as much as if they *were* blood."

"What's it like being unregistered?" Ashkir leaned his elbows on the table. "Living outside the wall?"

"Insecure." Scarlet didn't have to think. "No laws and a lot of predators. We were lucky. You need to get protection as soon as possible, if you want to live out there. If you don't have power, you need powerful friends."

"My adoption family's powerful." Ashkir dipped his finger in his drink and stirred the cooling liquid, before licking his finger. It could have been provocative, but that wasn't the message that Scarlet was getting. "They're not relaxing to be around, though. And Fallon's scary. Marcus, her husband, is never home, so she's the one who runs everything. Flora's terrified of her, and I think Serran hates her, even though he's her favourite. Serran's weird though, with his mood swings. Sometimes he's your best friend in all the world, then the next day, he'll behave as if you're his worst enemy. He beat me up, once, a couple of years ago. I had to spend a few days in a clinic. His mother had him whipped when I came out. She made me watch." He pushed his beaker away. "I know I'm lucky, but they're a strange family. I'd better get back."

Scarlet drained his drink. "If you ever want to go over the wall, just ask for me." He was joking, but for a moment Ashkir's face brightened.

"I'll remember that."

Chapter 6

Maeve carried a bottle of acetic acid over to the senior of the chemists, grunting as her ribs twinged. Most of the damage from Romero's beating had disappeared, but occasionally she had the sort of reminder that made her gasp out loud. It was lucky she healed quickly, and lucky that Scarlet had come along when he had. She was pretty sure that Romero had meant to kill her.

She handed her bottle over and went to help Tamsin, the other assistant, move stock from the lab to the pickup point. Bending didn't make her ribs feel any better, either, but she wasn't going to complain. This place was a million times better than her last two placements. It was almost like she had a real job. She wiped moisture from her forehead with the sleeve of her coverall. "It's so hot. And humid. Worse than this afternoon."

"Let's get a drink," Tamsin suggested. "We've finished with this for now."

Maeve rubbed her forehead again, pushing the damp hair away from her eyes, glad for a break. It might be better than working for Romero or Elise, but the job was hard work, boring and at the moment, painful. She followed Tamsin to the small room where the drinks were kept and sat down at a table. The night was muggy, most of the rain that had fallen during the day still hanging in the air. She was thirsty, but had hardly any money left from her wages after she'd paid an instalment to Scarlet for the cost of her indenture, and she didn't intend to waste it on a not particularly pleasant drink. She scowled as she drank some of the free purified water on offer to the workers. Scarlet would probably have let her off paying anything back, but Koo-Suki insisted. She wasn't any bigger than Maeve, but she had attitude. When she'd threatened Maeve with the knife, her eyes were almost as scary as Elise's. How had she got that way? And could Maeve ever learn to have the same effect on people? She'd wondered whether Scarlet might work as a protector, but that was before she met Koo-Suki. It was a shame though. She'd survived her childhood and teenage years by cosying up to various adults. She'd been a pet, a doll and a sex-toy. None of it had been fun, but at least she'd had some measure of protection. Until she'd reached eighteen and that bastard, Holbeck, sold her. Never again would she rely on anyone else. Use them, maybe, but never trust them. Rage had settled in her gut like a rock, after Holbeck's betrayal, keeping her awake when she should be asleep, coating her tongue with a sour taste that wouldn't go away.

She looked up as Tamsin joined her, a cup of coffo clasped in her hand. "Isn't it too hot for that?"

"Caffeine," Tamsin said. "I need the stimulant, and this is marginally better than those cold drinks. They taste like piss."

Maeve raised her eyebrows. "And you know this how?"

Tamsin grinned.

"Tamsin?" Maeve drew a pattern with her forefinger in the dirt on the table top.

"What?"

"How long have you been here?"

"A year. Since I was fourteen." She blew on the surface of her drink before testing the temperature.

"I wondered about Scarlet. Have him and Koo-Suki—"

Tamsin put her beaker down. "I hope you're not thinking what I think you're thinking."

"No." Maeve snapped. "Anyway, I don't know what you're thinking."

"Scarlet and Koo-Suki, and Mink as well, have been together since they were kids. Everyone knows that. They built this organisation up together. Anyway, Scarlet wouldn't be interested in you, so you'd be wasting your time. He doesn't have much to do with any of us. Koo-Suki manages production and staff. And Scarlet might look easy-going, but he's not an idiot."

Maeve frowned. "I'm not—"

"It doesn't matter anyway," Tamsin said. "If Koo-Suki thought you were even thinking that way, she'd murder you and bury the body. And you needn't think Scarlet would stop her."

"I just wondered. Are they exclusive then?"

Tamsin blew out a breath of exasperation. "Maeve, you should mind your own business."

"Are they?"

"I don't know," Tamsin said. "I don't think so, but Koo-Suki wouldn't have that sort of disrespect from people at our level. That's how she'd view it, you know?"

"Why's everyone so scared of her?" Maeve remembered the feel of the knife against her stomach.

"How do you think they got an operation like this?" Tamsin said.

"What?"

"Koo-Suki killed the previous boss."

"No!"

"I don't know the details, but one of the sellers told me he was a user. He tried to rape Scarlet when he was out of his head. Koo-Suki stuck a knife in him. She wasn't much more than eighteen."

"How old is she now?"

Tamsin shrugged. "Not sure. Quite old, I think. Twenty-five?"

"Scarlet's big. Why did she need to—"

"He can look after himself, but they're a team."

Maeve shifted to accommodate her aching ribs. "Bummer." She didn't want to spend the rest of her life shovelling Frenzi into consumer packs. Even when she'd paid her debts off, she'd barely have enough to get by. How did Tamsin bear it?

"Anyway, people aren't scared of Koo-Suki. They just respect her."

"So how do you find a protector, then?" Maeve needed a patron, preferably one who would help her gain citizenship, and there was no one like that around here.

"Why do you need a protector? We're part of the crew," Tamsin said. "We've got them all as backup. We get enough food, and clean water, somewhere safe to sleep, and credits. Most people don't have any of that. Seriously, Maeve, we're well off here. You don't need anyone else."

Maeve grimaced. Maybe things were different outside the wall, but she doubted it. Another job, that's what she needed, one where she would encounter people with legitimate power. People who might sponsor her citizenship. There was no way she was going to be a pleasagurl though, letting everyone have the use of her body for a pittance. She gritted her teeth. She'd find a way.

"What's wrong." Tamsin's voice broke her train of thought and she jerked her head up.

"Nothing. Why?"

"You had a really ferocious expression on your face."

"Just thinking." Scarlet, and by extension, Mink, were off her list, and Maeve wasn't even going to consider Koo-Suki. They weren't citizens anyway. She'd have to spend her few credits on going out. She wouldn't meet anyone here in the lab. Except the chemist and the technicians and none of them were of any use to her. She stood up. "Come on. We'd better get back to work."

As they walked back to the lab, she had a thought. "Do you think I could work in distribution?"

"Be a street pedlar?" Tamsin frowned. "Why would you want to do that. It's much safer here. I thought you were worried about protection."

"I like to be outside." It was true. She'd rather be outdoors than in the hot muggy underground lab. It might be just as hot, but the air was fresh at least, and the breeze would blow away the sweaty odours of anyone who came too close.

Tamsin shrugged. "Koo-Suki decides. You could ask her but I think she likes to use the young ones who've already got plenty of street smarts."

~~~

Koo-Suki was outside the caff, sitting alone at a table, and studying a hand-held info-screen, when Maeve went looking for her. A circle of light spilled from the small lamp on the table. She raised her head. Maeve slowed her steps, wondering if she was doing the right thing.

"Well? Work finished for the night?" Koo-Suki wore her sleek, close-fitting body armour, with a weapons belt around her waist. Her dark hair was a mass of tiny plaits spiking into a halo around her head, and her brown eyes were outlined in purple. She looked as purposeful and efficient as a woman who resembled a startled kitten could. No bigger than Maeve, she had presence. Was it her dark colouring, much more defined than Maeve's pale prettiness? Was it the well-used armour? Or was it the huge pistol lying on the table in front of her. She glanced down at her info-screen. Maeve shuffled closer.

"What are you looking at?" Koo-Suki's attention jerked back to Maeve.

"I wanted to ask you something." Maeve let her voice drop to breathy submissiveness.

"Come over here then. Don't just stand there." She put her info-screen down on the table, next to the pistol, and leaned back in her seat, eyes fixed on Maeve.

Maeve increased her pace until she stood on the opposite side of the table to Koo-Suki.

"What do you want?"

"I wondered if I could work in distribution instead of in the lab."

Koo-Suki frowned. "Why?"

"I like it outside. I'd work hard. Honestly." She widened her eyes and curved her mouth into a pleading smile.

Koo-Suki laughed.

"Please?"

"Don't try your whore's tricks on me," Koo-Suki said. "Save them for someone susceptible."

Maeve's face heated. She clenched her fists. "I'm not a whore. I've never been one."

"I thought you were working as a pleasagurl when Scarlet picked you up."

"I wasn't." She stamped her foot, knowing she was messing this up, but she'd always had a hard job controlling her temper, and just recently, it was like a sleeping volcano, in constant danger of eruption. "Two clients. I killed one and unmanned the other."

Koo-Suki sat up in her chair. "You said that before, but seriously? *You* killed someone?"

Maeve nodded, sullenly. "I told you."

"How did you do it?"

Koo-Suki obviously didn't believe her. "He left his knife next to the bunk." Maeve smiled as she remembered the surprise in the man's eyes as she'd plunged the knife into him. She couldn't be sure she'd killed him, but she certainly hoped she had. She'd left the tiny crib as fast as she could, when she saw how much blood came out of the wound she'd made. She'd been grabbed by one of the guards and dragged back to Elise, who'd told her exactly what was going to happen to her before she died.

"You can look after yourself then?" Koo-Suki smiled back at her.

"Yes."

"You're older than most of the outside team." Koo-Suki rested her chin on her fist. "You look harmless though." She laughed when she saw Maeve's surprise. "We don't want to scare the customers off. Imagine how they'd feel if Mink turned up, in a dark clearing, to sell them R'lax?"

Maeve tried to imagine it. From a distance Mink was scarier than Koo-Suki; he was tall and muscular, and she'd noticed that he had huge hands. His facial expression was forbidding, but his eyes weren't half as cold as Koo-Suki's. Still, if he offered to sell her chem, she'd run a mile.

Koo-Suki leaned back in her chair again. "Maybe we could try you out. The money isn't as good as the lab work though. Not at first."

"I don't mind." Maeve crossed her fingers behind her back.

"Okay." Koo-Suki picked up her comm again. "You can start tomorrow night. Be here at nine o'clock. I'll put you with one of the juvies." She bent over her work, paying no more attention to Maeve.

~~~

By the time Scarlet got home from the city, it was past four in the morning. The remnants of the orange drink still circulated in his system, making him twitchy and tired at the same time. The bedchamber was dark, and the bed was empty. Scarlet stripped off his body armour and boots, then the party skinsuit underneath it. He flung himself onto the bed, and closed his eyes. The door opened, and a dim light clicked on. Scarlet opened his eyes again. Mink and Koo-Suki came in together.

Mink tossed his face protector on a small table opposite the bed, and sat down. The mattress sagged. His cat-mutant slid through the doorway and jumped up next to him. The bed sank further. "How'd it go?"

"Pretty good." Scarlet sat up. "I think we've got a deal. A big deal too. We should get the formal order tomorrow."

"You stink of R'lax." Mink buried his nose in Scarlet's hair and sniffed.

"I can smell it from here," Koo-Suki said.

"Yeah." Scarlet pushed Mink away. "The place was completely fogged. Never seen so many people out of their heads. It'll be a great market."

"Did you enjoy the trip to the right side?" Koo-Suki started to remove her body armour.

"It was interesting," Scarlet said. "Rico Amarre gave me a drink. Something I'd never had before. Sort of stimulant, relaxant and aphrodisiac all at once."

"Mmm?" Koo-Suki kicked her boots off and pushed them under the bed. "You should have got a sample."

"Next time. I'd like to know what was in it. Someone mentioned diluted Wildwolf, but I don't know."

"Did you hook up?" Mink asked. "What with the aphrodisiac and all?"

"Nah." Scarlet shook his head and told them about the blond man and his weird family. "I think I had a lucky escape."

"You actually asked a citizen to join us if he wanted to?" Mink shook his head and lay back next to Scarlet. He patted the bed. "Come on Nyx." His pet mutant climbed over Scarlet and stretched out on Mink's other side.

"Not a citizen." The ceiling over his head spun in slow circles. All that smoke must still be affecting him. "He hadn't been granted rights yet. Anyway, I wasn't serious." He lay down next to Mink and closed his eyes.

"Your new pet came to see me today." Koo-Suki crawled into a space on the other side of the bed from Mink and Nyx.

"What are you talking about?" Scarlet kept his eyes closed. The moving ceiling made him queasy.

"That failed pleasagurl." Koo-Suki turned her back to him. "She wants a job change."

"I don't care," Scarlet said. "Let me go to sleep." His head ached. From the other side of Mink, a loud rumbling purr started up. It was weirdly soothing.

"She's a chancer." Koo-Suki relapsed into silence when Scarlet didn't answer.

Chapter 7

By the time Maeve had spent two weeks in her new position, she'd realised that street-pedlar wasn't an exact description of the job. Streets weren't involved. Wet steamy thickets played a large part in her life. Empty warehouses, and old ruined residences were there too, but they were usually buried in heaps of wet green stuff. She hadn't met anyone useful at all. Just loser users and underage pedlars. Still, it was early days and this was the bottom end of the market.

She followed Temmy along a narrow path and through a broken doorway. "Who the hell are we meeting here?" Mud clung to her cheap boots, weighing her feet down. Her cheap coverall stuck to her skin, wherever it touched her. She blew out a hot, impatient breath.

"Black Dorand." Temmy tossed the words over his shoulder and led the way down a passage to another broken door.

"And who in the whole of the fucking world is Black Dorand?"

"I'm Black Dorand."

Maeve halted in the doorway and stared at the speaker. He was a short, wide man, with a purple-red face made distinctive by the candlelight, a shock of white hair and a stubbly beard, covering his lower jaw.

"The acoustics in this place are interesting." He bared a mouthful of rotting teeth, in an unconvincing smile.

Maeve shuddered. Even from the doorway, she could sense the aggression oozing from his pores.

Temmy whispered in her ear. "Frenzi. He's been an addict for years. I can't believe he's still alive."

"Come in. I want to see what you've brought me."

"Go on." Temmy pushed her forward. "You've got the product."

That was another grievance. The boys made her carry the merchandise. All the time. None of them bothered. She wanted her own patch, but didn't dare approach Koo-Suki again. Not yet.

"Maeve – what are you waiting for?" Temmy passed her, grabbed her arm and jerked her after him, into a vast room, with a soaring ceiling. Patches of starry sky showed through the gaps. The place was lit by a miserable number of candles, giving the atmosphere a smoky scent; not unpleasant, but pervasive and mixed with the odour of R'lax. Black Dorand occupied a throne-like chair in the centre. Most of the light was around the him, but in the shadows behind the chair, other bodies stirred.

"You're a pretty little baby thing." He leaned back in his seat, blinking hooded eyes at Maeve. "Just the sort I like. Why are you wasting your time running chem for Koo-Suki and the gang?"

"I'm not—"

Temmy nudged her. "Don't argue with him, there's no point."

"If you want to join me," Black Dorand said, "I'll give you a job."

Two juvies, one male, one female, emerged from the darkness behind him and sat at his feet. He petted their heads roughly. "I'm a kind master, aren't I, puppies?"

The two answered in unison. "Yes master." They were naked, their half-starved bodies covered in cuts and bruises.

"No thank you." Maeve forgot to put the breathy seduction in her voice. This set-up looked worse than Claws and Romero.

"Give him the bag, Maeve," Temmy said.

She handed it over.

He checked the contents, before passing her a credit chip, which Temmy grabbed from her before she could look at it.

"Come on," he said. "We need to go."

"I'll ask Koo-Suki about you," Black Dorand said. "She's young, but she knows how to do a good trade."

Temmy led her out past a couple of young guards. "Take no notice of him. Koo won't sell any of our people."

Maeve glanced at him, but couldn't read his expression in the darkness. "I've only been here a few weeks. I don't think she likes me."

"Doesn't matter."

"Are you sure?" she asked. "I hate having to rely on other people. I really want my citizenship. That's the only security."

Temmy snorted. "I bet it's not. Anyway, you're not likely to get it, are you? None of us are."

"I will." Maeve pushed her way through a clump of wet spiky plants, her head lamp barely lighting the way. "Where are we going?"

"Short cut," Temmy said. "You shouldn't worry. Koo's okay. She'll look after you."

"Wait for me." A thin branch bounced back and hit her in the face. "Temmy? Wait, will you?" Twigs caught in her hair. She jerked her head free, wincing. "Why can't we go back the way we came? And what's that smell?"

Temmy crashed back through the bushes. "Let's turn round." His voice sounded funny.

"What's wrong?"

"You don't want to look. Come on."

Maeve pushed past him. The smell was weird. Disgusting and unfamiliar. Someone had slashed and burned the bushes, to make a small space. Part of the stench was wet charcoal.

"Maeve. Come back."

She ducked her head to let her lamp shine into the clearing. The blackened grass gleamed ruby under the beam from her light. She clapped her hand over her mouth and stepped backwards into Temmy.

"I told you." His voice was steadier now. "You shouldn't have looked. Come on. let's find someone."

"Was that a woman?"

"Come on Maeve." He grabbed her hand and hurried her along. "Suppose whoever did it is still around?"

71

"I don't think so." Whoever lay in that clearing had been dead for more than a day. She stumbled after him, trying not to trip. "Who would have done something like that? Could it have been Black Dorand?" She'd been around sufficient psychopaths to recognise one.

"Black... No of course it wasn't." Temmy paused when they emerged from the undergrowth. "Haven't you heard of the Silencer?"

"Silencer?" She couldn't remember hearing the name.

"Don't you watch the media? Talk to people?"

"Not about gruesome murderers." She jerked her arm free of Temmy, now they were on a proper path.

"He's a serial killer. Everyone knows about him."

Back at the caff, only Mink was around to listen to Temmy's description of what they'd seen. He frowned, the ferocious cast of his face making him appear capable of having killed the woman himself. Standing up, he grabbed his face protector and the gun lying on the table in front of him. He pulled the armour over his head and slipped the gun into his belt. "Come on. You can show me." He pointed a finger at a shadow creeping from underneath the table. "You stay here." Two green eyes blinked from the darkness, but the animal remained where it was.

Maeve hurried after him and Temmy. Mink turned his head. "You don't need to come, either."

It sounded like an order but Maeve ignored it. She didn't want to be by herself. The darkness outside the caff was full of menace. "I do need to." She jogged along behind them.

"What's wrong with you?" Mink asked Temmy. "I'm beginning to think you're a jinx."

"I was only taking a short cut," Temmy said. "I guess I'm just unlucky."

"It's less than two weeks since you found the last one," Mink said. "It looks like he's doing this more often. We've got to find him and stop this."

Temmy had found another body like that? Maeve pushed her damp hair back from her face. "Who's doing it?"

"Haven't a clue." Mink didn't turn round. "Keep up if you're coming with us. We don't want you to be next."

Maeve increased her pace.

"There've been four so far that we know of. If this is what Temmy said it was, it looks like the fifth. It started back in January."

Mink seemed willing to communicate, so Maeve asked. "Who are they?"

"So far, they've mostly been independent flesh pedlars. At least as far as we've heard. The Guard tried to link a murder in the city to these, but it didn't make sense. All the rest were fems, and the city one was male, but of course they think the killer's from outside the wall. That's why there've been so many Guards around recently."

Maeve slowed as they neared the body. She had a compulsion to look at it again, to check what she'd seen. Maybe if she saw it properly, she wouldn't keep re-imagining it. The foul familiar scent drifted to her nostrils.

Mink halted, looking down. He took a powerful pencil torch from his belt, switched it on and moved it over the body. "Nasty." He crouched down to study it, his gloved hand moving the head to one side.

Maeve turned her face away, but not before she caught a glimpse of gaping throat, and white bone. Something moved in the wound. She clamped a hand over her mouth.

Mink got to his feet. "Looks like another. We'd better get a message to the Guard."

"The Guard?" Maeve frowned. No one talked to the Guard. It was a bad idea to attract their attention.

"Anonymously. I'll sort it out." He pointed his bright torch at her.

She screwed up her eyes.

"You look a bit sick. I'll buy you a drink back at the caff. You too, Temmy. Let's get out of here."

~~~

Scarlet got back to the caff just after three am. Koo-Suki caught up with him as he made his way towards Mink's table. Temmy and Maeve were there too, sitting with Mink, empty beakers in front of them. That was odd. Scarlet glanced at Koo-Suki, who widened her eyes in an exaggerated expression of incomprehension. As they sat down, Mink waved the other two away with a small gesture of his hand. Nyx's head had been resting on Maeve's knee, and she hissed as Maeve stood up. Maeve rubbed her head, before leaving, the animal taking a few steps after her.

"What's going on?" Scarlet accepted the beer someone put in his hand, and took a deep gulp of it. "Why were you playing with the children?"

Mink's mouth twitched in a small smile, before flattening out again. "They found another body. Looked like the same killer as last time."

"Temmy *again?*" Scarlet took a smaller sip of his beer and put the beaker down. "What's wrong with him?" The boy was going to have nightmares.

"They were taking a short cut," Mink said. "I wonder if you should find him something else, Koo? Something inside for a while. He pretends to be tough, but he looked a bit sick."

Koo-Suki nodded. "I'll have a think."

"Your fem was a bit shaken too, Scarlet," Mink said.

"Not surprised. And she's not my fem."

Koo-Suki leaned her elbows on the table. "Do you know who this one was?"

"No." Mink shook his head. "It was a fem though. Young, thin and blond, again. The cuts were different, but her tongue was missing, like the others."

"Who the fuck is doing this? And why?" Helpless rage shook Scarlet. "It's on our patch. We've got to stop it. Next time it could be one of ours."

"I don't know." Mink rubbed his eyes. "Someone local must be involved or at least helping. No one else would know the places the bodies were left. Whoever did it has to be insane."

"You think?"

Mink nodded. "Or chem scrambled."

Koo-Suki scowled. "We have to find them, whoever it is. What about offering a reward?"

"What sort of reward?" Scarlet asked.

She rolled her eyes. "Credits of course. Most people round here would do anything for a few credits."

"That's a good idea," Mink said. "I'll spread the word."

Chapter 8

The street pedlars were supposed to work in pairs, supposed to have each other's backs. Temmy was conscientious about sticking to the rules, but the juvie she'd worked with for the last few days wasn't. "It's cos they don't trust us not to steal from them," he told her. "You'll be okay going back by yourself, won't you? I've things to do."

After finding the dead woman, Maeve wasn't too happy about wandering the night by herself, but there was no way she could refuse. "Yeah. I'll be fine."

On her way back to the flophouse, alone for the third night in a row, she spotted a man she'd never seen before, not one of the homs, or the juvies who worked the night shifts. He was walking along the pathway in the opposite direction to her. For a moment, Maeve panicked. He was tall, dressed in an armoured skinsuit with opaque eye protection, and looked older than most of the kids sleeping in the flophouse bunks. His head was bare, and blond hair curled to his shoulders, pale against the black of his armour.

She drew back into the bushes, her fingers contracting round the hilt of the small knife she carried in her belt. He walked past, slowed and stopped. He turned round. "Are you all right?"

She frowned, letting her head lamp shine directly into his shades.

"Should you be out here by yourself? Where's your minder?"

She took a step out of the bushes. "I'm not a bloody flesh-pedlar. Why does everyone think I am?"

The man held up his hands. "Sorry. You shouldn't be out alone though. It's dangerous."

Maeve edged closer, but kept her hand on her knife. "I'm fine. I can look after myself. Who are you?"

"My name's Marius. Let me escort you wherever you're going."

Maeve shook her head. She'd never heard of him. "It's all right. I'm going home. I live up the hill."

"Scarlet's patch?"

She nodded. "Is that who you're looking for?"

"Yeah. I just missed him. I'll see you on your way. You know there's a killer round about?"

"I heard." Maeve's skin twitched as he walked at her side. He was big, not like Mink, but big enough to make her nervous. She kept a good three feet between them and fingered the hilt of her knife.

He halted when they reached the path leading to the flophouse. "You should be safe from here."

She glanced up at the blank lenses of his eye cover.

He took them off, revealing tilted grey eyes. He had a nice face, friendly and open. His armour was clean and looked expensive. She wondered what he wanted with Scarlet.

"Can I buy you a drink?" he asked. "Tomorrow, maybe?"

"I work," she said. "Until the hour after midnight."

"That's good for me," he said. "Where shall I meet you?"

As she jogged up the hill, she thought about him. He didn't seem the sort of man who would beat her or kill her, but of course she'd carry her knife. Anyway, surely if he was going to kill her, he would already have tried. If she didn't take any chances she might just as well stay in her rut. She might just as well become a flesh-pedlar. Enough people mistook her for one anyway. She slipped into the flophouse and headed for her bunk. She'd make a bit of effort with her appearance tomorrow. He might be useful, might have contacts. Maybe he would know of a job that offered citizenship opportunities. She snorted into the flat pillow and fell into a deep dreamless sleep.

~~~

Scarlet and Koo-Suki waited in an empty room in an empty safe-house, well away from the city walls. Their offer of a reward, for information about the Silencer, had paid off. Scarlet leaned against the wall, hands in pockets. Koo-Suki paced. Her small head lamp bobbed back and forwards, casting a dim glow over the area, but not reaching the mould and the damp climbing the walls. Nothing could hide the smell, though. The place had been unoccupied for too long, and it was slowly decomposing. Soon, only the stones would remain.

The scrape of the sagging door pulled Scarlet out of his thoughts. He pushed himself away from the wall, rubbed a dark stain off the sleeve of his skinsuit, and turned his lamp towards the opening. Koo-Suki joined him, feet apart, one hand resting on her weapons belt.

Mink shoved the door wide open and dragged a man into the centre of the room, propelling him forward until he was standing in front of Scarlet, who directed his light beam up and down his body.

The man stared at the ground. He was at least six inches shorter than Mink. Half Mink's weight as well.

Koo-Suki nudged Scarlet. "He doesn't look like a murderer."

The man's head jerked up. "I'm not a murderer. Why would you say that?"

Mink cuffed him around the ear. "Speak when you're spoken to."

"But—"

Mink hit him again, harder this time.

"What's your name?" Scarlet asked. He was sure he'd seen the man before.

"Evesden Rickets."

"You were fingered as the Silencer."

"Silencer?" Evesden's voice rose to a squeak. "Me? I'm not..."

Scarlet folded his arms and raised his eyebrows.

"I couldn't do that," he said. "Kill people that way. It makes me sick to my stomach."

"How do you know how they were killed?" Scarlet asked.

"Everyone knows."

"We heard you were involved."

"No. Not involved as such. I just…" The man raked his hands through his stringy hair and rubbed his reddening ear. "I needed the credits."

"What?" Scarlet hadn't expected that.

"You killed them for money?" Koo-Suki's hand moved to the hilt of her knife.

"No." Evesden's voice rose again. "No. Not me. I told you I didn't kill them."

"What *did* you do?" Scarlet asked. Evesden was guilty of something.

"It was a contract. I was asked to show someone some quiet places. Out of sight. Places where no one goes."

"So he could butcher his victims in peace?" Koo-Suki took a step forward. Scarlet stopped her with a hand on her arm.

"They were dead already. He didn't kill them either. He was just told to get rid of the bodies. To dump them somewhere. Anyway, I didn't know what he wanted until I'd taken his credits. Then it was too late to argue."

Scarlet put a leash on his rage as he remembered the pathetic corpse in the park. Evesden Rickets knew what the Silencer was doing and had still helped him. He could have told someone, warned the locals. He was a pathetic excuse for a human being. "Who was he?"

"I don't know. Just some sort of bodyguard."

Scarlet nodded at Mink who slapped the side of the man's head, making him stagger. "Who was he?"

"I don't know. I told you." He rubbed his sore ear again.

"Are you sure?" Scarlet said. "I'll force it out of you if I have to." Next to him Koo-Suki pulled the large knife from her belt.

"Yes. Yes." Evesden's eyes focussed on it. "I've told you everything I know. He wore a full-face mask, and bulky body armour. He could have been anybody. I did get the idea he didn't like what he was doing."

79

"But he was male?" Scarlet thought he must have been. The murders weren't the sort of things most women would do.

Evesden's brow wrinkled. "I couldn't say. He was big. But he didn't do it anyway. It was his boss. I told you."

"For fuck's sake? You took a job like that from a perfect stranger?"

"I needed the credits."

"Can you remember anything about him? Anything at all?" Koo-Suki asked.

Evesden's eyes stayed on the knife. "I think he worked for a high-level citizen. His body armour was newish, and good quality, you know? And he offered a lot of credit. More than I'd ever earned before."

Scarlet threw his hands up. "I should kill you."

Evesden backed away, colliding with the bulk of Mink's body.

"But I want you to do something for me. If you do it, I might let you live."

"What? I'll do anything you want. You can't kill me."

"I can." Koo-Suki threw her knife on the air and caught it by the hilt as it fell.

Evesden opened his mouth, closed it again and gave Scarlet a pleading look.

"Later," Scarlet said. "We need him still, but if he gives us any problem, you can do what you like with him. I know you like your fun with a knife."

"What do you want me to do?" Evesden asked. "I'll do it. I will. Anything, but don't let her hurt me."

"Next time you hear from this client of yours, tell us," Scarlet said.

Evesden nodded his head obligingly. "Yeah. I will. But I showed him a few places. He might not come back for a while."

"Give us a list of the places."

After he'd finished, Mink steered him to the door and shoved him out.

Koo-Suki turned and punched Scarlet in the arm. "Fun with a knife?"

"I wanted to scare him."

"Why is it always me who's the bad guy?" She punched him again, muttering under her breath.

"I'll set someone to watch all the sites he told us about," Mink said.

Chapter 9

A week after they'd talked to Evesden, Scarlet, accompanied by three of his bodyguards, delivered a batch of Frenzi to a crew boss in Crouch End. The customer ordered the same again for the following month, as well a small amount of Screamer, telling Scarlet that the only other supplier in the area had disappeared a few nights ago, and hadn't been seen since.

"Dead, I should think," he said. "Probably murdered by one of his own people. You can't trust anyone." He hesitated, and lowered his voice. "Your people don't give you trouble, do they?"

Scarlet frowned. He had to lean closer to catch the words. "What sort of trouble?"

"Charis was down at the Old Factory last night," the man said. "You know it?"

Scarlet nodded. It was a drink and dance club in an independent area on the edge of his territory. He had no idea who Charis was, though.

"She saw Marius Tallis there."

"So?" Marius Tallis was second-in-command, and enforcer, to Paulinna, a racketeer who controlled the turf next to Stamford Hill. She distributed the same products as Scarlet, but acted as middleman, rather than manufacturer. The two crews co-existed in an uneasy peace and occasional collaboration.

"He was with one of your juvies. That little fem, that you fought Romero for."

"I didn't…" Scarlet sighed. There was no point in arguing over rumours.

"People have been talking about her, so Charis knew who she was." The man shrugged. "I thought you'd like to know. You've always been straight with me."

"Yes," Scarlet said. "Thanks. I'll deal with it."

What was Maeve doing with Marius Tallis? Did she even know who he was? He was an unpleasant piece of work, with a broad streak of violence running through his character, and a reputation as murky as the growing wetlands. He would definitely know who Maeve was, so what was he up to? They would have to talk to Maeve, or rather, Koo-Suki would have to talk to Maeve. The employees were her jurisdiction, so she could do any necessary conversing.

Koo-Suki narrowed her eyes, when Scarlet told her. "That fem's trouble. I could tell from the beginning. I'm the first to admire ambition, but she's in too much of a hurry." She sent one of the juvies, who worked around the caff, to go and fetch Maeve.

Ten minutes later Maeve hurried down the overgrown path, pale skin shining from the humidity. Her platinum hair escaped from its ponytail, the ends curling around her head like a halo. She wore a close-fitting black skinsuit of much higher quality than the ones she'd been given when she arrived. Scarlet ran his eyes over her small figure. Where had she found the credits? Koo-Suki was making sure she paid him back her meat money. She halted by the table, giving him a shy glance from beneath her lashes.

"Maeve?" Koo-Suki spoke sharply. "What did I say to you?"

She straightened and dropped the seductive moves. "Sorry, I didn't mean—"

"Never mind." Koo-Suki gave her a cold stare. "Scarlet has some questions for you."

Maeve kept her eyes on Koo-Suki. "What's wrong?"

"I'm told you were in The Old Factory last night," Scarlet said.

Maeve's eyes moved from Koo-Suki to him. "Yeah? I'd finished my work, so I went for a drink."

"You were with Marius Tallis."

"Marius? So what?" Her eyes darted back to Koo-Suki.

"You know who he is?" Koo-Suki asked. "He works for Paulinna Skit. He's a rival. You don't socialise with our rivals. He wants something from you. What is it?"

"He doesn't." Maeve's face flushed. "He's nice to me. He takes me places, and talks to me, and doesn't hit me. He gives me things."

"He's an enemy, Maeve." Koo-Suki leaned back and stretched her booted feet out. "Did he buy you those clothes?"

"What if he did? He loves me. He told me so."

Scarlet glanced at Koo-Suki. Maeve couldn't possibly believe that.

"He's using you." Koo-Suki rolled her eyes at him. "And he has a reputation for casual violence. He used to pimp his lovers when he got tired of them. He'll hurt you eventually. Drop him."

"No. I—"

"That wasn't a suggestion," Koo-Suki said. "If you spy on us for him, then you're both dead."

"I wouldn't—"

"Drop him."

Maeve scratched at the floor with the tip of her boot, her expression sullen.

"Do as I say." Koo-Suki made a shooing motion with one hand, and Maeve left, dragging her feet.

"Do you think she'll do as she's told?" Scarlet asked.

"I don't know." Koo-Suki picked up her beer. "Did she tell you how she ended up with Romero?"

Scarlet shook his head. "Not really. There was some trouble with a client. Claws said she killed someone. I didn't believe a word of it." He hadn't talked to Maeve. He'd got the impression she might have tried to latch onto him. He didn't need the aggravation.

"It's true, I think. She tried to kill her client. She said she managed it as well. I'm not sure I believe her, but there's something not right about her."

Scarlet grinned. "She's not as sweet as she looks?"

"She's not sweet at all. She's a little shark. If she wasn't bound to cause trouble, I think I'd like her. We should keep an eye on her."

Scarlet rubbed his chin. "I'll have a word with Temmy. She can go out with him for a week or so. He'll be glad to be back selling. He'll watch her for us."

~~~

Mink stalked into the bedroom. He threw his gun down on the table, where it landed with a clatter, before crashing to the floor.

Scarlet winced. Mink usually had the temperament of a houseplant. "Be careful. Suppose that thing goes off?"

Koo-Suki rolled onto one elbow and half-opened her eyes. "Can't you lot remember that this is a bedroom. That means sleeping and, occasionally, if I get lucky, sex. Keep the noise down."

"Evesden's dead." Mink dropped onto the edge of the bed. "And so's the man we set to watching him. What the hell's going on? There must be more than one person involved."

Koo-Suki sat up.

"Fuck." Scarlet stopped unfastening his armour and leaned a shoulder against the wall. "There can't be a *gang* of psychopaths on the loose." He glanced at Mink's face. "Our only lead. Who did we lose?"

"Wilmos."

"Fuck." Wilmos had worked for them for two years. "How—"

"Shot in the head with a laser pistol," Mink said. "At least that was quick. Evesden was stabbed in the gut. He bled out. It wasn't a good death."

Koo-Suki drew her knees up to her chest. "What are we going to do? We've got to stop this. Scarlet? You're the creative one."

Scarlet snorted and resumed undressing. Ideas? He was completely out of them. "Tomorrow. I need to get some sleep first."

"There's something else," Mink said. "One of our street pedlars was badly beaten tonight and left for dead. His partner found him, and came for me. I took him to the medic, the one who'll fix non-citizens. We had to pay, but he might have died otherwise. The partner says it was Marius who attacked him. He took his product

85

and his credits and tried to force him to tell the security codes for the distribution centre."

"None of the sellers know the codes," Scarlet said. Fury burned through him. "Who was the pedlar?"

"Yeah, but that didn't stop Marius beating him till he was too damaged to talk." Mink clenched his jaw. "I'm going to do the same to him. Our boy was fourteen and small for his age. It was Petey."

Koo-Suki lay down again. "Bastard."

Scarlet slid onto the bed. "We should talk to Paulinna. Marius answers to her." He closed his eyes, but he couldn't stop thinking of Wilmos, who hadn't deserved to die, not for keeping an eye on Evesden. Tomorrow he would try and find out who was responsible. Tomorrow, he would deal with Marius. Tomorrow, he would mourn the dead. Tomorrow, he'd go and see Petey.

Next to him, Koo-Suki slept the sleep of the righteous, and on Scarlet's other side, Nyx, Mink's mutant cat (or dog, or whatever) wedged her overwarm body between him and Mink. He thought about pushing it off the bed, but didn't want to risk losing a hand. He turned onto his back and stared up at the darkness, finally falling asleep as faint light glimmered through the cracks around the window coverings.

When he woke, the others were already up and gone. Scarlet dressed and went out to find them. He tracked them down to the caff, where they sat at a small table, Mink with a plate of rice and beans in front of him, Koo-Suki an empty beaker.

Scarlet joined them, resting his head in his hands. "I don't know what to do about this killer, other than warn everyone again. I'll send some of the juvies round later, to do that."

"Good." Koo-Suki nudged him. "That'll do for now, but I wonder how he's selecting his victims. Both the ones we found were pleasagurls."

Mink sat up straight. "Someone must know. Several someones must know. He's not disposing of the bodies by himself. He didn't

86

kill Wilmos and Evesden by himself. If he did kill them. It might have been one of his men, maybe the one who met Evesden before?"

"We'll find out. Anyway, we should warn everyone to look out for Marius as well. At least until we've spoken to Paulinna." Scarlet narrowed his eyes at an approaching figure. "Well, well. Look who's here now. Let's hope he hasn't stumbled on another corpse."

Temmy ambled towards their table.

"What do you want?"

Temmy grinned, completely unfazed by Scarlet's lukewarm reception.

"I thought you were watching Maeve?"

"I was. That's why I've come."

"What?" Koo-Suki snapped.

Temmy's eyes flew to her and back to Scarlet. "She's with Marius again."

"Stupid." Koo-Suki thumped the flat of her hand onto the tabletop.

"She did try to tell him she couldn't see him, but he wouldn't listen," Temmy said. "He took her back to his flop."

"So, she just rolled over for him? You're going to have to kill her," she said to Scarlet. "Before Marius does."

"Me?" Scarlet scowled, unsure if Koo-Suki was joking. "No way. We've got to do something about Marius though. It looks like Paulinna's planning to start a war."

"You think?" Mink asked. "It all seems a bit clumsy for Paulinna."

"He gave her credits," Temmy interrupted. "Lots of them."

"What the hell's he doing?" Scarlet raised a brow at Koo-Suki. "You have another talk with her. Don't kill her though? Please?"

Koo-Suki made a noise that might have been agreement, but might not.

"Watch Kuzu," he told Mink. "Don't let her kill Maeve. I'll deal with Marius."

"How?" Koo-Suki demanded. She grinned at Scarlet's instructions.

"I'll start with a serious conversation." Scarlet beckoned to the juvie behind the bar. "Talk about disrespect. Someone told him that

I had an interest in her. He's messing with me personally. And beating one of our boys? That's not right."

"But you don't have an interest," Mink said. "So, that shouldn't matter. The boy, though, that's—"

"Off course it matters," Scarlet said. "Disrespect escalates enough, it gets you killed."

"Let me kill him," Koo-Suki said. "Security's my job."

Scarlet sighed. "Stop messing with my head, okay?" He didn't like the idea of killing people, and Koo-Suki didn't either, whatever she said. She'd been silent for days after the time she'd killed another person. They'd never talked about it, and as far as he knew, she hadn't killed anyone since. He wasn't in the mood to joke about the situation, not after last night. If Marius was offering a formal challenge, they needed to send a clear message to his boss that she couldn't tread on their turf. "Kuzu? Make sure Maeve knows exactly what the issue is. We're not trying to spoil her fun. Tell her about Petey."

Koo-Suki folded her arms. "Right."

"Temmy?" Scarlet said.

"What?" Temmy had listened to the conversation with ever-widening eyes, but if Scarlet had to identify his mood, it would be one of excitement, not fear.

"Do you know if Maeve's meeting Marius tomorrow? And if she is, where?"

Temmy pursed his lips. "I can find out. We're working together tonight. Was it Marius tried to kill Petey?"

"So I'm told. Come back to me as soon as you know where he'll be." Scarlet took Temmy's wrist and transferred a small credit. Temmy grinned and ran off, disappearing into the trees.

"Why can't life be simple?" Mink's deep voice had a theatrical whine in it.

"Why's Paulinna suddenly getting aggressive?" Scarlet pulled his thoughts together. He wasn't addressing the question to anyone in particular, he just wondered.

"Maybe it's not Paulinna," Koo-Suki said. "Maybe Marius is doing this off his own bat. He's ambitious enough. He'll never get anywhere with Paulinna unless he deposes her."

"He wants my turf?"

"Our turf," Koo-Suki corrected.

Scarlet stretched his legs out under the table and accepted a beaker of coffo from the barboy. "Perhaps we need to have a talk with Paulinna. What do you think?"

"Yeah," Mink said. "Let's see what she has to say. If you kill Marius and he's acting under her orders it might be seen as an outright declaration of war."

"I'm not going to kill him." Scarlet's denial was automatic.

Koo-Suki's eyes narrowed. "We might have to. None of us can afford to look weak. You're right, though, Mink. Even if it comes to that, it's better we know what we're walking into. We can fix Paulinna if she messes with us."

"Maybe he just likes Maeve," Scarlet said. "She is pretty. If you like the type."

"Yeah. Right." Koo-Suki snorted. "That bastard hasn't got a sentimental bone in his body."

"I'll set up a meeting with Paulinna." Mink got to his feet. "As long as you do the talking, Scarlet."

~~~

Paulinna didn't appear dangerous. She was almost as small as Maeve, dark-skinned with a winning smile, and brown eyes that were usually slumbrous with promise. At the moment, they were sharp and predatory. "War?" She raised both eyebrows. "What gives you that idea?"

They sat in a small bar on the border between Crouch End and Muswell Hill, Scarlet, Koo-Suki and Mink on one side of a rectangular table, Paulinna and her sidekick, Amina, opposite. Each side had brought three heavily armed escorts with them. All the other customers had disappeared, and the bar's owner sat on a stool behind the counter, carefully ignoring his guests.

"Where's Marius?" Koo-Suki asked.

Paulinna gave her a curious glance. "Not here, obviously. Why?"

"He beat one of our street pedlars, almost to death," Scarlet said. "And he's been seen with one of our juvies. On our ground. Of course, he might be following his dick, but is that really in character?"

Paulinna grimaced. "No. He's a cold bastard. You should tell your fem...it is a fem, isn't it?"

Scarlet nodded.

"Tell her to be careful. He killed his last one, when he caught her running some Frenzi on the side."

"Harsh," Koo-Suki said. "But the stupid fem shouldn't have been caught. Anyway, if he kills one of ours, he'll regret it."

Paulinna raised her glass in a toast.

"So? What do you think he's up to?" Scarlet pulled his eye protection off and focussed his demon eyes on her face. He still wasn't convinced she was innocent of Marius's behaviour.

"Nice," she said. "Consider me scared. He's not here, is he? That should tell you something."

Amina leaned forward and whispered into Paulinna's ear. She was a tall, slender dark woman with soft doe eyes, who had been with Paulinna for less than a year. She wore top-range body armour and carried a pistol that was almost as thick as her thigh. A bit overkill in his view, considering the weapons lined up against the wall. Still, image was important. When she sat back, Paulinna nodded. "I've got a proposition. I don't think either of us want a full-on turf war, do we?"

"No," Scarlet said, "but that's not to say we aren't prepared to defend our territory."

"Marius has lost my favour," Paulinna said. "He tried to take something from me. At gunpoint. If he shows his face here again, he's dead. He knows that."

"I'm sorry," Scarlet said.

Paulinna waved his sympathy away. "Amina killed two of his supporters, but he escaped. I don't know where he is now. I thought he'd have moved into one of the unclaimed areas, but obviously not."

"Too lazy." Amina spoke up for the first time.

"Lazy?" Koo-Suki said.

"He wants ready-made markets, a ready-made workforce. He hasn't got the patience to build anything, and he hasn't enough credit to buy out an existing business. And he's a half-wit."

"If you kill him," Paulinna said to Scarlet, "I'll owe you a favour."

Scarlet glanced at Koo-Suki. A favour was a big thing from someone like Paulinna, but she wasn't a friend. In her own way, she was sneakier than Marius. He stood up, signalling to the escorts. "Okay. I'll do some investigations of my own. We'll be in touch."

He walked out with Koo-Suki. Mink lingered, to pay the bar-owner for the use of his space. The hoverboards were outside, with two more armed escorts.

"Well, that was interesting." Koo-Suki pulled her face protector into position. "What gave Paulinna the idea that we'd be her hired assassins? We're not that sort of organisation."

"We can talk back at the den," Scarlet said. "I don't want to hang about here. Come on Mink."

Once they were back on their own territory, in their own caff, Scarlet called one of his young pedlars. "Fetch Maeve."

The juvie disappeared into the night.

"What are you thinking?" Mink signalled to one of the juvies, who brought over a trio of beers and a tube of R'lax.

"Maybe set up Maeve to trap him," Scarlet said. "I want to talk to him before we do anything drastic. Maybe he's using Maeve to cheer himself up after his fall-out with Paulinna. Maybe we'll just have to give him a beating and throw him off our turf."

Koo-Suki rolled her eyes. "He's still disrespecting us. And I think Paulinna has a nerve, trying to get us to do her dirty work."

"Mmm," Mink picked up his drink. "We can't be sure she's not just playing us. She's held that territory for a long time. She's a tricky one. Still, we should do something about Marius. He nearly killed little Petey. I've a mind to end him just for that."

Scarlet nodded.

Koo-Suki squinted into her own drink. "Would Maeve betray him? When I was her age I wouldn't have. It's romantic to protect your lover."

"I was your lover when you were her age," Scarlet pointed out.

"And me," Mink said.

"My point exactly," Koo-Suki said. "And did I betray you?"

Mink snorted. "You never had a romantic bone in your body."

Koo-Suki punched him in the arm.

"You were loyal though," Scarlet patted her thigh, comfortingly. "But we're different, we're family. We rise or fall together. Maeve's a loner. She probably thinks Marius can help her get established. She's looking for security, and who can blame her?"

"Me," Koo-Suki said. She wiped her mouth. "All right, I get that. She wants a better life. Fine, but not at our expense. We have to protect ourselves. I told her not to mess with us. I warned her."

"I wouldn't trust her, even if she offered to bring him to us wrapped in chains." Scarlet rethought his suggestion. "He's her lover. What sort of person would do that? At the least, her loyalties will be torn."

"Okay," Koo-Suki said. "We'll just talk to her."

"I'll talk to her," Scarlet said. "You scare the shit out of her."

"Her?" Koo-Suki snorted. "She's not scared of anyone. She's an idiot."

Chapter 10

"Where were you last night?" Scarlet asked Maeve. One of his men had brought her to the caff, before she left for her job. "I sent someone to find you."

"I finished my work," she said.

"That's not what I asked."

"I went to a bar with a friend." Her mouth set into stubborn lines.

"You're still seeing Marius?" Scarlet settled back in his chair. Maeve perched on the edge of a stool opposite him, wearing a high-quality skinsuit in midnight blue. It showed off her slight figure and contrasted with her colouring. The last one she'd worn had been black. Her pale silky hair was pulled into a tail on the top of her head, and hung down her back, a streak of creamy blonde. She was cute, but he wondered where she had found the credits to buy the skinsuits.

She stared at her tightly clasped hands. "I'm sorry." Her voice was a husky whisper. She raised her head and looked at him through long dark lashes.

He frowned. Last time he'd seen her, her lashes had been pale, as pale as her hair. Another expense she needed to account for. "We told you not to see him."

"But I love him."

Scarlet sighed. He doubted that very much.

"And he loves me."

"Maeve?"

She met his naked eyes without flinching.

"We told you to drop him. I don't care whether you love him or he loves you. You've disobeyed a direct order."

"You said I wasn't property." She scowled at him.

"What?"

"If I'm not, then you can't tell me what to do."

"No." Scarlet jabbed his forefinger at her. "But I can throw you out. Will you survive without protection?"

"I can look after myself." Her eyes slid away from his. "And Marius will look after me."

Scarlet narrowed his eyes. "He won't be able to look after himself, let alone anyone else. He's made an enemy of his old boss, and if you think Koo-Suki's scary, then you need to meet Paulinna."

"He's going places." Some of the defiance had faded from Maeve's voice. "He's got credits. He gives me presents."

Scarlet had a good idea where Marius thought he was going, and that was into his shoes. It wasn't going to happen. "He nearly killed one of our sellers last night."

"I don't believe you," Maeve said. "Who?"

"Petey." He'd visited Petey, earlier. The boy wouldn't be able to walk for weeks.

"He's just a kid," Maeve said. "Marius wouldn't do that. You're lying."

Scarlet got to his feet and leaned forward, resting his hands on the table and thrusting his face towards her. "I'll let you think about it. Consider your options, that's all I'm saying."

She stood up, shifting from one foot to the other. "I don't want to go independent." Her eyes pleaded with him. "But I want citizenship. And Marius…"

Scarlet hardened his heart. "Think about it. And while you're thinking, you might consider Petey. Go and see what your lover did."

Her eyes flashed with anger. "Liar." She ran down the path and into the woods, her pale hair swinging.

"What did she say?" Mink appeared from the darkness, followed by Koo-Suki.

Scarlet turned his chair round, and straddled it, resting his arms on the back. "She's an idiot. *Marius loves me,*" he mimicked. "I told her to think about it. She doesn't want to be thrown out, so she can't be that serious about him. She didn't believe he'd beat someone up."

"So?"

"We can't trust her to help us deal with him. Temmy's following her. I've got a couple of men looking for Marius. I'd like a word with him."

"Before you kill him?" Koo-Suki asked.

Scarlet grimaced. "I hope I don't have to." The memory of Petey's small battered body, flooded his mind. He'd never killed anyone personally before, but he might screw up the motivation to finish Marius off. "I want to know what he thinks he's doing. We can't let ourselves be fucked over by him *or* Paulinna."

Mink pointed at the point where the trees encroached into the clearing around the caff. "That's one of our men, he's waving at you, Scarlet."

"He's been looking for Marius for me." Scarlet beckoned him over.

The man hurried to their table. "I found him. He's holed up on our turf, right up by the old pits. Where the marshes start, at the edge of the wetlands."

"Good. Worth me heading up there?"

"He's got armed minders with him," the man said. "He was going down to meet that fem of yours after midnight. I heard him say so. She's got a loose mouth, Scarlet. She's been telling him all sorts of things about our setup."

Mink swore.

"She doesn't know that much," Scarlet said.

"She's told him where our factory is, and where the workers sleep."

"How do you know that?"

"The men he's attracted are a bunch of no-goods," the man said. "Looser mouths than your fem."

"Do you know where he planned to meet Maeve?"

"Yeah. Abney's bar. He's only taking one man with him."

Scarlet stared at the table top, thinking. Why did Marius want to know where the staff accommodation was? "Come on Mink. We'll go and have a chat with him. Before Maeve arrives. Koo? You want to come as well?"

She shook her head. "I've things to do. You two should be enough. See you later." She disappeared into the night.

Mink pushed himself to his feet. "Get someone to delay Maeve," he told the messenger. "And organise a couple of men to come with us. Armed."

Marius was already in Abney's bar when Scarlet's party arrived. He sat at a small table with his minder. He was perfectly groomed, his armoured skinsuit was the latest design from the city markets, and his blond hair hung in a beaded plait down his back.

"Pretty, isn't he?" Scarlet whispered to Mink. "I could fall for him myself."

Mink's mouth twitched in amusement. The two of them pulled chairs up to the table. Marius's head jerked towards them in surprise.

"Not expecting us?" Scarlet asked. Everyone knew Marius was not very bright. He had been muscle for Paulinna, as well as entertainment. His reputation was for thoughtless brutality, not strategic thinking. Or any sort of thinking.

"No. Why would I be? What are you doing here?"

"We're here to see you," Mink said.

"You've been making free with what's ours recently," Scarlet said.

Mink nodded his head. "That's right."

"I don't know what you're talking about."

"I hear that you've broken with Paulinna," Scarlet said. "She doesn't seem very happy with you."

Marius's gaze drifted over Scarlet's shoulder to assess the threat from his three men. "That bitchfem Amina told you that? She never liked me. And she's got Paulinna in her pocket."

"Right. So that's why you're messing with our space?"

"I'm weighing up my options." Marius sipped his drink, his eyes never leaving Scarlet.

"And you've been romancing one of our pedlars. Picking her brains." Scarlet let his voice drop to a threatening tone.

"Picking her brains?" Marius laughed. "Maeve? She told you that? What brains? She's just a failed pleasagurl. Good to look at, good for a fuck, but that's all."

Scarlet wished Maeve could have heard him. It would have cleared up any illusions she had about Marius's intentions. "Why were you asking her about our business then? Gets you excited, does it?"

Marcus's brow creased.

"And you beat up one of our boys."

"Me?" Marius said. "No, I didn't. It must have been someone else. I wouldn't waste my time on a kid."

"Why do you want to know where our peoples' flop is? And I heard you're gathering an army." Scarlet glanced at Mink. "What do you think of that? On our territory?"

Mink shook his head. "Sounds bad." He rubbed his knuckles, decorated tonight with duster rings. "Sounds hostile."

For the first time Marius looked alarmed. "Not to use against you. And the flop? Mink, I was just chatting to the fem, for fuckssake. Making conversation. Scarlet, you can't imagine that I—"

"I imagine nothing." Scarlet stood up, convinced that he'd been right about Marius's intentions. "I want to talk to you. Alone." A pulse thudded in his temple. He might really have to kill the man. He glanced at Marius's companion, whose hand edged towards his weapon. "Leave that."

The man placed his hands on the table.

"I'll want to talk to you as well."

The man paled as Marius gave him a warning frown.

Scarlet nodded to his own men. They removed the weapons from the table top. "You first."

Mink hauled Marius's man to his feet and dragged him to the door.

"Make sure he stays put." Scarlet pointed at Marius. The armed escorts took up position on either side of him. "And take his weapons off him."

Marius's mouth opened as though he wanted to say something, then closed again as he realised there was no point.

Scarlet followed Mink and his captive round the corner of the building.

Mink slammed the man against the rough wall. "Scarlet? You want to talk to him?"

Scarlet moved in front of the man and stared at him. His eyes often made people keen to talk. The man turned his head sideways.

"What's your boss gathering an army for?" Scarlet asked him.

The man shrugged and spat out of the corner of his mouth.

"Nasty habit." Mink polished his knuckle rings with the end of his sleeve, before removing them and punching the man in the gut.

When he finished choking, he gave Scarlet a sour look.

"You owe Marius no loyalty," Scarlet said.

The man grimaced. "He promised to pay us. Big credits."

"Has he?"

"No."

"Then he hasn't bought you yet," Scarlet pointed out. "Has he?"

The man squeezed his eyes shut in thought.

"Do you want Mink to hit you again?" Scarlet asked.

"No." The man held up both hands. "No. It was a stupid idea, but my job isn't to ask questions."

"Go on."

"We were going to come after you and him, and Koo-suki."

"Seriously?" Scarlet said.

"Marius said you were complacent. Soft. Flabby. You'd be easy." The man shook his head in disbelief. "I'd heard different but—"

"Flabby?" Mink sounded insulted.

"Not me. I didn't believe it." The man gave him a nervous look. "That fem of yours? The one he'd been romancing, she told him where your place was, where the different stuff was made."

"Maeve's been with us less than a couple of months. She knows nothing," Scarlet said. Marius was living up to his reputation for stupidity.

"Kuzu's going to kill her," Mink said.

"Yeah." Scarlet laughed. "She might be better going independent. More chance of staying alive." He stopped laughing abruptly and pointed at the man. "Get out. Go a long way. If you come back, I'll kill you."

"Or I will." Mink held up a fistful of metal.

The man sidled along the wall and disappeared into the shadow of a ramshackle building on the edge of the marshlands. Scarlet watched him go. "That was easy."

"We're going to have to deal with Marius," Mink said. "We might have to kill him."

"Yeah." Scarlet flicked a flying insect away. He'd never killed anyone before. A range of alternatives flashed through his mind. He dismissed them. "Maybe. We should probably let Maeve see. Let him tell her how he was using her, first."

"Right," Mink said. "Knock some sense into her. She won't live long if she doesn't smarten up."

"Come on." Scarlet went back to the bar and gestured to the men to bring Marius out.

"You stay here," he said to one of the escorts. "Tell Maeve we've taken her lover to the old burial place in Abner Park."

"What?" Marius struggled in the grip of the two men. "Why there?"

"You don't get to ask questions," Mink said.

"No. Just answer them," Scarlet said. "And you can explain to Maeve, exactly why you were interested in her." He led the way along the narrow path, through the marshy ground and decaying buildings, towards the old cemetery. As they approached the broken gates, Marius twisted free, pulling a knife from inside his chest protector and lunging at Scarlet, who pivoted away, so that the knife glanced off the armour of his sleeve. Before he could retaliate, Mink punched Marius in the side of the head. He crumpled to the ground.

"Get up." Scarlet nudged him with one foot. He didn't move. Scarlet kicked him harder.

"Shit, Mink. You've killed him."

"I barely touched him." Mink crouched down next to the collapsed body. "No. There's a pulse. He's going to be out for a while, though." He stood up again.

Scarlet glared at the two escorts who looked sheepish. "What the fuck do you think you were playing at? Are you functional or just decorative? You let him grab a knife. You were supposed to search him."

"Sorry Scarlet." The older one spread his arms out in apology. "I don't know what happened. He just—"

"Never mind." Scarlet frowned down at Marius. Blood dripped from the point where his forehead met his hairline. The side of his forehead was dented. "Mink? Look at his head. Did you break something?"

"Maybe. He must have brittle bones or something."

"Nice punch. You're still wearing the rings."

"I forgot. Didn't have time to think." Mink rubbed a speck of blood off his fingers, with a broad leaf plucked from one of the shrubs.

What to do now? Scarlet glanced again at Marius. "Do you think he'll wake up? His skull looks like it's fractured."

Mink bent down again. "Doubt it. Shit. Shit. What now?"

Scarlet's eyes narrowed. "Wait here," he told the escorts. "I want to check something. Come with me, Mink." He pushed his way into the graveyard, through the undergrowth, dodging the broken remains of headstones, until he came to a clearing. It was surrounded by small trees and an explosion of plant life. The centre was a large square, made of paving slabs, with a flat stone tomb in the middle.

"What are we doing here?" Mink sounded plaintive as he pushed past Scarlet and surveyed the space.

"Let's put Marius on here, then we can see what we're doing. When Maeve comes, she'll spot him straight away."

"Why?" Mink's face screwed up in confusion.

"He's likely going to die, anyway," Scarlet said. "There's no way he's going to tell Maeve anything now." He pushed a branch aside, ignoring Mink's loud curses as it sprung back into his face. "I don't want to kill Maeve, not after the hassle of getting her off Romero, but we need to do something about her. If people think she betrayed us, and we do nothing, it makes us look dud."

"I suppose so."

"You know I'm right."

"So, what's your plan?"

"She sees him here. She sees us finish him, and she'll tell people. She'll be more careful in future, and we'll have shown we don't take betrayal lightly."

"I hope you know what you're doing," Mink said. "She strikes me as an 'act first, think later' sort of fem."

Scarlet ignored him and gave his instructions to the escorts. One waited for Maeve at the entrance to the cemetery; the others concealed themselves in the shadows of the graveyard.

Scarlet hung back with Mink in the darkness of an ancient half-dead yew tree. In front of him, less than a couple of meters away, the stone sarcophagus rose like a sacrificial altar, illuminated by the pale rays of an almost full moon. Its corners crumbled, and the stone cross at one end was missing both its arms. Marius's body sprawled across the surface, face up to the sky.

"Who's going to finish him off?" Mink muttered.

"You started it." Scarlet said. "I'll finish him." His stomach clenched, but it was only fair.

The cemetery was almost peaceful. Only the normal rustlings of small nocturnal mammals disturbed the quiet. Once they stopped talking, he could have been completely alone. Mink was invisible in the darkness, and the escorts were at least fifty metres away. Abner cemetery had escaped most of the destruction of the war years, and was high enough to escape the flooding that had devastated London before the wall had been built. It had been designated an area of historical interest, but it was outside the walls, so very few people ever set foot in it. And no one came after dark. It was as wild as the rest of outer London, just the sort of place that the Silencer might dump his bodies. Despite the heat of the night, Scarlet shivered.

Where was Maeve? He stared at the sarcophagus. A black slug glided over the top edge. It had to be at least six inches long.

The ferns rustled, the sound merging with the rattle of small stones. Someone was coming. He leapt onto the top of the tomb, to stand with his legs astride, one foot on either side of Marius's body. It was impossible to tell if he was still alive.

Maeve emerged from behind what had once been a marble angel, propelled by a push from one of the escorts. She paused, muttered something to the escort, and squeezed past a miniature temple. When she saw Scarlet, she hesitated, hands upon her hips. "Scarlet? What do..." She spotted the figure stretched between Scarlet's legs. "Who's that?" Her voice held curiosity rather than fear.

Scarlet bent, and grabbing Marius's long plait, dragged his head up so that Maeve could see his face. Strands of thick blond hair fell forwards, obscuring his features. Scarlet pushed it back with his other hand, revealing the ruin of Marius's forehead. A snorting breath came from him. He *was* still alive.

She froze. "What have you done? You've killed him?"

"Not yet." Scarlet released Marius's hair, letting his head thud to the stone. The anger he'd managed to suppress rose in him. How dare she make a fuss over this lowlife, brainless, boy-battering pond scum? He hadn't saved her life for this. Did she have no sense of self-preservation? Didn't she care that he was a killer? Didn't she care that he'd almost killed Petey? "You know who he is then?"

"Marius." She didn't move, but her body quivered with the urge to rush forward.

"He's an enemy. You were supposed to stay away from him. We warned you. Did you think we were joking?"

"He's not my enemy." Maeve folded her arms. "Leave him alone."

"That's what you think. Anyway, he's trespassed here. Tried to take what's mine. I can't let him get away with that."

"I'm not yours."

"I wasn't talking about you." Scarlet scowled at her. Pretty boy Marius had interfered with his business and almost murdered one of his pedlars. He probably wouldn't have thought twice about killing Maeve either. It would have served her right. He kicked the body hard with one foot, feeling something break beneath his boot. He flinched.

"No. Don't. Scarlet, please." Maeve edged between the weathered gravestones. Her face was pale, bloodless in the moonlight. Fear had wiped away her elfin prettiness.

Scarlet forced himself to smile at her from his perch on the sarcophagus. Maeve was lucky. Anyone else in his position would have killed her. He nudged the unconscious figure with one foot, gently this time, and bent to pull a knife from the sheath in the side of his boot.

The slug had paused in its journey, pulling its horns in and arching its back. Scarlet picked it up and placed it on the ivy around the base of the cross. He didn't want to stand on it.

Maeve's mouth opened but nothing came out.

"Look Maeve?" Scarlet showed her the knife. "Marius disrespected us. We can't let anyone get away with it. You know that. He took what was ours. Tried to take more."

"Yours?" Maeve's face tensed with rage. "I was never yours." She rocked on the balls of her feet, ready to jump.

"Mine." He didn't mean it, but she annoyed him. "Ours. Who got you out of Romero's crib? Who stopped him from beating you to death? Who owns your loyalty? You haven't paid back the flesh-cost yet."

103

"I know." Maeve took another step forward. "I know. But you said I was free. Please. Put that knife down."

Scarlet stooped and dragged his knife across Marius's throat, trying not to think about what he was doing. He jumped off the tomb, avoiding the spurting blood, as Maeve rushed forward. She bent over her lover's body trying to stop the stream of blood with her small hands. Maybe she really had loved him, but if so, she was an idiot and he'd saved her from a world of disillusion. She was lucky she wasn't facing Koo-Suki.

He dug his knife into the soil, and wiped it on the leaves of a fern, the muscles in his legs trembling. The black slug had moved from the ivy, back onto the stone of the cross. Scarlet dragged in a lungful of air, then another.

Maeve looked up. "He was my chance. My way out. He was going to help with getting my citizenship. You've spoiled it all. I'll get you for this." Her breathy voice was harsh with fury.

"Marius? Citizenship?" Scarlet forced himself to laugh. "You believed that?"

She stamped her foot. "You'll be sorry." She spun round and ran back the way she'd come.

Scarlet slipped the knife into the side of his boot.

"You did that like a pro." Mink joined him.

"I feel sick." He walked to a raised grave and sat down, elbows on knees, head in his hands.

"You've missed your way in life." Mink patted his shoulder. "You should have been a vid star. Come on, get up. We should go."

Scarlet stayed where he was and rubbed a small mark on his sleeve. "Is that blood?"

"Just mud. Come on Scarlet. You can't stay here."

Chapter 11

Maeve stamped along the marshy path, back towards the flophouse. She had nowhere else to go. Disappointment and rage wrestled in her gut. Marius was dead. Of course, she knew he'd lied about loving her, but he'd still been good to her, buying her presents, offering to help her find a job with potential prospects. Now she had no hope of citizenship. Fury at Scarlet sent her heartrate to the sky, made her want to scream at the night. She shoved a wet yew branch out of her way, barely noticing as it slapped back across her chest. All those lies about Marius. She hadn't known him for long, but she knew he wouldn't beat a child. *Would he?*

She took a deep breath and crouched down to wipe the palms of her hands on a deep patch of moss growing over a heap of stone. They were sticky with Marius's blood. Once she'd scrubbed them clean, she closed her eyes, seeing again, the pool of dark blood on the stone under her lover's body. Her eyes stung with unshed tears. Marius had been her first step to a better life. She opened her eyes again, rubbing them until she was sure she wouldn't cry.

When she reached the fork in the path, she paused, reluctant to go into the flophouse. Other people would be there, and she didn't want to talk to anyone, or even see anyone. Her heart still pounded against her ribs. What was she going to do, now? Scarlet would pay. Mink and Koo-Suki too, but Scarlet was the one who'd killed Marius. She clenched her fists.

Once in the flophouse, she stamped to her bunk, uncaring whether she woke anyone else. She pulled the thin cover over her head and tried to breath herself into sleep. It was mid-morning when she woke, still tired and wrapped in angry misery. She dressed in her new blue skinsuit and headed for the back door of the caff, hoping to avoid everyone. Two of the juvie chem pedlars sat at a small indoor table, but Maeve grabbed a serving of cereal and carried it to an unoccupied table on the other side of the room. She ate it slowly, letting depression settle over her.

The sound of a chair scraping against the stone floor pulled her out of her thoughts. Tamsin sat down opposite her. Maeve scowled, willing her to go away.

"New skinsuit, Maeve? Don't look like that. I haven't seen you for a while." Tamsin plonked her coffo beaker on the table. "Did you hear about last night?"

"What?" Maeve jerked to attention. Scarlet hadn't had time to let people know he'd killed Marius and surely no one had found the body yet. No one went in Abney Park cemetery, especially at night. "Who told—"

"Another body," Tamsin said. "Right in our territory. And they say it's a citizen. From inside the walls and just dumped here, where anyone could find it. The others were all hidden. The Guard is everywhere. They're questioning Scarlet, Mink and Koo-Suki right now. Can you believe it?"

At the mention of Scarlet's name, rage erupted in Maeve's stomach again. He had said she was free. It looked like that was fine as long as she didn't do anything he didn't like. She was almost as much a prisoner as she'd been with Romero. She squashed the small voice that said she wasn't being used as a sex-slave, that no one had threatened to chain her to a bunk until she festered in her own wastes. No one had left her to die, serving the sort of clients who didn't care about wallowing in filth. No one had threatened to skin her alive. "Why? Do they suspect them?"

"Nah. They're going to talk to everyone," Tamsin said. "At the moment, they're being polite, but everyone's ready to run if that changes. We're prepared."

"Run? Do they really think one of us is the killer?"

"I hope you've got an alibi?" Tamsin said. "I heard you had a way with knives."

"Oh, shut up." Maeve pushed her cereal bowl away. "Why's there such a fuss about this one?"

"Citizen?" Tamsin said. "Didn't you listen to me? She's a registered citizen."

"What the hell was she doing down here then?"

"Don't know," Tamsin said. "Maybe he just dumped her here."

Maeve stood up. "Got to go." She ambled out of the caff, chewing on her thumbnail. What would happen if the entire organisation ran? Should she go with them? Would she be allowed to? Would Scarlet and the others throw her out? She had a small amount of credit left from the gifts Marius had given her, but it wouldn't last long. At least she had the skinsuits. She wouldn't look like a complete loser if she had to find new work or protection.

Two men in the dull black armour of Central Law Enforcement blocked the main path leading from the caff. Two more guarded the way out, into the woods. All four carried light anti-personnel weapons. One of them raised his gun as Maeve passed him. She rolled her eyes. Who was going to attack law enforcement in full daylight? It was an easy way to get the entire region flattened, emptied of human life and re-formed as wilderness.

Koo-Suki, Maeve and Scarlet sat at one of the outdoor tables, surrounded by more Law Enforcement figures. A man and two women sat opposite, one of the women leaning forward, talking. Maeve was too far way to hear, and she turned onto the path leading away from the caff. She wasn't sure where she was going, but she didn't want to see Scarlet. Her hands curled into claws as she thought about him. She would try and kill him if she had to see him. Then Koo-Suki would cut her into little bits with that knife she waved about. Eyes on the ground, she crashed into a solid object.

"Watch it." Two large hands in black gloves descended on her shoulders, steadying her. "Where do you think you're going?"

She looked up. The enforcement officer was at least a foot taller than her, and like the ones at the caff, he wore full body armour, and a helmet with face protection and dark glasses. He looked like something from one of her nightmares. "I'm sorry, Sir." She used her breathy childish voice.

"Where are you going?" he asked again. "No one's supposed to leave."

"I didn't know." She twisted her hands together and gave him a pleading look. "I only just woke up. No one told me." His dark glasses made it impossible to tell whether he believed her, whether he was preparing to arrest her, or whether he was softened by her pleading. She was glad she was wearing the nice skinsuit; it showed her off to the best advantage.

"Come on." He took her arm and tugged her after him. Fairly gently.

"Where are you taking me?" Everything she'd heard about the security forces ran through her mind. "I haven't done anything wrong."

"Then you've nothing to worry about." He led her back to the caff and to a table away from everyone else. Scarlet, Koo-Suki and Mink had moved to a smaller, round table, and were alone. As Maeve passed, she met Koo-Suki's gaze. Koo's eyes narrowed in warning. Maeve glanced at Scarlet, who ignored her. She clenched her teeth. She would get him.

"Sit down." The enforcer released her arm and pushed her onto the bench. He sat down next to her, a bulky intimidating presence. "Do you know who's behind these killings?"

"No. Of course not." Maeve gave a tiny shiver, not enough to be theatrical, but enough so that the officer would notice. "I'm sorry."

He took off his face protector and dark glasses, and smiled reassuringly at her. "Why would you? This is just a formality. We have to talk to everyone."

He was younger than she expected, probably only a few years older than her. "It's horrible," she said. "Everyone's terrified."

"We'll catch him," the officer said, "but in the meantime, you should be very careful."

"I will be." Maeve examined him through her dropped eyelashes. She'd always thought that the Guards asked questions with their fists. They were nightmare figures to most unregistered people outside the walls. This one was polite.

"I need to ask you some questions," he said. "Just routine."

"Okay."

"Where were you last night?"

Maeve bit her lip. "I was out by the old New Road. Where it meets the main path."

"What time?"

"From ten until half-past midnight."

"Were you alone?"

"I was with Temmy, one of the others."

"Temmy? I think we've already talked to him," the officer said. "He told us he was with a fem. I guess that's you."

Maeve nodded.

"And after that? Just to be sure you're clear?"

"I went to a bar up near Abney Park."

"Don't look so worried," the officer said. "The body was miles away from there. I think you're clear. The boy's story confirms yours. If you remember anything else, give me a call." He touched his chip to her wrist and lowered his voice. "Call me anyway. I'll buy you a drink."

Maeve hid her surprise behind a smile. "Thank you, Sir." She would definitely call him; it was the first time, since Holbeck, that anyone with citizenship had shown an interest in her. He might be just as useful as poor Marius. Maybe more.

As she walked away, Koo-Suki called to her. "Maeve? A word please."

She stopped.

"Maeve. Here. Now."

She dragged her feet as she approached the table with the three murderers.

"Sit down." Koo-Suki patted a seat next to her.

Maeve slid into it, perching on the edge and turning a resentful gaze on Scarlet.

"You were passing information to our enemy." Koo-Suki fingered her knife, ignoring the presence of the City Guards. Her voice was low.

Maeve kept her own voice to a murmur. "It wasn't like that. It wasn't an interrogation. We were just talking. He didn't need to kill him." She pointed at Scarlet. "We were only getting to know each other."

"You tell yourself that if it helps," Koo-Suki said. "Me? I don't care. I'm not interested. You disobeyed our orders. If you do that again, you'll be as dead as he is."

Maeve's face flushed with rage. "He didn't have to kill him," she repeated.

Scarlet shrugged as though he didn't care.

"He was an enemy," Koo-Suki said. "He wanted to take over our operation. If that doesn't bother you, then maybe you'll care that he told Scarlet he'd been using you. He called you a failure, that you were just a pretty fucktoy."

Maeve clenched her fists and half rose from the chair.

Mink on her other side grabbed her arm and pulled her back down.

"Liar." She spat the words at Scarlet. "He didn't say that."

Scarlet's expression was hidden behind dark glasses.

"You need to be more careful who you mix with," Mink said.

"Liar." She glared at Scarlet. "You're lying." Her voice rose and one of the law enforcers turned to look at her. "He wouldn't say that."

"Keep your voice down." Koo-Suki hissed the words at her. "And show some respect."

"Watch who you talk to in future." Scarlet waved a hand in her direction. "Go away, now."

Maeve's legs trembled as she walked away. She wanted to grab the knife from Koo-Suki and sink it into all three of them. She hated every one of them. They'd all been in on killing Marius. And they were wrong. He wouldn't have called her a fucktoy. Her gut squirmed with rage, the anger climbing through her body. As soon as she was outside, she staggered into the long grass and threw up her breakfast. Afterwards, she pressed a hand against her hollow stomach and took a few breaths of the damp muggy air, in an effort to calm herself. It didn't work. She would find a way to get even. There was always that Guard, the one who'd asked her to call him. She'd do that later, when everyone had gone out to work. That would teach Scarlet. Koo-Suki and Mink, as well. Maybe if she gave him information, the officer would help her, maybe find her a new job. She didn't want to stay in this one, even if they'd have her. She stalked off down the path. She'd call him now.

Chapter 12

The City Guard dispersed as darkness fell, but tension still filled the settlement.

"Is it worth meeting Claws tonight?" Koo-Suki asked as Scarlet pulled on his body armour. "Wouldn't it be better to leave it for a few days?"

"I'll be careful." Scarlet said. He had promised Claws the first delivery of Frenzi, and wanted to be sure it got to him. The Guard might start poking about in the warehouses, if they got bored, possibly seizing the product, and selling it for themselves. "They're not interested in small fry chem pedlars. Not yet. The chem, maybe, but not us."

"Are you sure Claws won't have gone into hiding?"

Scarlet shrugged. He was curious about whether the Guards had bothered Claws's crew. Besides, he was restless. It was impossible to relax. He didn't feel guilty about killing Marius, but he couldn't help thinking about the blood, the dent in his skull, and Maeve's face, when she realised he was dead. Work would take his mind off it all. "I've nothing else to do. We don't lose anything by going."

"Fine. Take a good bodyguard."

He nodded. "I'll take three." He chose three men who'd worked for him for a couple of years, all of them reliable, and as far as he could tell, loyal.

Claws's organisation hadn't been bothered at all by the murder enquiry. They were further from the city than Scarlet's base. "We didn't have a dead citizen on our turf," Claws said. "How come you don't know who's doing it? You aren't losing your grip, are you?"

All three of Scarlet's escorts fingered their weapons. Scarlet removed his glasses. "Try me and find out."

"Just joking." Claws shifted uneasily. "Thanks for the Frenzi. We'd like the same amount next month and I'll see you next week for the DeathDreamer."

On the way back Scarlet stopped at a new popup bar, to drop off a small amount of Dreamer he'd promised to the owner.

"Thanks." The barman took the bag with the Dreamer shots and brought them all beers. Scarlet leaned back in his chair, sipping on the beer and watching the action in the room. Most of the customers were beer drinkers but there were a couple, in a dark corner, who were definitely on something stronger. The Dreamer probably, as they lay back on stained, sagging couches, eyes half-closed, breathing heavily. He couldn't understand why people did this – took themselves out of life. He'd never been tempted by his own product. R'lax smokies were the farthest he went. It was the same for Mink and Koo-Suki, but maybe these people had such awful lives that...

A scuffle at the door drew his attention and he squinted through the smoky dimness. "Temmy? What the hell are you doing out here?"

Temmy pushed past the doormen and rushed to his table, breathing heavily. Scarlet and all three of his escorts got to their feet.

"I ran all the way." Temmy bent over, trying to catch his breath. "Koo-Suki sent me. She said to tell you not to go home."

"She said what?" Scarlet offered Temmy his beaker of beer.

Temmy took a long gulp. "The Guards are looking for you."

"Me? Why? They spoke to me this morning."

"They think you're the Silencer."

"What?" Scarlet's voice was completely flat, his mind an empty space. Around him, his three escorts stiffened.

"That's what they said. While they were talking to Mink, Koo-Suki told me to find you."

"But why should they think—"

Temmy's breathing was almost back to normal. "I don't know."

Scarlet took back his beaker and finished off the beer. His mind still couldn't process the information. He patted Temmy's shoulder. "Okay. You've passed on the message. Go back to Kuzu and tell her I'll be in our safe place by dawn." No one apart from the three of them knew where the safe place was. Hopefully, he'd be able to get there. Hopefully, Koo could tell him what was going on.

Temmy's face screwed up with worry. "Be careful, Scarlet. If the Guard catches you—"

"They won't." Scarlet was fully aware of what the Guard would do if they caught him and he had to quell his own rising panic. He didn't want to scare the boy and he definitely didn't want to show weakness in front of his escorts.

Temmy hesitated.

"Go on." Scarlet made a shooing motion. "Kuzu must be worried."

Temmy slowly turned away.

"Keep yourself safe," Scarlet called after him, fighting the urge to run immediately. "Tell Kuzu and Mink to take care. Tell them to get out if they can. Tell them I'll see them soon."

"Scarlet?" The escort nearest to him sounded nervous. "Why would they be coming after you? You can't be the Silencer. You've never—"

"Thanks." Scarlet forced himself to grin at the man, who lowered his eyes in embarrassment. "I don't know, but I guess someone pointed them in my direction." He picked up one of the half-full glasses and sipped at the contents while he thought. "Who'd do that though? None of our people would speak to the guards. Anyway, if people round here thought I was the Silencer, they'd have a whip round and pay for my assassination themselves."

"What are you going to do?"

Scarlet put the empty glass down. "We're all going to leave now. You'll escort me to the edge of our turf, then go back to the den. You'll tell Kuzu or Mink that I've followed our plans. As far as you're concerned, I'll disappear."

The escort frowned. "We can't just leave you."

"You can if I order it. I'm ordering it."

The escort's frown deepened.

Scarlet ignored him, and carefully fitted his head protector over his crest of hair. "Come on. We should go" He led the way to the crossroads where the main path met with several minor ones. All the paths disappeared beyond ruined buildings, into the scrubby woodland. He halted. "This is where I leave you. Keep safe."

The senior of the escorts, Jayden Sith, his name was, set his feet apart, bristling with outrage. "I'm not going. My job is to protect you. You pay me to do that."

"You shouldn't know where I'm heading. Then if anyone asks you, you can tell them you don't know. Suppose they use a truth drug on you?"

Jayden gestured at the others. "You go now. Do as he says. I'm staying."

Scarlet waited until the sounds of their departure died away, leaving only the rustlings of the night. He fingered his gun, aware that Jayden's eyes had darted to it before returning to his face.

"I've been with you since you set up in business for yourself," Jayden said. "I know you aren't the Silencer. That's the stupidest thing I've ever heard. Anyway, I know what my job is and I know you're not going to kill me for doing it."

Scarlet hesitated. Jayden had always been reliable. He moved his hand away from his weapon. No way could he shoot a man who'd been nothing other than loyal. "Then you know more than I do." He supposed he had to trust someone. "Come on then, if you're coming." Turning away, he headed down a narrow muddy track between two rows of broken buildings and almost completely blocked by a tangle of thorny branches and small trees. A long lethal offshoot, from some low-growing plant, wrapped itself around his calf, dragging at the hi-tech fabric of his skinsuit. "Fuck." He unwound it, and stepped over.

"Are you sure you know where you're going?"

Scarlet inspected his leg, brushing at a loose fibre. Fortunately, his clothes were still intact. "Yeah." He set off again, more cautiously.

A moment later, the path cleared. It was still narrow and muddy, clogged by rubble, but most of the growth had been hacked away. He, or Mink, or Koo-Suki, took it in turns to check the path, to make sure it was difficult to find, and to keep it free of too much growth. He waited for Jayden.

"Have you no idea who might have fingered you?" Jayden asked.

Scarlet considered. "Not really. It could have been anyone. Romero? Paulinna? But why me, and not Mink or Kuzu? They must know the others won't let it go. If we hadn't killed Marius, I'd say it was him, but he's dead, so no, I've no clue." A tingle of suspicion pushed at his thoughts.

Three hours later they arrived at his destination. He'd taken a roundabout route, hoping it would confuse anyone who might follow. The safe place was in a part of outer London which had once been smart and desirable. It was as overgrown and ruined as everywhere else now, and the place he was heading for was a broken down mid-terraced house in a row of slowly collapsing buildings. The local crew boss demanded a mass of credits for the use of the place, but even he didn't know its exact location.

Scarlet pushed his way past two lanky shrubs, descendants of the original ornamental garden, and picked his way over piles of rubble. He dodged a giant sharp-edged grass-like thing and waited for Jayden to join him.

"Looks nice. Homely."

"A flamethrower might improve the outlook." Scarlet bent and pulled away a wet, moss-covered flagstone, waiting while a colony of long, multi-legged invertebrates fled to safety. He wiped off a layer of soil, exposing a plaswood trapdoor underneath, and held his palm against the square in the centre until he heard a quiet click. Grasping the handle, he dragged it upwards, revealing a rectangular hole in the ground. A flight of well-maintained plastone stairs led down into the earth. He ushered Jayden ahead of him and closed the trapdoor, reactivating the lock. At the bottom of the steps, a substantial plaswood door blocked the way. Scarlet reached past Jayden, using his palm to unlock it. "Go on in." He followed Jayden through. The door swung closed, sealing itself.

Jayden looked over his shoulder. "Is that the only way in and out?"

"What do you think? We'd be like rats in a trap. Over here." Scarlet pushed past into another room, one which had three doors leading from it. One of them was solid plaswood. "That leads into a tunnel. Hope it's still dry. It comes out in a big area of marshland; the sort of place that gives you time to disappear. Mind you, if you don't know where you are, you're likely to disappear into the swamp and never be seen again."

"You built all this?"

Scarlet nodded. "Most of it." He and Mink had done some of the work, but they'd employed a small team to excavate the tunnel. "Not personally. We brought some contract workers here in blindfolds. They didn't know where they were. The people who used to build tombs in the old days killed their workers, and buried them in the building. Mink didn't want to do that, so we used blindfolds."

Jayden grinned. "Yeah, right."

Scarlet opened another door. "Bathroom. No running water though, just a chemical latrine. We'll need to get rid of it when we leave."

The third door opened onto a small room which was lined with shelves, stacked high with crates. "Food and water. Emergency rations, but hopefully we won't be here for too long." He rummaged in one of the boxes and produced a small barrel-shaped container. "Look, we got beer. Not cold, but it'll do." Finding a couple of beakers, he passed a drink to Jayden. "Come on." He led the way back into the first room, sat on a long, padded bench and took a drink of his beer. "Nice, isn't it?" Reaction was setting in and the hand holding the beer shook. He put the beaker on the floor.

"I'd get a bit claustrophobic if I had to stay too long."

The air was musty, but breathable. The place hadn't changed since Scarlet had last been in it, a few months ago. It was dry, which was a miracle, but the plastone walls and floor seemed to have kept out any ground water. A small generator in one corner would give them central light if they wanted it, but Scarlet preferred to use his head lamp and save the generator. He stretched his legs along the bench, leaned back and prepared to wait. His nerves were alive with impatience, firing up his flight or fight response. There was no one to fight, and nowhere to run. He bent down and carefully picked up his beer. After a moment Jayden sat on the other bench.

Chapter 13

Scarlet woke from a half-doze, heart thudding, unsure what he'd heard. Jayden was on his feet, weapon ready in his hand. The door opened.

Koo-Suki strolled into the room, holding her small laser pistol loosely at her side. She raised her eyebrows at Jayden. "Glad to see you're ready for anything." A smile stretched her lips but didn't reach her eyes. "Scarlet? I thought only the three of us knew about this place? Isn't that what we decided?"

Scarlet shrugged. "It was either bring him with me, or kill him."

"Right," Koo-Suki said. "Jayden, get me a beer, will you? Close the door behind you."

Jayden left the room.

"What's going on?" Scarlet shifted sideways to face Koo-Suki. "Is it true? They think I'm the Silencer? Where's Mink?"

The smile faded from her face, leaving it strained. "We couldn't both get away at once. Mink's hard to hide. The Guard's everywhere. They're keeping an eye on everyone. I swopped clothes with one of the pleasagurls. They've turned up in droves, been hanging around the Guard, hoping for a hook-up. I don't know whether they really believe you're the killer, but they're definitely looking for you."

The micro-skinsuit Koo-Suki wore was not her usual style. It was cheap, flimsy, and left her arms and legs bare. "You came out here without armour?"

"I didn't have much choice," she said. "I managed to keep the boots, but I didn't want to be stopped."

"Is Mink okay?"

"He was. He'll look for an opportunity to get away"

"What happened?" Scarlet asked. "What put the idea into their heads? We don't know anything much about the murders. Why do they think I killed them?"

"Maeve's missing," Koo-Suki said.

Scarlet stared at her. His earlier suspicions circled round his mind. "You think she—"

"I don't know. Why would she go missing just now, though?"

"She might have wanted to get away from any reminders of Marius."

Koo-Suki grimaced. "She didn't like us very much. Especially you. You didn't see the look she gave you, yesterday morning."

"I saved her life," Scarlet protested. *Maeve?*

"Yeah. No good deed, and all that."

"Fuck. So, this is all my fault?" Scarlet couldn't believe Maeve would have done this.

"No. It's her fault, if it was her who pointed the finger. She has a temper and her off switch doesn't work. You might have noticed."

"But she won't get away with it. If anyone finds out, they'll kill her without asking questions. You don't shop people to the Guard. You just don't."

Koo-Suki fingered her pistol. "I'll kill her myself if I find her."

Scarlet rubbed his forehead. "Yeah." He didn't think he'd be able to change Koo-Suki's mind on that, and thinking about it, he wasn't sure he wanted to. He'd rescued Maeve from murder by Romero, and she'd tried to wreck his life. If it was her. He still wasn't sure he believed it. "What now?"

"First things first. You need to get away," Koo-Suki said. "They're not going to stop looking for you. You know what'll happen if the Guards get you down to Security Central. Even if they find the real Silencer, it'll be too late for you."

Scarlet grimaced. Everyone knew what happened down there. Not many people who entered, ever left again. It might be different for citizens, but Scarlet wasn't a citizen. Fear arrowed through him. "What about you and Mink? Will they take you in?"

Koo-Suki shook her head. "I don't know. We're getting out as soon as possible. Everyone's had the message passed to them. By the day after tomorrow, the den and the flophouse will be empty and the factory dismantled. Mink's going to be the hardest, but he'll manage."

"Shit." Scarlet rested his head in his hands, digging sharp nails into his skull.

"You need to change your appearance. Everyone knows what you look like. I told you those eyes were a huge mistake." Koo-Suki punched his arm. It was a discussion they'd had many times. He liked his red eyes, but Koo-Suki was right; they were distinctive.

"Credit." He dragged his fingers through his thick crest of hair, tugging on the beads. One came loose and rolled across the floor. "I'll need a lot. So will the rest of you."

"Not a problem," she said. "Mink transferred everything we have into a new secured account. He did it as soon as the guards showed up. He also transferred a pretty hefty amount to your personal chip."

Scarlet blew out a breath. That would help. "You can't go back. If they can't find me, they'll have you and Mink down in the cells facing a full interrogation within a day. I wish you'd brought Mink with you. What if he—?"

"He wasn't worried," Koo-Suki said. "He said he'd be fine. And you know Mink. He looks slow, but he's got a mind like a mantrap."

"I hope so."

The door opened and Jayden appeared, juggling three beakers of beer. "Not too soon, am I?"

"No," Koo-Suki said. "Thanks." She took her beer.

Jayden put his own beer on the floor, and picked up Scarlet's bead, handing it back to him. "Yours?"

"Thanks." Scarlet closed his eyes and rolled it between his fingers and thumb, before hurling it at the wall. "Fuck. I can't believe she'd do this."

The rest of the day passed slowly. When Koo-Suki yawned for the third time, Scarlet stood up. "We should get some sleep, while we can. Jayden? You keep watch. I'll relieve you later."

Scarlet might as well have taken the first watch. Nagging worry kept his mind active, and he couldn't settle. His life was over, or at least, it had changed drastically. *Maeve? Why?* It wasn't just Scarlet, whose life was messed up, it was Koo-Suki, Mink and the rest of the crew, from the chief chemist to Temmy and the other juvies. He turned onto his side and stared at Koo's body, on the other bench. She seemed to be asleep. The air in the underground room was heavy with damp heat. His skin was sticky, and some strands of hair had worked lose from his crest to cling to his skull. He sat up, took a deep breath and picked up a pack of tepid water. "You sleep," he told Jayden. "I can't." *Where was Mink?*

Koo-Suki woke a couple of hours later and the two of them rifled through the crates in the storeroom, looking for food. The boxes were full of military rations.

"This might as well be sawdust," Scarlet grumbled.

"I'd kill for coffee," Koo-Suki said wistfully.

It was midday before the door opened again. Mink walked through. He had a bag over his shoulder and was dressed in skinsuit body armour and full facial protection. His giant pet glided into the room after him, head pressed against his legs.

"How did you get here?" Koo-Suki asked. She jumped off the sofa and wrapped both arms round his waist. "I was worried."

"Me too," Scarlet said. He slapped Mink's shoulder. He even rubbed Nyx's head.

"I brought coffee." Mink opened the bag and pulled a flask out. "You'll have to share it."

"I love you." Koo-suki grabbed the flask and opened the mouthpiece, making a small sound of pleasure as she drank. "Real coffee." She passed the flask to Scarlet.

Mink sat on one of the benches, rubbing his hands over his face. "We've got big trouble Especially you, Scarlet. And you look awful."

"Thanks." Scarlet pushed his disintegrating hairstyle away from his face and handed the flask back to Koo-Suki. "What's happening?"

"That last body probably wasn't the Silencer," Mink said. "Even the Guard can see that. It was a hom, and older. It wasn't killed with a knife either."

"Does that mean—"

"They're still looking for you for the other murders," Mink said. "They're not going to give up on that."

"So, what do we do?" Scarlet's mind had seized up.

"The first thing is to get you somewhere safe," Mink said. "You can't stay here. I've talked to someone who helps people disappear."

"Who?" Scarlet asked.

"Two of them," Mink said. "The first one to help you change your look. The other charges a fortune to get people out of trouble. We won't tell her who's after you, or the price will skyrocket."

"If she doesn't know, she must be the only one," Koo-Suki muttered.

"What about you two?" Scarlet said. "You know the guard'll come after you, if they don't find me."

"We'll be long gone," Mink said. "We're not going back to the den. I've got the crew salvaging equipment and stuff. Too many people depend on us now. We can't just leave them. We'll stay low, get the operation up and running somewhere else, and then we'll come and find you. Anyway, they might catch the real culprit before then."

"Not if they're wasting resources looking for me," Scarlet said gloomily. He felt useless.

"I'm going nowhere until I've murdered that baby-faced witch-whore from hell," Koo-Suki said. "It couldn't have been anyone else."

"Forget her," Mink said. "If she's stupid enough to talk to the Guard she's not going to last long."

"What a waste of my effort," Scarlet grumbled. "I wish I'd let Romero kill her. He'll be laughing himself into a coma now." He grabbed the flask from Koo-Suki and drained it. "When do I have to go? And where?"

"You're seeing Manny now," Mink said. "He's the nearest cosmetician I could find who wasn't a butcher. You need to get your eyes and hair changed. They're the things that make you stand out."

Scarlet groaned. He loved his scary eyes and his edgy hair, but supposed he'd rather be alive and boring than a fashionable corpse. He dragged his hands through the remains of his cobalt-tipped crest. It was beyond saving, anyway.

~~~

Manny's place was more than an hour's walk away, a small concrete bunker on the outside, a modern cosmetic enhancement facility within. Mink gave Scarlet a push when he held back. "For fuck's sake, Scarlet, it's just hair. And it's a complete mess at the moment, anyway."

"And eyes. It's my image."

Manny took one look at Scarlet and his gloomy hound dog face sagged further. "This is him?"

Mink nodded.

"No challenge. No challenge at all. I can give him contact lenses to slot over his eyeballs. They'll cover up all the red, and if I use an amber filter for the irises, they'll look brown, natural for his colouring. No one will know they aren't his own eyes."

Scarlet grimaced. "Do I really—?"

Mink slapped him round the head. "You can take them out if you ever want the demon look again. Personally, I think you shouldn't."

"Personally, I think you should keep your opinion to yourself."

"And if I cut his hair and curl it, that would make a big difference." Manny raised a questioning eyebrow. "Any hack could do that. And how about his nose? I'll do you a good deal on it. Change it from straight and long to short and tilted. He'd look cute, with the curly hair."

Scarlet squeezed his eyes closed and pinched the bridge of his straight nose. "Mink?"

"I don't think that'll be necessary," Mink said. "If you have the eyes and hair fixed and wear a cheap skinsuit, it should work. I'd go for cropped hair though."

"Thank God." Scarlet opened his eyes. "A crop," he said to Manny, "and no curls."

When he'd finished, Manny held a mirror up for him. Scarlet inspected his image, feeling depressed. He looked ordinary, not himself. Maybe he should have had the nose job, just to complete his misery. "Thanks. What do you think, Mink?"

Mink studied him. "Nice. You look pretty with those bushbaby eyes."

"I'll punch you if you don't shut up."

"Most important though, you don't look like serial killer, Scarlet." He paid Manny the agreed number of credits and took Scarlet's arm. "Let's go."

"What's the hurry?"

"We should get away from here. Manny won't say anything immediately, but I don't trust him not to tell somebody you were here. He probably won't, but..."

"Yeah." It didn't do to trust anyone. Everyone had their own survival as their first priority.

"The woman who's going to make you vanish is coming to us," Mink said. "I'll collect her, she'll be blindfolded and confused, so she'll have no idea where she is. Then she can take her time talking us through the options."

"How's she making me vanish?" With his present luck, she'd probably bury him in an unmarked grave.

"She didn't say, but she's got a sky-high reputation. New name? New location?"

"Are we all going?"

Mink shrugged. "I don't know what she'll suggest, but we should sort out the business before we disappear. A lot of people depend on us."

Back in the safe-place, Koo-Suki and Jayden stared at Scarlet in amazement.

He glowered back. "I know I look boring and ugly. This was Mink's idea." Mink had gone out to collect the woman who could make people disappear.

Jayden laughed.

Koo-Suki patted his cheek. "You look gorgeous. That haircut shows off your cheekbones." She giggled.

"You think it's funny?"

Koo-Suki's laughter stopped suddenly. She folded her arms. "No. I don't think it's funny. I think it's a disaster. Your beauty treatment's the least of our problems. Anyway, you do look good. Sort of androgynous and soulful. I always hated those red eyes."

Scarlet grunted. He knew he was vain, but everyone had a small flaw somewhere, and if he bumped into Maeve again, he might kill her himself. Anyway, it was better to concentrate on his appearance than to think about his murky future. "What happens when the guard discovers both you and Mink are missing?"

"I don't know," Koo-Suki said. "They'll look for us I guess, but neither of us are as well-known or as distinctive as you, and we've already put our move into action. They might question a few people. No one close to us though. They've scattered."

Scarlet flinched. 'Question' usually meant pain and possible death. He lay down on the bench, closing his eyes and testing the sensation of the new contact lenses. Manny had told him that within a day he wouldn't know they were there. They would last at least a year, he'd said.

When Mink returned, he brought a woman with him. She wore an opaque face-covering, which Mink removed once he'd guided her to one of the benches. Her skin was dark brown, her eyes were blue, and she could have been any age between thirty and sixty. She studied Scarlet. "You're the one who needs to disappear?"

"Yeah."

"Where to, what from, and how long for?"

Scarlet had no idea. "Somewhere safe, I suppose."

"The Guard is after him." Koo-Suki said. "If they don't give up soon, we might all have to follow him. So somewhere he can start a new life if he needs to."

The woman raised an eyebrow. "Why are the Guard looking for you?"

"Someone told them I was the Silencer."

The woman looked alarmed. "You aren't?"

"No. I'm not," Scarlet snapped.

"Of course, he isn't," Mink said. "If he was, I'd break his neck, myself."

The woman shrugged. "Okay. I'll lay out your options. Then I'll tell you which I think is best. The Guards don't give up easy."

Scarlet nodded, his stomach churning.

"The first and cheapest option is to hide out in a different part of outer London. Personally, I don't think that's a good idea given your situation. As I said, the Guard's relentless. You'd always be looking behind you and someone would betray you eventually."

"Right," Scarlet said. "So that's out. What else?"

"We could set up false citizenship, and settle you in London, inside the walls."

"That sounds good."

"It wouldn't hold up for long," the woman said. "It's not the best choice unless you only need to hide for a few days."

"What *would* be the best choice, then?" He wished she would get to the point.

"Your best option would be to get out of Britan altogether, at least for a while."

"Out? How?" No one he knew had ever left Britan.

"We could ship you to the Americas. They don't have any agreement with Britan, but they don't like the British. They don't like incomers. I wouldn't recommend it."

"Why suggest it then?" Koo-Suki paced across the room. "None of your options look good."

"I'm letting you know your choices," she said. "I wanted you to know you have alternatives."

"What else?" Scarlet said.

"I've got a citizenship alias that might be a good match for you," she said. "It only came up today. It's for a level one security guard on a space shuttle trip. You get off planet, the guards won't look for you there. It's the most expensive option."

"Space shuttle?"

"To the hub for the Sector 3 outer galaxies. You'd be a substitute for a sick crew member."

Scarlet pursed his lips, his breath whistling from between them. He'd always had a yen for space travel, but it was an impossible dream for people like him. "I don't believe you. No one gets on those. Not if they don't have citizenship." Not unless they wanted to sign on as indentured labour on some mining asteroid, and few people were stupid enough to do that. At least Earth servitude came with free, breathable air.

"It's a job that already exists. We just have to get the id changed, and that's what I'm good at. There is a caveat, though."

"What's that?" Scarlet was sure it would be a major caveat. Anyway, what had happened to the citizen who the job belonged to? How sick was he?

"The job lasts until the hub. You'll be paid, but then if you don't get another job, you might have to sell yourself into indenture." She gave him a nervous smile. "I'm sure you'll find something."

Indenture? That was the mining asteroid thing. Good jobs, off planet, never went to the unregistered. Just like good jobs on planet. "Can I come back here?"

"Only if you pay a fortune, or find a job on a home bound shuttle. I wouldn't expect your citizenship papers to hold up forever either. And do you want to come back, if the Guard's still looking for you?"

Scarlet frowned. It didn't sound like that good a deal.

The woman glared at him. "Look Scarlet, you're in serious trouble. You don't have much time. If it was me, I'd get off planet."

"How do you know who I am?" His disguise couldn't be that good. He'd ruined his image for nothing.

The woman sneered. "Get real. Three of you? On the run from the Guard. Who else could you be?"

Scarlet rubbed his hands over his face. He glanced at Koo-Suki, then at Mink, who stood, one shoulder propped against the wall, shaking his head slowly. "What about the others?"

"What about them?"

"Will they be able to join me?"

"Those two? Not now." The woman pursed her lips. "These opportunities don't come up that often. The next one I'll save for them. For a price."

"Will there be a next one?" Koo-Suki asked.

The woman shrugged.

"Jayden?" Mink waved at the escort. "Stay with our guest a moment. We need to confer." He led the other two into the inner room.

"What?" Scarlet was defensive.

"You should take it," Mink said. "Who knows what opportunities you might find, once you're out there. If you stay here, it's obvious what's going to happen."

"But what about you and Koo?"

"We'll be okay," Koo-Suki said. "Neither of us are as distinctive as you and neither of us are wanted serial killers."

"Thanks." Scarlet stared at the wall, his eyes stinging. The new contact lenses. He rubbed at them.

Koo-Suki came up behind him, wrapping her arms around his waist. She rubbed her face against his shoulder blade. "You'll come back, or we'll come after you. We'll stay in touch. There's a message service that goes with each shuttle. If you can't come back, we'll find you."

"That's right," Mink said. "I've always wanted to go into space."

"Okay." Fear of ending up a low-level labourer on an airless asteroid lurked at the back of Scarlet's mind. He pulled himself together. "Let's tell her and get her terms. Then, if there's time, we need to discuss the business." He pushed the door open. The woman glanced up.

"We'll take it," Mink said. "Let's talk terms."

The price was as steep as they'd expected, but the credit in Scarlet's new account covered it. He wasn't leaving his partners destitute. "When do I leave?"

"Tomorrow," the woman said.

"That soon?"

"You can't afford to wait," the woman said. "Me, or one of my people will meet you at the main junction of the Middle Road. We'll sort out your citizen registration and take you to the shuttle port. Give me your comm data and I'll send you the details of your new identity."

Chapter 14

Mink, Koo-Suki and Scarlet arrived early at the Middle Road junction, a precaution, in case they were walking into a trap.

"Benaiah," Scarlet grumbled. "She's called me Benaiah. What sort of a name is that?"

"Benaiah Scarlet. She's kept part of your old name," Koo-Suki said, "so stop going on about it."

"Boring Benaiah," Scarlet muttered, quietly enough that Koo-Suki couldn't hear him. She was twitchier than he'd ever seen her. Twitchier, even, than him.

A couple of people passed by on foot, both young, both men, dressed in ill-fitting, battered armour, but the road was even quieter than usual. After another hour, an armoured smallcar appeared, gliding west along the Middle Road. It was fitted with New-Life algal structures along its flanks, an energy converting feature that marked it as belonging to the military. The vehicle made no sound as it approached.

Scarlet retreated further into the bushes. "That's an official transport. The Military Guard. We've been betrayed. Let's go. Now. I knew that woman was—"

"Wait." Mink gripped his forearm.

The transport drew to a halt, hovering a few inches above the path. The side slid open and the woman from the day before jumped out. Her eyes narrowed as she scanned the bushes.

Mink stepped forward.

"Where's my passenger?" she asked.

"What do you think?" Scarlet whispered at Koo-Suki. "Should I trust her?"

"If she betrays you, I'll chop her into a thousand pieces. I told her so, yesterday."

"Seriously? And they tell me I'm melodramatic. I'm glad you're on my side." Scarlet hugged Koo-Suki, clinging to her small, strong body, for a long minute, before he stepped out of hiding. "Right. I'm going. Wish me luck."

"Where, in all hell, did she get that vehicle?" Mink muttered to Koo-Suki. "Go on Scarlet. I'm as sure as can be that she's honest. She's got a good reputation. She wouldn't want to lose it. It's her income."

Scarlet hugged Mink and then Koo-Suki again. He didn't want to go, didn't want to leave them. He didn't know how to be alone.

The woman beckoned. "Finish with the goodbyes, will you? We need to leave."

Scarlet pulled free of his friends, walked to the smallcar, and climbed into the front passenger seat, leaning out to call to Mink and Koo-Suki. "Don't forget to let me know what's going on with you. As soon as you can." He pulled the door closed.

"I thought you were going to chicken out," the woman said.

"No." Scarlet took a deep breath. "Why would you think that?"

She shrugged and gestured towards the man seated in the back of the vehicle. "You can call him Gaven."

"Is it his name?"

"To you, it is. He'll take you to the shuttle, show you where to check in."

"What about the citizenship?" There was no point in all this if Scarlet couldn't prove he had a right to work.

"Hold out your wrist," the woman said. "Gaven? Please?"

The man pulled out a comm-pen and pointed it at Scarlet's extended wrist. He felt a brief shock as the data hit his chip, and then nothing.

"What is it?" Scarlet asked. "What level?"

"Level two," the woman said. "It's a good one. You'll have the right to work in security, manual labour, that sort of thing, for as long as it lasts. Benaiah Scarlet has worked as private security for the past three years."

"Where did you get the name?"

"I had to think of something. I opened a dictionary and stuck a pin in. Don't you like it?"

"Not much." Benaiah? He sounded like a vid character. "And how long—"

Gaven shrugged. "Months to a couple of years. Most likely it'll be good for at least a year."

A year was long enough to come up with ideas. It would have to be. "How will I know if it's wearing off?"

"Your wrist, where your chip is, will start to tingle. There's a three-day delay after that."

The vehicle cruised over the top of the lush forest. He could see for miles, as far as the distant black snake of the river Thames. Years of unchecked woodland growth hid most of the ruins of outer London, but within the ring road, the shining buildings of the city stood out, the materials for the rebuilding chosen to resemble marble. Darker patches showed where attempts had been made to keep some sense of London's long and picturesque history. Black plasteel walls followed the winding river, keeping it contained, keeping it from drowning the city. The smallcar veered towards the Thames, following it west, before swinging away again, northwards, in the direction of London's main travel hub.

The space port was protected by a solid black plasteel wall, just like the one that contained the river. Its threatening grimness reminded him of Security Central. A film of sweat soaked his brow as he realised how narrow his escape had been. Suddenly, he couldn't wait to get away from Earth.

The smallcar descended to a fortified gate at the spaceport's entrance. Guard towers rose at regular intervals around the high wall. Men clad in heavy body armour stood in front of the gate.

"Why so much security?" Scarlet muttered. "You'd never get on one of the shuttles without being caught, so why all this?"

"Terrorism," Gaven said. "Some people think the space program's too limited. If everyone doesn't have the opportunity, then no one should. It's true that any planet worth colonising is limited to those who can pay, but blowing the place up won't change that."

Two guards approached the car. The woman lowered the window, and held up her wrist for the id scanner. A guard checked it. "Your passengers?"

Gaven held out his wrist.

Scarlet hid his trepidation as he held out his own.

The guard scanned him. "What's your business?"

"I work here," Gaven said.

"I'm here about a casual job on one of the shuttles," Scarlet said.

The guard opened the gate for them. The smallcar glided through, crossing an open space towards a row of buildings. It slowed to a halt.

The door slid open. "Go on, get out. This is where I leave you," the woman said.

"Thanks." Scarlet jumped out of the car after Gaven. The door closed, the smallcar rose, rotated through one hundred and eighty degrees and headed back to the perimeter.

"Hurry up. You don't have time to daydream." Gaven's voice pulled him out of his trance.

"Where am I going?" he asked.

"You can register over there." Gaven pointed to a long low building, a hundred meters away. "Your data says you have a position as a security professional on shuttle 27, travelling to intergalactic hub 3. It's an entry level job, so you should be all right."

That meant absolutely nothing to Scarlet other than that it was a long way away. "Hub 3?"

"It's the jump off point for the third unexplored region," Gaven said. "It serves a couple of the Earth-like colonies and a few mining operations, as well as being the headquarters of one of the exploration forces."

Scarlet thought about that for a moment. "Could I get a job there?"

Ahead of him, Gaven's narrow shoulders lifted in a shrug. "How should I know? I've never been there." He pushed open a door into a reception area, a room lined with manned desks. "Number fifteen," he said to Scarlet. "That's where you check in. He'll tell you where to go. Good luck."

"Wait." Scarlet wasn't ready to be abandoned by his last link to his life. "Thank you."

"No need to thank me." Gaven lowered his voice. "I've been well paid."

Scarlet watched him slip away, through the door and across the concourse. He turned back and scanned the room. Counter fifteen was about twenty metres away. A woman leant on the counter surface talking to the duty attendant. As Scarlet approached, she straightened and stepped aside.

The attendant shifted his attention to Scarlet. "ID please."

Scarlet extended his wrist. "I'm here—"

The attendant motioned him into silence. "Just a minute." He scanned Scarlet's wrist, passed the data to his desk unit and looked up. "Benaiah Scarlet? You're for shuttle twenty-seven. Bay ten. You'll need to report there in the next hour. She departs in four hours. You're late." He frowned, but it looked more of a habit than annoyance.

"Where's bay ten?" Scarlet asked. "I'm new on the job."

"Sula?" The attendant nodded at the woman who still leaned against the side of the counter. "You're going over there? Take him with you, will you?"

Sula straightened. "Sure. I'm late as it is. See you next time I'm down." She beckoned to Scarlet. "Come on. I'm shuttle twenty-seven, too. We'd better check in."

Chapter 15

Scarlet darted sidelong glances at Sula, as she led the way to the shuttle bays. She was smaller than him, a couple of inches taller than Koo-Suki, but without the hard leanness. More like Maeve, he supposed. His step faltered as he thought about Maeve and what a huge mistake he'd made. Koo-Suki was right; you couldn't save people who didn't want to be saved. Stopping Romero killing her had been the right thing to do, but the first time she disobeyed orders, he should have thrown her out.

Sula became aware of his inspection and gave him a questioning look. She was pale-skinned, red-haired and dressed in a light-blue coverall. "First time on this transport? I haven't seen you before."

"First time in space," Scarlet said.

"Really?"

"I've been in security for a while," Scarlet said, telling the story that the woman had drilled into him. "Mostly for rich individuals. I was bored and a friend recommended me for this."

"Nothing exciting about the hub shuttles," Sula said.

"Maybe not," Scarlet told her, "but it's different. A change."

"I suppose."

"What about you?"

"Hydroponics," she said. "I've done a bit of work on the hub-station before, but I'll be staying a while this time. They want to expand their terraforming. The place is a miserable junkyard hotchpotch, but more and more people are living on it, so it needs updating. They'll be building a new pod-string onto it in a couple of years. Lots of work for us engineers." She made a sharp left turn. "Are you doing the return trip?"

"No. I think the regular crew member's booked for the return journey," Scarlet said. "I'll be looking for another job."

"Seriously?"

He nodded.

"You're mad."

"Why?" He didn't like that, especially as it reinforced his own view. "If they're expanding, won't they need more security?"

"They might, but you're taking the risk of being stranded without a job."

"But, can't I—"

She slowed her pace. "Most opportunities, you'll find, involve a one-way ticket to one of the mining colonies." She gave him a comprehensive head to toe inspection. "You won't have any problem getting taken on by a mining crew."

"Why one way?"

"It's a scam. Basically, it's indentured servitude. They don't call it that, but they charge you for the fare out to the colony, they charge you for your keep and you end up with a pittance. They even charge you for the air you breathe. You'll never save enough to cover your fare back."

"Does no one work there voluntarily?"

"Doubt it," she said.

Scarlet had the credit that Mink had transferred to his account. He'd not tried to access it with his new identity, but he'd been told it should work. It wouldn't last forever, though.

"Having second thoughts?" Sula glanced over her shoulder.

"And third." He gave her his most charming smile. "Too late though, I've signed the contract."

"Maybe you'll find something. If I hear of anything, I'll let you know."

"Thanks."

"Here we are." She led him to the foot of a black plasmetal staircase, which ascended to the open door of a horizontal entrance tube. "We need to find the second officer."

"Who?"

"Human Resources is one of his roles. He'll check you in and tell you your duties." She jogged up the steps. The second officer sat behind a desk at the far end of the tube, a large man, in sleek closefitting armour. A stungun lay on the surface of the desk. "You're late."

Sula rolled her eyes. "I'm here, aren't I? It's three hours till take off." She held out her wrist and the officer scanned it.

"Go on then. You're in bunkroom 13."

Sula squeezed past the desk and disappeared round the corner. The officer turned to Scarlet. "What's your excuse? I don't know you, do I?"

"I'm a last-minute recruit. A replacement for the permanent security junior." He held out his wrist for the scanner.

"You're in bunkroom 13, too," the officer told him. "Drop your things off there, and go and find the head of security. You should be helping check people in in the next hour, and you're not in uniform yet. Come and see me once we're underway."

Scarlet tried an experimental smile and got a slight twitch of the lips in return. He counted that a success and edged past. Bunkroom 13 was a dormitory at the end of the corridor, with six shelf-like bunks crammed into it. Five of them looked to be claimed. He tossed his bag on the sixth and went to search for the head of security.

The walls of the narrow corridor were studded with closed doors. He tried one; it was sealed. Hearing voices, he turned down a side corridor. The closest door stood open, and inside the room, two men in grey and silver uniforms were deep in conversation. He paused.

Both men turned. "Can I help you?" one of them asked. His tone of voice suggested he'd better have a right to be here.

"I'm looking for the Chief Security Officer," Scarlet said.

"That's me." The man gave Scarlet a thorough inspection. "Are you the substitute junior?"

"Junior Security Officer?" Scarlet asked.

The man nodded. "What's your name?"

"Benaiah Scarlet."

The man's eyes widened. "Really?"

"Yeah."

"Pretty boy." The other man raised an eyebrow at the Security Officer. "You'd better hope he's a hard worker."

"I am, Sir." Scarlet's work ethic had never been criticised but, in his old life, who would have dared? And pretty? Perhaps his makeover wasn't as bad as he thought.

"Call me Chief," the Security Officer said. "Come with me. You need a uniform." He stalked out of the room, without waiting for Scarlet, who hurried after him.

The Chief opened a cupboard door. Shelves were piled high with grey fabric, boots and breathing apparatus. After an assessing look at Scarlet, he selected a roll of dark cloth. "Put it on and hurry up."

Scarlet stripped off his skinsuit and pulled on the uniform. It was similar to that of his new boss, but with less silver. The Chief opened another cupboard and extracted a weapons belt. He handed it to Scarlet who fastened it loosely round his waist.

"Here." The Chief handed him a taser stick. "You know how this works?"

"Yes, Chief."

"Don't use it without permission. I'll have to justify it and if I do, I don't have a problem with putting the blame on you. Which is where it will probably belong anyway."

Scarlet smiled uneasily.

"Now. Your duties. Our cargo will embark in the next hour, and you'll be there to meet them. You'll check them off against the list and ensure that we have no more and no less than we expect. Is that clear?"

"Absolutely, Chief," Scarlet said.

"Make sure their wrist chips agree with the list. No cutting corners. Right?"

"Right, Chief."

"Economy passengers don't have much space. You'll take them through the safety procedures before we lift off, show them how to use the hammock restraints. We don't want any broken bones. Come along, I'll show you how to do it."

Scarlet almost had to run to keep up with him. The economy berths were small enough to give Scarlet claustrophobia, but he listened to his boss's instructions, and went through the procedures with him.

"Once we're on track, we check on the passengers every couple of hours. We've a rota for their mealtimes, and they're allowed out for an hour of exercise every day. I'll let you have the timetables. We've a hundred and sixty economy berths in ten bunkrooms, and twenty luxury staterooms. You can leave the luxury passengers to me. We're a small crew, so you'll do some domestic duty as well as the rest. Hygiene. Meal supervision. All right?"

"Right, Chief."

"Good. What's your security experience?"

"Earth only," Scarlet said, hoping he wouldn't have to trail out the parcel of lies he'd prepared.

"In what field?"

"Personal civilian protection," Scarlet said.

"A bodyguard?" The Chief groaned. "Oh well. A trained monkey could do your job."

Scarlet followed the Chief back down through the vessel to the desk where he'd checked in. The second officer had gone. "This is where you'll receive the passengers," the Chief said. "Once they're on board, you'll patrol the dormitories and make sure they're all strapped in for lift-off. Finish that, then go to your own bunk and secure yourself. When we are on trajectory, come and find me, and I'll go through the emergency procedures with you. How to use the breathing apparatus, and the vacuum suits, things like that."

"Right Sir," Scarlet said. That didn't sound too onerous, although he wondered what would happen if there was an emergency before he'd been shown the procedures. A sudden, horrible death, he imagined. He sat behind the desk. "Where's the scanner?" He was talking to himself, but the chief gestured to his waist. "Everything you need is in the belt. I'll leave you to it." He hesitated. "It's your first time, off Earth?"

"Yes."

"If you find me, after you've checked the dormitories, I'll get you a berth with a window. You should see us lift, get the view of Earth as we leave."

"Thanks." Once he left, Scarlet groped at his belt, which held a number of pockets and holsters. He'd have to examine them later. He found the scanner and leaned back in the chair. There was a small info screen in the counter, and Scarlet played with it for a minute, before finding the passenger list. He waited.

All the economy passengers arrived at once, milling around the base of the shuttle, before forming a queue. He scanned their wrists, checked the lists and told them where to go. There were exactly one hundred and sixty of them, assigned to bunkrooms 1 to 10. The second Officer guided them away, while Scarlet dealt with the twenty staterooms and their occupants. There were thirty-three of those. Once they'd all been shown to their rooms, the entrance tube disconnected, and the door slammed closed.

Chapter 16

Maeve lay on her side, on a broad sleeping platform, in a very small room. She propped herself up on one elbow and looked down at her companion. His name was Simen and he was a member of the Civilian Guard. She'd given him Scarlet's name, suggested he might be the Silencer, and started this whole business. The den had been broken, the crew had fled, and she was in deep trouble. Why, why, why, had she done it?

Early morning light leaked through the shutters and showed the solid shape of his body, outlined by a thin cover. He still slept, his breath coming in small snores. In his sleep he looked young and ineffective; not the sort of man to propel her upwards, to security and safety. At least he'd brought her back inside the city walls. She was safe from Koo-Suki, for the time being.

She sank onto her back and stared up at the ceiling.

She'd heard whispers that Koo-Suki wanted to kill her, and when Maeve thought about it, she couldn't really blame her. If only she hadn't lied about Scarlet. After a couple of years of keeping her temper under control, she'd completely lost it again. Trying to kill the pleasar client didn't count; he was a rapist and her survival was at stake. Holbeck had deserved her fury, but Scarlet hadn't. He'd saved her life. She breathed out a sigh of frustration. She hated to admit it, even to herself, but Marius was a user and a thug, and now, because of him, she had a whole sector worth of enemies. Not to mention a serious case of a guilty conscience. If she got out of this mess, she'd just have to make a bigger effort to think before she acted. Shame twisted her stomach and she shifted back to her side.

Next to her, Simen stirred. His hand settled on her waist, hot and damp, but he hadn't completely woken. Hopefully, he'd stay asleep for a while longer. She needed time to think. Simen's accommodation was single use, level one citizenship, and while the concierge might turn a blind eye to a young man's fun time, eventually she would throw Maeve out. The room was tiny, even for a single person, with space for the bed and a small desk. The hygiene facility was in a cupboard. Simen had bought a temporary entertainment permit for her, but it was time-limited, and when it ended, she would be illegal again. If she left the city, Koo-Suki would find her. She might forget about Maeve after a while, but not yet. She closed her eyes. Finding a job had to be her number one priority if she was to stay within the security of the city walls. Maybe the search for Scarlet would die down soon. If he escaped, maybe everyone would forget about her. If he was caught, it wouldn't be only Koo-Suki she had to worry about. All his friends would hunt her down. Why had she done it? She groaned aloud.

Simen snorted, stretched, and sat up. "Ugh. What time is it?"

"No idea."

He checked his info-screen. "Shit. I'm late." He scrambled off the bed and dressed. "What will you do today?"

Maeve sat up and rubbed her eyes. "I don't know. Maybe go round some of the agencies. Look for work?"

Simen fastened his weapons belt. "You won't find anything. Not without citizenship."

"What will I do?" Maeve was talking to herself, rather than to him.

"I wish I could help. You need citizenship, though, and there's nothing I can do about that."

"You could marry me," Maeve suggested without much hope.

He raised his eyebrows. "Even if I wanted to get married, I'd need permission to marry a non-citizen." He shook his head. "I wouldn't get it. And my own position would suffer. Honestly, Maeve, I'd like to help you but that wouldn't work."

Maeve forced herself to smile at him. "I was joking." She'd hoped, even knowing it was a vain hope. "I can't go back though. Koo-Suki's promised to kill me."

"Do you think she means it?"

"Yeah," Maeve said. She drew her knees up to her chest and rested her head on them. "Have you seen her?"

"Cute. Small."

Cute? What did he know? "She's a maniac. Everyone says so."

"I think you're turning her into a bogeyman. She's just a woman. An unlicensed one."

Maeve glowered. What did he know? He'd never tried to live outside the walls. "Lots of people want to kill me."

Simen's forehead creased. "If you're really worried about the death threats, I know of an agency that takes illegals. It finds them work in the city."

"What sort of agency?"

Simen avoided her eyes. "An escort agency. It would give you time, but it's not somewhere *I'd* want to work."

"Why would they take someone without citizenship?" It sounded a bit like her original agency. Elise's.

"Some of their clients have interesting tastes. Illegal, so they can't use citizens," Simen said. "I shouldn't tell you this, but a few of the Guard take bribes to turn a blind eye."

"How do you know about it?"

"One of our cases," he said. "A citizen was killed there. Turned out it was a dispute with another citizen." He frowned again. "Forget I mentioned it. It's a snake pit." He headed for the door.

"Wait," Maeve called.

"You shouldn't—"

"I'm desperate. I'll try anything. Please?"

Simen's frown deepened. "I'll take you down there when I've finished my shift. Five o'clock this afternoon. If you're hungry, you could visit the river area. There're loads of cafés and food stalls. Have you enough credit?"

"Yeah. I'm okay." Maeve sank back onto the bed. How did she get herself into these situations? One moment of rage and spite and she'd wrecked her own life as well as Scarlet's. She closed her eyes again, trying to think of a way out of the trap she was in. Ten minutes later, she gave up, thinking she could ask around the agencies, maybe have a look at the place Simen had mentioned. She pulled on one of the fashionable skinsuits that Marius had bought for her, raked her fingers through her hair, and headed out, into the muggy heat of the morning.

It took her half an hour to walk from the housing complex to the river front, and by the time she got there, the rain had started. Most of the walkways headed downhill towards the Thames, where bars and cafés clustered together along the land side of the River Path. Many of them fronted apartment buildings, accommodation for high level citizens. Maeve checked the credits she had left from her employment with Scarlet, and her relationship with Marius, and decided she could afford breakfast in one of the cafés. By the time she'd finished, the heavy downpour might be over. She chose a café which overlooked the Thames and took a seat under the awning, listening to the satisfying racket of the rain on the canvas. A server joined her immediately and she ordered coffee and pastries, the sort of food it was hard to come by in the outer zones, especially if you didn't have much credit. She stared at the river while she waited. It was full from the summer rains, dark and turbulent, swirling against the protective walls, as though it was waiting for an opportunity to escape and overwhelm the city. Its power and strength were evident in the visible spirals of current. She was sure she saw the fin of a river shark as she stared, but it disappeared before she could be definite.

"Fem?" A voice dragged her attention back to her surroundings and she looked up to see a Civilian Guard standing over her. She had to force herself to remain calm.

"I need to see your data," He smiled in a manner that should have been reassuring, but made her tremble. "You know we had a murder in the city recently?"

"Yes." She held out her wrist. "I'm visiting. I'm a registered temporary entertainer."

The guard ran his scanner over her wrist. "That's correct." The respect in his voice had disappeared. "Who are you visiting?"

"Simen Tinns. He's in the Guard."

"I know him." He ran his eyes over her. "Lucky Simen. If you have time for someone else, I'm available."

"Thank you." Maeve let her lips curve into an appreciative smile. "But I don't want to upset Simen."

"You won't upset him."

"I need to check." She played with a strand of hair and widened her eyes at him, wishing he'd go away and leave her alone.

He took her wrist and transferred his details. "Call me." He moved to the next table.

Her coffee arrived, fragrant and steaming. The pastries were delicious, flaky and filled with sweet almond paste. She closed her eyes, savouring the rare pleasure of luxury food, and her mood picked up. Things would work out. She was still alive, surprising when she thought about it, so her luck couldn't all be bad.

Simen returned home at five, that afternoon, still in uniform. He removed his helmet. "Did you have any luck with the agencies?"

She shook her head. "You were right. None of them would even interview me. You will take me to the one you mentioned, won't you?"

"If you're sure. I don't like it. Seriously Maeve, I've been thinking about it. It's shady."

"Please. I'm desperate. I've not got a lot of options."

"Fine. Don't blame me if you get into trouble." He scowled at her. "I'll take you for something to eat afterwards."

They walked down to the river, along the fashionable walkway and then back up a street which wound between some mid-level residential units. Behind them were a couple of restaurants, a bar and a place that looked like a dance club.

"This is it." Simen held his face up to the camera.

The door swung open, the doorman's face freezing when he registered Simen's uniform. "What can we do for you, Sir?"

"I want to see Shila," he said. "Nothing official. She doesn't need to worry."

"Fine. I'll call her. Just go through."

Maeve followed Simen along a dimly lit corridor, to a door at the far end. It opened automatically, a crescendo of pulsing music bursting out, louder than anything she'd ever heard. She clapped her hands over her ears.

Simen pushed his way through tightly packed dancers to the bar, Maeve behind him. He leaned across the counter and said something to the server, who nodded and spoke into his comm.

Simen leaned his back against the bar. "She's coming down. She'll see you."

Maeve dragged her hand through her loose hair and took a deep breath, knowing she looked her best. Her midnight-blue skinsuit was probably the nicest in the place, but it would stink of R'lax for the next week. Smoke hung in the air, coiling, multicoloured in the light from the dim lamps. Clients reclined on couches around the edges of the room, or swayed slowly on the dance floor. Maeve would have bet that at least some of the dancers were under the influence of Muzak. A man danced alone at the edge of the floor, his body boneless and snakelike in its movements. His hair was as extreme as Scarlet's, a great crest of blue around his head. *Scarlet.* Had they caught him yet? Guilt slammed into her again.

She tugged on Simen's arm.

He lowered his head to listen.

"How's the search for the Silencer going?"

"What?"

She repeated the question closer to his ear.

"They haven't found him yet. They're still looking though. His friends have disappeared as well; the woman who wants to kill you and the big man."

"Mink and Koo-Suki?" Maeve swallowed, wondering where they were. She fingered her throat nervously. "I'm wondering if I might have made a mistake. Maybe it wasn't him. Are you sure—"

"Simen Tinns?" A woman pushed through the crowd around the bar. "This way. I can't hear myself think in here." She led them to a door at the back of the bar, and into a small office. The door closed and the noise stopped. "You want to talk to me?"

"Yeah. My friend's looking for work."

The woman looked down at her. "This?" Almost as tall as Simen, her height was emphasised by the stilt shoes she wore. She was in late middle-age, elegant, expensively dressed in a fluid, clinging gold sheath, her bare arms tattooed with images of snakes and lizards, and corded with muscle. Maeve didn't like the look of her at all.

"This is Maeve. She's unlicensed."

The woman assessed Maeve again, with cold thorough eyes. "Have a seat." She gestured at a couch, waiting until they were seated before she took the chair opposite. Maeve studied her surroundings nervously, and glanced back at the closed door.

"You're looking for a job?" A slit in the gold cloth of her skirt opened, as the woman crossed one long muscular leg over the other.

Maeve nodded, unable to take her eyes off the reptilian tattoos covering the woman's thighs.

"And you're an illegal."

"I'm unlicensed." Maeve raised her head, almost missing the flash of interest in the woman's eyes.

"I see. You realise that puts you in a difficult position?"

"Yes." Maeve chewed on her lower lip. "But I hoped—"

The woman held up one hand. "If I offer you a position, it will be a low level one. You'll be paid, but not much, and you'll be expected to deal with the less pleasant clients, if you're asked to."

Maeve grimaced.

"They'll be the ones the licensed pleasars can afford to turn down. Do you understand?"

"I think so." It looked like she was back in the sort of situation she'd escaped from before, but at least this time she *would* be paid. "Is there any chance of gaining citizenship?"

The woman pursed her lips. "I'm not supposed to employ illegals, so I can't sponsor you, but you might meet someone who will."

Maeve nodded, hope flaring.

"You might not last long enough," the woman said. "I make a point of honesty with the staff. We do our best to keep you alive and in good health, but I'm promising nothing. You're disposable."

"I'm desperate," Maeve said.

"I'll give you a contract to look at," the woman said. "I guarantee you won't get anything better. Not without citizenship. Come back tomorrow if you want to try out for the job."

Afterwards, Simen bought her dinner at a riverside bar. "What did you think?"

"I don't know." Maeve's appetite was non-existent. She poked at the protein on her plate. It was substantial, subtly flavoured and expensive. She needed to eat it. She put her fork down. She'd skimmed through the contract, but it hadn't helped her reach a decision.

"You know what I think," he said. "But what else can you do?"

"Nothing." Maeve stared blindly at her plate. "I don't know why I'm even pretending I have a choice. I've minimal credits, no legal existence and a psychopathic knife-chick on my heels."

"That answers your question then, doesn't it?"

"It's all so unfair." She picked her fork up and dug at the food. She couldn't afford to wallow in despair. She had no other options, and this didn't have to be for ever. Just until they caught the real Silencer. The money was rubbish, but she'd get a room, and a food allowance, and the agreement could be terminated instantly by either side.

"Just be careful," Simen told her. "You can always refuse clients if they make you nervous."

"They should be more nervous of me." Maeve put her fork down again and glowered at her plate. She hated everyone.

"What?"

"Never mind." Simen was law enforcement. He probably wouldn't understand why she'd stabbed her first client with his own knife.

"I feel responsible." Simen's plate was empty. He leaned back in his seat. "You're so young. You're too sweet. You don't know how bad some people can be."

"Yeah. I'm pure sugar." There was no point in showing how insulting she found his description. Maeve knew exactly how bad people could be.

"Seriously Maeve. You need to keep your eyes open. Shila has some nasty clients. There are a couple you should avoid at all costs."

"Yeah." Maeve picked her fork up and prodded her food. It sounded like those were the sort of clients she'd be given.

Chapter 17

Maeve held her face up to the retinal scanner outside the club. She clutched a small pack which held two of the skinsuits Marius had given her, as well as some of the cosmetics she'd bought herself with his credits. Thank goodness this job offered accommodation. She had nowhere else to go, but it was a relief to get away from Simen. He meant well, and he was the most generous man she'd ever met, but his vocal concern about the job amplified her own anxiety. He wouldn't listen to her, when she said she might have made a mistake about the Silencer. She didn't want to see him again.

The door finally slid back and the doorman loomed in the space. "We're not open yet."

"I'm here to see Shila."

Both his eyebrows arched in exaggerated surprise. "Shila? She expecting you? I'd better check. What's your name?"

"Maeve."

He turned away and muttered into a handheld comm. Maeve shuffled her feet.

"You're here about a job?" He stepped aside. "You'd better come in."

She squeezed past him into the corridor. "Where do I go?"

"Someone will collect you soon." He leaned against the wall and stared at her.

The youth who came for her was tall and slender with perfectly symmetrical features. His skin had an olive tinge in the artificial light, his eyes glinted green, and dressed as he was, in a long loose robe, he might have been male or female. She guessed at male. He beckoned her from the far end of the corridor. His voice, when he spoke, was deep. "Come with me."

He walked with a distinctive limp, through the empty bar, and into the back office. Maeve followed.

Shila looked up. "So? You decided to join us?"

Maeve nodded.

"I'll give you a list of the rules. Make sure you stick to them, or you're out. We've a queue of non-citizens who would take your place in a second. I'm giving you a chance as a favour to the City Guard."

"Thanks." Maeve clasped her hands behind her back.

"I don't suppose you've many options, have you?"

"Not many, no."

"What did you do? Kill someone you shouldn't? Steal from your owner?"

"I was free," Maeve snapped. "I lived outside the walls. I just made a bad enemy."

"Careless." Shila walked round the desk to face Maeve. "Watch how you speak to me. I'm a tolerant woman, but I won't have disrespect."

"Sorry." Maeve stared at the floor.

"Griff?" Shila glanced at the youth. "Fetch me some coffo. Bring some for her as well. Sit down, Maeve."

Maeve sat.

"Let me tell you about the job."

"Where will I work?" Maeve hadn't noticed the presence of street pleasars in the inner city, not like in the illegal zone.

"You'll work here, from the bar. We have a catalogue of staff our patrons can scroll though. You'll be included in that. You'll be out in the club the rest of the time. You might catch someone's eye that way. I suppose you can dance?"

"Not professionally."

"Doesn't matter. You just need to show yourself off."

Maeve nodded, doubtfully. "Why not take someone with citizenship?"

"Most of our staff are citizens, but we don't want any trouble with our clients. The licensed staff might sue if they get damaged. They have legal protection. You don't. You know that, right?"

"Yes." She didn't like the implications of the warning. It sounded as though Shila expected her to get hurt.

"The back pages of the catalogue showcase those of our employees who'll do things most of the staff won't."

Maeve grimaced. "What sort of things?"

"Anything, from pander to fetishists, to rough sex. Some of the clients like to beat their partners, some like to be beaten. The hardcore sadomasochists go to more specialised places. Most of ours will just be strange; a bit bizarre in their demands." Shila rolled her eyes. "We have one level five citizen – male – who likes pale fems with scars. He likes to lick them. Nothing else. It has to be fems and they have to have white skin and pale hair. Timi makes most of her income from him. She pays her way with the scarlicker, and doesn't have to take any other clients if she doesn't want to."

"I could handle that." It would be massively better than Maeve had hoped for.

"We'll see. We'll try and start you off with the harmless ones. Don't want to waste my time on a corpse."

Maeve flinched. "What's the pay?"

"You get your room and your food. You give fifty percent of your fees to me, and you'll be charged for the tools of your trade. Costumes, makeup, toys. You can keep any tips."

Maeve had expected to give Shila more. "How much will my fee be?"

"You'll be booked through a handler, who'll set the fee depending on the service."

"Right." Maeve had resisted this sort of position while she was in the institute, hoping something better would come along. Bitterness swamped her. She was almost as badly off as she had been with Romero, but at least Shila would pay her.

"You'll appeal to a lot of our clients. The ones who like youth. How old are you?"

"Eighteen."

"You don't look it. I'd have taken you for fifteen at most."

Maeve shrugged.

"We don't force our staff to do anything they don't want to," Shila said. "We have enough applicants banging on our doors, not to need to. I'm warning you, though, if you don't earn enough to cover your costs, with a bit more for profit, I'll throw you back to the streets. This is a business."

"I'll do my best."

Shila's eyes narrowed. "How do you feel about people who like pain?"

"They can please themselves, but I don't like it. I don't want to get hurt." Maeve was running if serious damage was on the agenda. She already had Koo-Suki looking to kill her, and probably the rest of her old crew, as well.

"What about causing it?"

"Yeah. I could do that." She wouldn't enjoy it, not in cold blood, but she could do it.

Griff returned with their coffo and Shila got to her feet. "I'll leave you two together. Griff will find you an appropriate costume. Griff? Make the most of her youth. Exaggerate it." She closed the door behind her.

Maeve sipped at her coffo and eyed Griff as discretely as she could manage. "Do you work in the club?"

"I manage the staff," he said. "Shila's my ma. I did the sort of work you'll be doing, until my leg was damaged. I still take an occasional client. Fetishists."

Maeve narrowed her eyes, trying to see the family link between the two. "You don't look like her."

"Adopted."

"I see." She didn't. How could Shila make her own son work in the dangerous end of the sex industry?

154

"I'm in charge. You do as I say and you'll be fine." He eyed her skinsuit. "Nice, looks expensive, but it won't do for this place." He opened a cupboard door and pulled out a short cream translucent tunic. "This'll work for you. Put it on."

Maeve sighed and stripped off her skinsuit, rolling it up and forcing it into her pack, before pulling the tunic over her head. She assessed her image in the full-length mirror, as Griff took a small brush out of his bag. She didn't look young and sweet. She looked young and stupid.

"In future you'll do this yourself," he said. "Pay attention."

He painted iridescent blues and greens round her eyes and thickened her lashes. Standing back, he assessed the result. "Brows?"

"What?"

"No. I don't think so. You look a bit weird with those pale brows. I think weird will work well. You look like a fairy child."

Maeve leaned closer to the mirror. The face paint looked good from a distance, but close up, it was garish and exaggerated.

"Do you think you can do that next time?"

Maeve nodded. "Where do I get the stuff?" Her own cosmetics were more subtle.

"I'll show you where you'll get yourself ready in future. We keep some stock there. Eventually you might want to buy your own. We can sell you the stuff you need. Come along, let's get you out, onto the floor. The bar opens soon."

"I start right now?"

Griff took her arm. "Do you have a reason to wait?"

Maeve suppressed the urge to put her hands over her ears when he opened the door to the dance floor. The music already pounded through the room, bouncing off the walls. She's be deaf if she had to work here for long. Griff steered her to the far side of the dimly lit space, where a platform ran along the wall perpendicular to the bar. Three youths and two young women leaned against the wall chatting.

"Get up on the stage. If someone requests you, you'll be called. You'll take it in turns with the other staff to go out to the dance floor."

Maeve climbed the steps to stand at the end of the row, next to one of the women. She was the smallest person there. The woman beside her was tall and unnaturally thin. She had dark skin, light blue eyes, and pale hair. She glanced down at Maeve. "New?"

"Yes."

"Good luck."

~~~

Maeve hated being stared at. Nothing good ever came of it. She hated waiting, and not knowing who might request her company. She hated wondering whether she would earn enough to pay her way. She'd been taken off the platform by one client so far, so at least she'd made some money, even if she had to give it all to Shila. She folded her arms and leaned against the wall, glaring at the dance floor.

The youth, next to her, stuck his elbow in her ribs. "Don't slouch, and stop scowling. You won't get any customers like that and you'll annoy Griff. You don't want him smacking you about."

"Thanks." She supposed she'd been lucky. Her single client had been hyped up on some illegal aphrodisiac and had only wanted instant relief. He'd staggered off afterwards, grimacing in discomfort, his dick already stiffening again. People were a complete mystery to Maeve. The ones in here were legal, most of them had plenty of credits, and the majority had medium to high level citizenship, so they were secure, safe and had the right to a good life. Most of them would have generous breeding rights as well. They could have a family, two children of their own. What was wrong with them? She kept her face clear of the deep contempt she felt.

A hand on her bare foot jerked her back to reality.

One of the licensed fems stood under the platform. "You're new, aren't you?"

Maeve nodded.

"I need a favour. I'll owe you."

Her neighbour shook his head. "Don't do it. She's only asking you because everyone else would say no."

"What do you want?" Maeve squinted down into the smoky darkness.

"I've double-booked," the woman said. She was tall, blonde, muscular, and dressed in a couple of straps of black faux-leather. Around her neck, she wore a heavy metallic pendant, heart-shaped, on a synth leather string. "Just a mistake, but I'll be in trouble if Griff finds out. Would you take one of my clients?"

"Can I do that?" she muttered.

"You can, but Griff won't like it," the youth said. "Not without permission. If Shila gets to know about it, you could be in real trouble. Mind you, it's a good idea to keep the licensed staff happy."

Maeve didn't care about Griff, but she couldn't imagine that a client who'd booked the woman in front of her would be satisfied by herself. She jumped off the platform. "What sort of client?"

"He likes being abused," the woman told her.

"Do I look like a dominatrix?"

"I'll lend you a whip and a couple of other things. I've some spare restraints. Come on. I'll give you a quick lesson. It'll be worth your while."

"How?"

"We'll split the fee."

"Okay." If she was being paid to beat a client, then she was safe from one who might pay to beat her.

The woman led her through the door behind the bar, and once in the corridor, through another door into a small room, impressive if you liked torture chambers. Maeve didn't. The walls were black, with metal rings fixed to them. The bed was a narrow bunk with posts at each corner. The posts also had metal rings embedded in them. Next to the bed stood another post with rings at the top.

"Look in that drawer," the woman said. "You'll find some stuff."

Maeve opened the drawer. A coiled synth leather whip lay at the front. There was a face mask that encompassed a gag and blindfold, a pile of chains, a pair of shackles, a paddle and a knife, as well as some things she didn't recognise. She picked up the knife, weighing it in her right hand. It was lightweight, small. She touched the edge with her finger. A thin line of blood oozed from the broken skin.

"Hey. Careful with the knives," the woman said. "They're sharp."

"Too late," Maeve muttered. She sucked at her finger and put the knife down again, taking the synth whip instead. After a second's consideration, she took the mask as well, laying them both on the bed. She'd never used a whip before, never even seen one close-up. She inspected the hilt, finding the activation button and moving it to the on position. When she unfolded the lash and cracked it at the whipping post, it surged with electricity, making a satisfying sound as it connected. It had a range of power settings.

The woman took it off her. "It's easy to use, but you need to be careful." She flicked it to its full length, showing Maeve how to control it. "Try it again."

Maeve cracked it a couple of times, aiming at the bedposts.

The woman frowned. "It's better than a manual whip. Easier. Practise with it, while I go and collect the client." She looked over her shoulder as she left. "And put the knife back in the drawer. I don't want you using that on a client. Not if you don't know what you're doing."

Maeve set the power button to maximum and aimed the tip of the whip at the wall. It showered sparks as it connected. She lowered the power and tried again, hitting the exact spot she'd targeted. Dead easy. She folded it and tapped it against her leg as she waited.

The door opened and the woman came back, leading her client on a chain. He was completely naked except for the metal collar round his neck and a set of heavy shackles on his wrists. Maeve could barely hide her contempt. He was born free and he wanted to play this sort of game. *Why?* He needed to try it for real.

"What's your name?" she asked.

"George, but—"

"Not you." She cracked the whip in his face, missing by a millimetre, more by luck than skill. "I don't care what *you're* called. I meant you." She nodded at the woman.

"Tooley," she said. "George is one of my slaves. He's displeased me, so I'm passing him to you."

George dropped his gaze. "Please Mistress, I didn't mean—"

She drew back her arm and slapped his face with her full strength. "Shut up."

A frown lingered on her face as she drew Maeve to one side of the room. "You do know about safe words, don't you?"

"There are no safe words." She slapped the whip against her thigh, grimacing as the sting penetrated the thin cloth of her tunic.

"If he uses his safe word, you stop what you're doing instantly," Tooley said.

Maeve glanced at the man. "Of course. I know that. What's your safe word, Master no name?"

"Asparagus."

Maeve rolled her eyes. "Chain him to the post for me."

Tooley gave her a sidelong smile. "Bossy, aren't you?"

Maeve glared at her.

Tooley jerked on the man's chain and attached his wrist shackles to the rings at the top of the post. She shortened the chain until he was on tiptoes. His face was a mixture of discomfort and excitement. He had an erection.

Maeve stroked the folded whip over the skin of his back. Some raised bumps suggested that he had scars, but the light wasn't bright enough for her to be sure. Maybe he'd taken a whip fetish too far.

"Aren't you going to use the mask?" he asked.

She slammed the folded whip against the back of his thighs. He whimpered.

"Did you speak? Don't do it again. You're not getting the mask. I want to hear you scream."

Tooley frowned again. "You *will* be careful, won't you?"

"Of course, I will." Maeve gave her a shy, seductive smile and stroked the man with the whip again. A shiver ran through him.

"He's paid for half an hour," Tooley said as she left. "Keep the whip on the lowest setting. And leave the knife alone."

Maeve stood behind the man, unfolding the whip and allowing it to make its powered crackles as she did so.

When Tooley returned, she had a man and a woman with her. The woman was obviously her double-booked client, adorned with the same sort of shackles as Maeve's shivering ecstatic customer. The man was dressed in an iridescent skinsuit that must have cost as much as every single item Maeve had ever owned. He was tall, fair and fashionable, handsome, save for the discontented line of his painted mouth.

"Little girl with a big whip." The corner of his mouth twisted in half a smile. "I like it. Give me the whip."

At Tooley's small nod, Maeve handed it to him.

He cracked it once, moved the power up a slot, and brought it down on the client's back with twice as much force as Maeve had used.

The man screamed. Blood oozed from a line of broken skin.

"Like that, do you?" He moved the power up another notch.

"Don't, Serran," The client sounded scared. "Please don't do that."

"Sir?" Worry leaked from Tooley's voice. "Give me the whip. Please?"

The man switched the power off, stroked the folded whip over the client's buttocks and handed it back to Maeve, amusement on his face. "Untie him."

Tooley unfastened the shackles and the client fell to his knees, catching himself on swollen hands.

"Get up." The man he'd called Serran sounded impatient. "Put some clothes on, will you? I'm in a hurry."

The client pushed himself to his feet and held out his wrist to Maeve. She stretched hers out, registering the ping of the credit transfer. The two men and the woman left the room.

Tooley grimaced. "I didn't like the look of that man. The client's friend. I was scared he wouldn't give the whip back. If we'd had to call security, we'd both have been in trouble."

"We could have got it off him, between us," Maeve said.

"How much did George give you?" Tooley asked.

Maeve shrugged. She'd left her scanner with her skinsuit, in the locker room.

"You'll give me half," Tooley said.

"No." Maeve folded her arms. "You're getting half the fee. I keep the tip."

Tooley glared. "I get all the fee."

"Half." Maeve pulled the knife out of the drawer, slashed at the air in front of the other woman. She'd earned her fee. "That's what we agreed."

Tooley gaped at her.

Maeve put the knife back in the drawer, reminding herself that she was supposed to think before she acted, nowadays. "Look. I don't want to cause trouble. You did me a favour. This time, you keep the fee, but next time, we split it."

Tooley chewed on her lip. "Okay. There might not be a next time though."

"There will." Maeve kept her eyes on Tooley until the taller woman nodded.

Chapter 18

When Maeve arrived for work the following day, a Civilian Patrol Guard walked down the street towards her. As he passed, he whispered, "People are looking for you. Mink knows where you are. Koo-Suki knows where you are."

Maeve froze. "Wait."

He walked away, ignoring her. She felt sick. Was that man really a Guard, or had Koo-Suki smuggled one of her people into the city? How much danger was she in? Stiffening her spine as she walked to the changing room, she racked her brains trying to decide what to do. Should she leave now and try to find another similar job? *Impossible.* She'd never have found this one without Simen's recommendation, and while she hated it, at least it kept her fed. Anyway, Koo-Suki was just a woman, a small woman with a big reputation, and a knife. Maeve shivered, remembering the feel of the knife point against her stomach, but she knew how to use a knife, as well. She just needed to be on her guard.

"Shila wants to see you." One of the other women was stripping off her street clothes. "As soon as you get in."

Now what? Maeve wondered. This was already a bad day, and it had barely started.

Shila's eyes were flat and cold. "I heard you did an unapproved job yesterday?"

Maeve nodded, letting her expression fall into curiosity. "Yes. It was a favour. Is that a problem?"

"Not the first time." Shila's smile didn't warm her eyes. "If you do it again, there will be penalties."

"I—"

"Financial penalties. You'll find yourself working for nothing for a week. And I'll make sure you get the worst of the clients."

Maeve took a deep breath. "So, what's the correct response to that sort of request?"

"Pass it by Griff. We take our percentage and everything's fine. We don't get our cut, and we aren't happy." Her smile fell away. "There's another thing. One of the clients from last night liked you. I've had an interesting request for you."

"What sort of request? Does the client want me again?" She hoped so; it had been easy work. "George?"

"No. His friend wants to buy you out as a present for his brother."

"What?" She'd not heard of that sort of arrangement before. "Which friend? And how does that work?"

"He pays me for your time. Pays your keep, pays your part of the fee. You go and work for him exclusively."

"He buys me?" There was no way she would agree to that.

"Not you," Shila said. "He buys your contract."

"I can still leave, if I want to?"

"I wouldn't," Shila said. "Not after the client's paid. He's not a particularly nice man."

"So, I can't walk away," Maeve said. "And I'm unlicensed. What if he's violent? I have no rights. I don't like it."

"It'll be a profitable deal for you."

It sounded more like it would be profitable for Shila. Maeve would take the risks, Shila would rake in the credit. "But—"

Shila leaned her elbows on the surface of the desk. "If he was buying you out for himself, I'd say you'd be right to worry. He's a hellraiser, a vicious piece of shit—"

Maeve interrupted. "Was he the blond one? Serran something?"

"That's him. Serran Willim. He's on the way to becoming a complete narco-freak."

He was the one who'd taken the whip to his friend. "I don't think—"

"He's buying your contract for his brother. The brother's eighteen this birthday. I've met him, just once, but he seems a normal sort of boy." Shila tapped her fingers on the desk. "I'd advise you to accept.

The family are second level citizens, so if they like you, they might keep you on. It's a possible route to citizenship for you, and you said that's what you wanted. The fee to you personally will be good, and no one's going to arrest you as an illegal while you're working there. I can't see a drawback. Can you?"

Maeve stared at the floor while she weighed up her options. "How long is the contract for?"

"Four weeks and you'll be provided with accommodation, food, clothes, whatever you need."

"How much do you make?"

"That's none of your business," Shila said. "Your business is whether you accept or not. I'm telling you, if you turn it down, you won't have a future with us. You'll be back on the streets."

"So, I've no choice then." If the situation was bad, she'd leave, with or without permission. She was used to running. The contract was no worse than her present job, and it might get her away from a potential attack by Koo-Suki. "When would I start? And when will I be paid?"

"You'll be paid at the end of the job. He'll collect you tonight. You can wait here."

Maeve gave her a sarcastic smile." Do I need to change into that godawful outfit?"

"No. He'll tell you what to wear when he arrives." Shila left, the door hissing closed behind her.

Maeve sank into her chair and propped her feet on the desk, unsure how long she'd have to wait. After half an hour, Griff arrived with her bag. She took her feet off the desk and opened her eyes.

"Making yourself at home, are you?" he asked.

Maeve shrugged, unfastening her bag to check her stuff. Both her spare skinsuits were inside.

"Serran Willim is a strange one," he said. "I've heard rumours about him. Nothing good. You'll be working for his brother, but even so, watch him. That's all I'm saying."

She closed her bag, rolling her eyes. "Do I look like a fool."

"Ma's bringing him along in a couple of minutes," Griff said. "Seriously, Maeve, be careful. He's got a reputation for violence. Everyone says he's plain mean. Vicious."

She narrowed her eyes. "I don't have much choice, do I? Your ma told me I wouldn't have a job if I said no."

"I know, but—"

The door opened, cutting off whatever he had been about to say. Shila walked in, together with the man from last night. Maeve re-assessed him through her long lashes. He was tall, athletic, and blond. He'd lined his pale-grey eyes in deep indigo blue, and stained his eyebrows in the same colour. Definitely handsome, but his mouth had a cruel line to it, mixed in with the discontent. His facial skin had been depilated and polished until it gleamed.

"What happened to the white virgin look?" he said to Shila. "I liked the contrast between the sweet little girlie and the big whip."

"You told me you'd dress her yourself."

"So I did." His mouth twisted into a thoughtful smile. He beckoned to Maeve. "Come over here."

Maeve stood up.

"Turn around."

She spun in a slow circle.

"I'd like to see her in dom gear." He turned to Shila. "Have you anything that might fit her?"

Shila turned to Griff with a raised brow.

"I'll have a look," he said. "She's pretty small. Our dominatrixes tend to be a lot bigger. The clients like them that way." He backed out of the door.

Serran circled Maeve, making her skin prickle with nerves. When he stood in front of her again, he placed a finger beneath her chin, tilting her face up. "Open your eyes."

Maeve obeyed, while keeping her expression blank.

"Very nice. Do you dye your eyelashes?"

Maeve blinked in confusion. "Yes. Just recently."

"Pity." His cold grey gaze held hers. "Do you know who your parents were?"

"My parents?" No one had ever asked her that before. Of course, she didn't know who they were. She'd been found in a doorway, a few hours old, a few hours from death. "No."

"Looks like you had some gene manipulation. Your colouring's unusual."

Maeve smiled, uncertain whether that was good or bad.

"I've found something." Griff reappeared with a pile of black synthetic leather. "Maeve? Try this on."

Maeve eyed the clothes with distaste. People in the city didn't seem to worry about exposing their bodies, or going around almost completely naked. Probably because no one was likely to shoot them, or to view an expanse of naked flesh as a possible home for a knife blade. She took a piece from Griff, relieved to see that it was slightly more substantial than the thing Tooley had worn. It was a very short skirt which barely reached the top of her thighs. On Tooley it would have been a wide belt. The second piece was an arrangement of straps that criss-crossed her breasts and fastened at the back of her neck. She wriggled it into place, and laced up the footwear, flat sandals with straps that wrapped halfway up her thighs. She snuck a glance in the mirror. She looked like something from a fantasy holoshow about prehistoric warrior maidens.

"That'll do." Serran laughed. "You look ridiculous. Ash won't know what to do with you."

"Ash?"

"My baby brother. It's his birthday, you know. I need to give him a present." Serran walked round her, his brow furrowing. "She needs something else. Glitter? And have you got a bow. A big shiny one. She *is* a present."

"Of course." Griff disappeared again, returning with a spray tube of silver glitter and a wide silver ribbon.

Serran squeezed the tube. Maeve closed her eyes in time to avoid getting the spray right in them. When she opened them, her bare biscuit-coloured flesh sparkled. She wondered if it would come off when she washed.

"Put the bow round her neck."

"Hold still." Griff tied the wide ribbon in a bow.

Maeve clenched her jaw.

"Come on, girlie. Stay close. I don't want to lose you." Ignoring Shila and Griff, Serran took her back to the club, with its ear bruising music and smoky atmosphere. He headed to the bar and picked up a copy of the catalogue of services. He glanced sideways at her. "I want the dom from last night. What was her name?"

"Tooley." Maeve was surprised. He didn't look like the kind of man who paid to be whipped.

Leaning on the surface of the bar, he leafed through the infodoc, past the section on recreational drugs, until he found Tooley's picture. "It's interesting to turn things around. She's the sort of woman I like. Not a little nothing like you." He glanced sidelong at Maeve as he pressed the button for Tooley. "You'll be perfect for Ash, though."

Tooley appeared almost immediately.

"Next Monday night," Serran said. "I'll want you for two hours. I'll pick you up here."

Tooley was dressed again in her synth leather with a whip slotted into her belt. "You need to talk to Griff," she said.

"I'm talking to you. Monday night, I said."

Tooley's eyes avoided his, but she nodded.

"Fetch me a drink before you go," he said. "I'll have a beer."

Tooley wasn't a server, but she nodded again. "Yes, Sir." She hurried away.

Serran pushed Maeve to a small table at the edge of the floor, and sat down, gesturing to her to do the same. When Tooley brought his beer to him, he drank it quickly and ordered another, together with some R'lax. He gave Maeve a R'lax smokie. "Stay put." He strolled to the dance floor, stopping to talk to people, selecting an occasional partner and dancing a little.

Maeve dropped the R'lax in a disposal slot and tried to find a comfortable position on the narrow bench. The cheap synth leather chafed her skin. She slipped a finger under the strap that circled her right breast, trying to pull it away from her flesh. It snapped back as soon as she released it. She leaned forward, resting her elbows on the table and stared at the dance floor. The longer she had to wait, the more nervous she got. At last, Serran returned, beckoning her to follow him.

Outside the club, two uniformed bodyguards fell into step behind him. He ignored them and strolled towards the river. Maeve followed, between him and the guards. She wondered where they were going and if she dared ask. Best not, she'd find out soon enough. She didn't want to attract Serran's attention. He made her nervous, in the same way that Elise had made her nervous, and Elise had been an out-of-control sadist.

They turned onto the River Path, passing a couple of government buildings, impressive and imposing in their fake antiquity, before coming to a high and solid gate, constructed to resemble wrought iron. A real, human gatekeeper sat in a small kiosk on the other side.

The gate opened as Serran approached.

"ID, please, Sir." A guard stepped into his path, a note of pleading in his voice.

"You know who I am."

"Sir? You know your father's orders. I need an id for the woman, as well. I can't let you through without them."

"Do you like your job?"

"I'll have to call your father." The pleading note drained from the guard's voice, leaving resignation behind.

"Don't bother." Serran extended his wrist.

"Thank you, Sir."

As Maeve moved to follow him, the guard stopped her. "You too."

Maeve held out her arm for the scanner.

"Sir?" The guard frowned. "Do you know she's unregistered?"

"Of course, I do, you idiot."

"Your father—"

"Has he said anything specific about lowlife whores?"

Maeve thought of protesting the definition, but guessed that's what she was now. Lowlife though? *The lowest.* She mentally shrugged off the description. It was just a handful of words.

"No, Sir, but—"

"Well, wait until he does. If you still have a job. If it's up to me, you won't." Serran grabbed Maeve's wrist and dragged her after him.

The front door opened to reveal another guard. This one ignored them. All the guards had to be for show, Maeve thought, everyone knew it was safe inside the city walls, for registered citizens, at least.

Serran dropped her wrist and strode across a wide hall, floored with real marble in a streaky grey-white colour. It glittered in the light from the overhead lamps, just like Maeve's silver-sprayed skin. She scratched at a patch of glitter on her arm and hurried after him. A white staircase rose from the centre of the hall, spiralling around a corner and disappearing upwards. Serran climbed three flights to a spacious landing. He held his wrist against the panel on one of the doors. It swung open on an inner lobby with four more doors leading off it. Another guard stood against the wall, still as a statue. His eyes slid towards Serran, rested on Maeve, and skittered away again.

Serran pushed one of the doors open and shoved Maeve through, ahead of him. Light gradually filled the space.

Maeve looked around. She'd never seen anything like this before, at least not in real life. The floor she stood on was soft and made of some sort of pale pink fabric. Three grouped couches were each big enough for a tall man to lie full length on, and were upholstered in a slightly darker shade of the fabric on the floor. As the light grew, shutters gradually moved to cover floor to ceiling windows.

Serran threw himself onto one of the sofas. "You." He pointed at one of his guards. Both had been so silent, Maeve hadn't realised they were still there. "Go and get Ash. You can all leave afterwards." As both guards turned away, he changed his mind. "Get me a drink first. A golden dream. And one for her." He indicated Maeve, who stood just inside the door, waiting to be told what to do next. Serran ignored her and checked his comm.

The guard brought two glasses containing a pale orange liquid, handing one to Serran and one to Maeve. She glanced at it doubtfully, wondering who Ash was. Probably the brother.

"Drink it. You'll never get anything as good as this again."

Maeve tasted it. It was alcoholic, warming, and as she swallowed, a pleasant languor washed over her body. She swayed and took another sip.

The door opened, and a young man stalked in. His dark eyes were wary, and his golden ringlets stuck out from his head in a tangle, as though he'd just crawled out of bed. He dragged one hand through them, pushing them away from his face. Loose white trousers hung low on his hips. His chest was bare, smooth chocolate brown skin, over visible ribs. "What do you want? Everyone's been in bed for hours."

"Happy birthday." Serran surveyed the newcomer over the rim of his glass.

"It was yesterday." The youth folded his arms. "It's four in the morning. I was asleep."

"I've brought you a birthday present." Serran pointed at Maeve. "Her."

Maeve slowly focused on the two of them. The drink had a soporific effect on her. Heat pooled between her legs.

The youth's eyes widened as he looked at her properly for the first time. "What?"

"A present. I bought her in a club down East."

"A person? A human being?"

"Not a citizen, so not a real human being. A pleasar. All tied up with a bow, just for you."

Strength drained from Maeve's legs, and without waiting for permission, she sat on one of the empty couches. Her glass was empty. Her feet didn't reach the ground. The room spun around her head.

"Are you mad? Ma will kill you." The youth's eyes left Maeve and returned to Serran.

Serran smirked. "No, she won't. She might be annoyed with you, but she'll think I'm a generous and good brother. I hope she doesn't have you beaten." His expression said something very different.

"Take her back where you got her. Just look at her. She's covering the sofa in that glittery stuff. And is she consenting age? She looks about fifteen."

Maeve wanted to argue but the floating feeling wouldn't let her.

"I'm not taking her back. I suppose I could kill her if you don't want her." Serran stood up. "No one would blame me. Anyway, they told me she was eighteen. And where're your manners?" His fists clenched at his side. "Don't you like my present?"

The youth took a step backward, holding up both hands. "Look, Serran, I can't keep a pleasagurl in the house, you know that." His voice was conciliatory.

Serran's fists unclenched. He slapped the youth across the face, hard enough that he staggered sideways. "Say 'thank you'."

The youth rubbed his cheek. "Thank you." There was no emotion in his voice.

Serran ran the ball of his thumb down his brother's cheek and rested it on his lips, rubbing back and forth. "Take her away, then. I'm bored with all this."

Maeve's head spun. She was warm, happy and aroused. A faint unease settled in her stomach. Why wasn't she more worried? Hadn't Serran said something about killing her? That drink must have had seriously good chem in it. Perhaps she should find out what it was and spend her remaining credits on it. Her life was pretty awful, so why didn't she just drug herself into oblivion? She realised that the youth was talking to her. *Ash?* His name was Ash. He was Serran's brother.

He frowned at Serran. "What have you given her?"

"Just this." Serran held up his own drink. He put it down and dragged Maeve out of the depths of the sofa, shoving her towards Ash, who caught her, set her straight and took two steps backwards.

She swayed where she stood, her body a column of molten surrender. She hummed under her breath.

"Golden Dream. Too good for her, I suppose." Serran smirked at his brother. "Make the most of it while the effects last."

"Come on, whatever your name is." The youth stamped to the door.

Maeve stumbled after him, stopping when she lost momentum. Ash took her wrist and hauled her through the door.

"And don't try and get rid of her," Serran shouted. "Or I'll beat you till you can't crawl, let alone walk."

"Fuck." The youth halted as the door closed behind him. "What the fuck am I supposed to do with you?"

Maeve considered the question, but it was far too hard to think of an answer. She wanted to lie down. Preferably with someone else. Ash's features blurred into a dark sphere.

"Sober you up first. Follow me."

Maeve weaved after him until he held up his palm to a door. It swung open.

"Sit down." He pointed to a sofa.

Maeve sat, staring at him. He was pretty. Thinner and younger than she preferred, but he would do. Heat throbbed in her loins. Alarm poked at the back of her mind. She'd never felt like this before. People lusted after her, not the other way round. What was happening to her? She closed her eyes, wriggling uncomfortably. The leather straps irritated where they touched her skin. She moaned. Her body was on fire.

Voices made her open her eyes again. A woman, someone new, stood next to a floating tray. She poured a rich brown liquid into a real porcelain cup and handed it to Ash.

"Thank you." He carried it over to Maeve and held it to her lips. She pulled her head back.

"It's just coffee." He frowned down at her. "With an antidote to that stuff Serran gave you. Here. Take it, will you?"

Maeve rolled a tiny volume around her mouth. It didn't taste like any coffee she'd ever had before and she said so. Another wave of heat washed through her. She took a second sip. It couldn't be worse than the orange drink. Unless Ash wanted to kill her. Her head was already clearing, although her whole body still pulsed in time with her heart. She handed the empty cup back to Ash. He gestured to the servant who filled it again.

"How do you feel now?"

Maeve squeezed her eyes closed and rested her head against the back of the sofa. "Okay." She still felt a little displaced, sideways of where she should be. Opening her eyes, she blinked rapidly. Her vision blurred. She covered her mouth with one hand, holding the nausea down. "I'm fine."

"Where did Serran find you?" He eyed the synth leather straps, barely covering her body, with an expression of distaste.

"In a club just off the river walk."

"A sex house you mean?" Ash said. "I bet it's that place he took me to a while back."

Maeve thought about protesting but couldn't be bothered. The aftermath of the drugged drink left her weak and defeated. Maybe drugs weren't the way she wanted to go. "You don't want me, then?"

Ash rolled his eyes. "Of course, I don't want you." He handed her the second cup of coffee. "A child that Serran dragged home? How old are you?"

"Eighteen."

"No way."

Maeve shrugged. "How old are you?"

"Eighteen."

"Huh." Maeve paused. "What happens to me now?"

"Why should I care? That's up to you surely."

Maeve stared at the dark brown liquid in her cup. "He paid the club owner for me."

"Slavery's illegal."

Maeve laughed, a forced humourless sound. "Easy for you to say. They call it indentured employment, and you end up paying them for it."

"What's your name?"

"Maeve."

"How long had you been in the pleasar house?" He took another cup from the woman servant and waved her away. She left the room, taking the tray with her.

"It was a dance club," Maeve said.

He raised one eyebrow.

"Two days," Maeve said. The silver bow scratched the underside of her chin. She put the cup down and worked at the knot with both hands. "Anyway, I can't go back. Someone wants to kill me."

Ash sighed. "You'll have to stay here a couple of days anyway, until Serran's forgotten about you. He's not nice if he's thwarted. I'm tired of him using me as a punchbag."

Relief washed over Maeve. Two or three days to make new plans? Better than nothing. Maybe Ash could help her. She glanced sideways at him. Maybe not. Her mind still wasn't working properly. She'd think about it later.

Chapter 19

Maeve woke up bewildered, not sure where she was. Sharp pain shot through her head, then faded to a dull throb, as she struggled into a sitting position. The sofa she'd slept on was bigger than most beds she'd encountered. She blinked, as a shaft of light stabbed through her brain. Her eyes felt dry and sore. She rubbed them and blinked again.

On the opposite side of the room, a wall of glass let the morning sunlight in to flood the room. It was too much, and she pulled the thin coverlet over her face, while she struggled to build a picture of the previous night. The blond man, Serran, had brought her here. His brother had given her coffee. She'd been drugged. That's why her head hurt. She lowered the coverlet cautiously. This must be the brother's space.

Her sofa faced the windows, but if she half-closed her eyes, she could bear the light. She twisted round, inspecting the rest of the room. A small table stood against one of the walls, with two upright chairs pushed under it. The opposite wall had a sleeping platform, partially concealed by an ornate hanging curtain. The room was silent.

She hopped off the sofa, tripping over a large silver bow, and pulled the bed-curtain back. A hand-embroidered coverlet lay neatly on top of the platform, but there was no sign of anyone having slept there. Maeve frowned, and tried one of the two doors in the room. It wouldn't budge, the lock pad next to it looked like it needed an id or a palm print to operate it. The other door led to a washroom, with a shower cubicle, a basin and a toilet. She used the toilet, fascinated by the amount of water that ran into it when she pushed its button, and took a long drink straight from the tap on the basin.

Leaving the washroom, she tried the other door again. It still wouldn't open. Panic rose in her throat. Why had she been locked in? She peered out of the window wall but it faced onto a small internal courtyard, at least three floors below. It was beautifully kept; the paths swept and the circular lawn trimmed to a green carpet. A spreading mango tree shaded a bench in the centre of the grass, but she couldn't see any human life at all. She was trapped. Resting her forehead against the cooling glass, she took a few calming breaths. They didn't help. The strap holding her clothing together tightened round her neck. She slipped a finger under it, easing it away from her windpipe. Someone must come soon. She tugged at one of the straps crossing her breast. The synth leather had to come off. *Now.* She couldn't bear it a second longer. It took her ages, the straps all needed unwrapping and the ones that compressed her breasts fastened behind her back. Eventually the awful thing fell away, leaving a ghost of its structure in the red marks that punctuated the glitter on her skin. She sat on the sofa and picked at the silver, watching flecks fall to the pale floor.

The door opened and the youth from the night before walked in. His eyes widened as they focussed on her naked, glittering body. He stared at the pile of synth leather on the floor. "Go and have a shower."

"What?" No way was she letting him tell her what to do. Had he told her he was eighteen, or was she just imagining it? If so, given that he'd just had a birthday, he was at least a month younger than her.

"There's that awful trashy glitter everywhere. Go and wash it off."

"You locked me in." She glowered at him.

"Go and wash."

Maeve scratched at the glitter.

"Now, for goodness' sake." He pointed at the door to the washroom.

"Okay. Only because it itches, though." If he thought he could bully her, he was in for a disappointment. She turned round at the washroom door, folding her arms across her breasts. "And it was your brother's idea to cover me with that horrible stuff."

"I don't care whose idea it was. Just wash it off. Go on."

He was sprawled on the sofa when she came out of the shower. "Put some clothes on. I'm not interested."

"Where are my things? Your brother took them." He was a spoilt child. Not worth wasting her charm on. Even if she had the energy to conjure it up.

"How should I know?" He shrugged irritably, got up and pulled open a drawer beneath the sleeping platform. "Here. You can wear this."

She caught a pile of slippery sapphire fabric. "I want my own things." The skinsuits Marius gave her were of much higher quality than anything she'd be able to afford for herself.

"We'll find them. Put that on for now."

Maeve shook it out and slipped it over her head. It was an opaque tunic, with a wide neckline and no sleeves, much too big for her. It was long enough to cover her knees.

"That's better. Are you hungry?"

Maeve was definitely hungry. The tunic slid off one shoulder. She hitched it back up. "I want my things."

"I told you I'll find them. Later."

"Are you going to let me out of here or am I a prisoner?" She walked to the window and rested her palms on it. "And what did you say your name was?"

"It's Ashkir. You can go if you want to, but I'd rather you stayed until Serran forgets about you."

"I'll think about it." Maeve had no intention of sharing her hopeless situation with him. Better if he thought she was doing him a favour.

"Fine. Do you want something to eat while you think? I'm hungry, even if you aren't."

"I suppose so."

He pressed a button next to the id lock, and a moment later, a woman appeared, dressed in a dark blue uniform coverall.

"Get us something to eat, please," Ash said. "Bread? Protein? And some coffee."

The woman nodded. "Right." She stared at Maeve.

"What are you looking at?" she snapped.

The woman ignored her. "Ash? Does your mother know you've a pleasagurl in your rooms? An underage one?"

"I'm eighteen," Maeve muttered.

Ash rolled his eyes at the servant. "How would I know? It depends if Serran told her."

"Serran?" The woman's face morphed into an expression of distaste.

"She's a gift from him," Ash said. His voice was filled with sarcasm. "A birthday gift."

Maeve was beginning to feel she was an object they were talking about, rather than a responsive human being. "I'm sitting right here."

"It speaks." The woman arched her brows in exaggerated surprise.

Maeve bared her teeth.

"Go and get the food," Ash said. "I'll deal with my mother."

The woman shook her head at him and left.

"That's a servant?" Maeve said. "You should sack her." The woman hadn't behaved like she imagined a servant would.

"She's my guard as well, so she's protective."

"She was rude."

When the woman returned, she put a tray on the small table, waiting while Ash and Maeve sat. "Is that satisfactory, Sir?"

"Thank you." Ash waved her away.

"You'd better get to your parents before Serran does," she said. "And if I were you, I'd get that creature out of the house."

"Mind your own business." Ash broke off a piece of bread. "You're not me, and it's complicated."

The servant pursed her lips, gave Maeve a stare of disgust and left.

Maeve grabbed at the bread more quickly than was polite, but she was absolutely starving. "I don't remember much about last night," she said. "Why did Serran give you something you don't want?"

Ash swallowed his mouthful and snorted. "He's stirring things up. He hates me. He's not keen on Flora either - she's our sister - but he seriously hates me. Bringing an unlicensed sex worker into my parents' house is not going to go down well, but he won't be blamed." He picked up a single walnut. "You *are* unlicensed, aren't you?"

Maeve swallowed her food. "Yeah." As she began to feel human again, her worry resurfaced. "If I leave, will Shila have to give the credit back to Serran?"

"Shila? What credit?"

"He paid Shila to take me out of the club for a month. I don't understand how the indenture thing works. I just know that she thinks I owe her." She glowered at the food on the table. "It's not fair."

"Nothing's fair. Life's not fair."

"So?" Maeve said. "What about the credits? Shila's going to kill me if she has to give them back. She'll blame me."

"Serran might not even remember," Ash said. "I wouldn't worry."

Easy for him to say. "I don't want to go back." Maeve gave him a sideways glance, thinking she might as well ask. "When I go, could you help me get across the river?"

"Why would you want to do that?" Ash's forehead wrinkled. "There's nothing over the other side. Some level one citizen housing and a few factories. That's all. The rest's swamp land and old flooded housing complexes. There's Security Central, of course."

"I need to get away. Someone wants to kill me." She hoped Ash wasn't as malicious as his brother, or she was really in trouble. "And I don't want to work at that club any more. I want a job as far away as possible."

"You won't find work over there," Ash said. "It's bad enough for low level citizens. There's no way you'll find anything without a license. How would you survive? Suppose the Guard catches you without a permit?"

Something would come along. Against all the odds, she was still alive, wasn't she? She rested her elbows on the table. "You don't look like your brother."

"That's because I'm adopted. A charity case."

"Did they give you citizenship as well?"

"In theory," he said. "I haven't got the confirmation yet. They told me it would be high, to reflect the family's own status."

"That's good isn't it?"

He snorted. "If it ever happens. I might leave the city myself."

Maeve's head snapped up. "Don't be ridiculous. You've got it made here."

"That's what you think."

"You don't know what it's like living without any legal standing." Maeve's voice rose. "Do you think I want to be a pleasar? Do you think I want to wear those ridiculous outfits and service anyone who's got enough credits? Do you think I like being called a whore? I'd love to be in your position."

He lowered his eyes. "It's not much fun here, either. Imagine living with Serran for years?"

"You've managed it till now. You'll get your citizenship soon and then you can go wherever you want. I can't believe you're whining about a few days."

"Why don't you shut up? You don't know anything."

"I know you've got a whole lot more options than I have." Maeve's face was hot with indignation. If only she had the chances he had. She'd let Serran do whatever he wanted, if it meant a chance for freedom and security. For citizenship.

"Maybe."

"Where's your brother? I need my things."

"I haven't a clue. He sometimes disappears for days. He might be in his rooms, or he might be with his nasty friends in some bar somewhere."

"Can't you look?"

He sighed. "I'll ask one of the servants."

Maeve stretched out full length on the sofa, her mind circling her problems over and over again. South of the river still sounded like an option. It had distance in its favour, but Ash made it sound very unattractive. She should try and stay here as long as they'd let her. Koo-Suki didn't have a chance of coming anywhere near her while she was in this luxury stronghold. Neither did the Guard, or anyone else. She sat up and wrapped her arms round her knees. Ash was reading something on his info-screen.

"Tell me about your family?" she asked.

It took a moment before he realised she'd spoken, and he raised his head from whatever he'd been studying.

"My family? You mean the Willims?"

She nodded.

"What do you want to know?"

"Who lives here. What they do."

He put his info-screen down and leaned back. "We all live here. My adopted father owns the place."

"What's he like?" Maeve really wanted to know whether he was the sort of person who would let her stay or the sort of person who would throw her out immediately.

"You must have heard of him. He's Marcus Willim."

When she shook her head, he added, "Wealthy, top level citizen? Part of the legislative council?"

Maeve closed her eyes thoughtfully. That sounded slightly familiar. They'd been taught the main political facts about the council back at school. She hadn't paid much attention then.

"He wants Serran to follow him into politics, but so far he hasn't shown much enthusiasm," Ash said.

"Is he likely to throw me out?"

Ash shook his head. "He doesn't pay much attention to the household unless it makes problems for him."

"Who else?"

"My sister. My mother of course. She's a legal worker and my sister followed her into the profession. My mother's the one who would throw you out."

"That makes three of you." Maeve frowned. "Three siblings?" Surely even the rich and influential had to obey the population laws.

"I told you I'm adopted," Ash said. "They took me in as part of the climate refugee campaign and by-passed the regulations that way." He said it as though he'd learned the words off by heart and now had no problem reciting them without emotion.

"Is that all? It seems an awfully big apartment for just five people."

"Marcus owns the whole building. Some other relatives have apartments here as well. Then there are the servants and guards. Most of them live in."

"What about you? What do you do?"

"I'm just starting my legal training. My mother says there's always work for another lawyer." He grimaced.

"Don't you like it?

"Not much." He turned back to his infodisk.

"What are you doing?"

"Studying." He looked up. "I need to do this. I've exams coming up. My mother says if I don't pass, there will be repercussions. Her idea of repercussions tends to be painful. Do you read?"

Maeve glared at him. "Of course, I can read."

"There's a reader over there. Help yourself. And keep quiet."

Chapter 20

Two days later, Maeve was still reading. She hadn't left Ash's room, but at least she'd been fed, and for the time being, she was reasonably safe.

She looked up when Ash rushed into the room, letting the door swing closed behind him. "What?"

"My mother's coming to see you."

"Shit. Is she going to throw me out?"

"I don't know. Serran told her about you." Ash raked both hands through his short golden hair. "I'm surprised she hasn't been before."

"What should I do?"

"Stand up and look respectful when she walks in. Don't speak unless she speaks to you first."

Maeve's heart thudded. "Are you scared of her?"

"Yeah, a bit."

She perched on the edge of the sofa, sitting on her hands to stop herself chewing on her nails. Ash sat opposite, looking as tense as she felt.

The door opened, and a woman strode in. She was almost as tall as Serran, and was dressed in an ornate version of the law society uniform, ankle-length black robes embellished with gold embroidery. Her dark blonde hair was bound in multiple plaits, all pulled to the back of her head, and her makeup was a simple enhancement. She had Serran's mouth, and ice-grey eyes. Maeve jumped to her feet, even though the woman behaved as though she hadn't seen her.

Ash rose more slowly. "Good morning, Mother."

"Good morning Ash." She inclined her chin towards Maeve. "Is that the girl Serran told me about?"

"Yes. She was a present from him."

His mother's brows arched in surprise. "He didn't tell me that. You're on good terms with him, again?"

Ash's expression didn't flicker. "I hope so."

"Why did he buy you a woman?" His mother studied Maeve. "She looks a little young, don't you think?"

Ash shrugged. "I didn't ask him. I didn't want an argument."

"No." The woman's gaze swung between Ash and Maeve. "I'll talk to him, but it's good that he's making an effort. Where did he get her?"

"He bought her indenture," Ash said. "For a month. I didn't like to reject—"

"You can't keep her in here," his mother said. "You need privacy for your studies."

Maeve's heart almost skipped a beat. Ash's mother talked as though she was a domestic animal, and it sounded like she was going to throw her out.

"She can have a bed in one of the servants' rooms. We've plenty of space."

"Thank you." Ash didn't look surprised.

Maeve's heartbeat settled into its normal rhythm.

"We shouldn't upset Serran. He's far too sensitive. He'd be hurt if you got rid of his gift. Is that one of your tunics she's got on?"

Ash looked at her. "Yes. I don't know what Serran did with her things."

"She can wear a house uniform. Send one of the servants to bring her one and get them to find her somewhere in the quarters. Honestly, Ash, what were you thinking of?"

"Sorry," Ash muttered.

The woman turned to Maeve, her eyes scanning her from the top of her ponytail, right down to her bare feet, lingering on the silver gel on her toes. "What's your name?"

"Maeve." Maeve wondered whether she should curtsey or call the woman Sir or Marm.

"How do you fill your days, Maeve?"

Maeve looked around the room for inspiration. "I've been reading."

"That's very nice." The woman sounded as though she was talking to an infant. "But you're not really good value, are you? Not if you were brought here as entertainment for my son?"

Maeve stared at her toes.

"How much of your time did Serran buy? Four weeks?"

"Yes, Marm."

"You'd better make yourself useful. I'll talk to the house servants about letting you do some tasks while you're here." Now she sounded as though she was doing Maeve a favour. "You can read in your spare time." Her attention returned to Ash. "If you want her for anything, then that's a priority. After you've finished studying, though. How's that going?"

"Okay."

"Good." She swept out of the room.

"Whew." Ash rubbed his forehead.

"Yeah." No wonder Ash was scared of her. She was like a chill wind sweeping through the building.

"I'm sorry about the extra work."

"What extra work — I wasn't doing anything," Maeve said. "I'd rather be busy." She liked the idea of working with the servants. If she made herself useful, maybe there would be opportunities.

Fifteen minutes later, a woman in a blue utility coverall came to the door.

Ash let her in.

"Marm Willim sent me," she said. "I've been told to find her a bed downstairs."

"Fine Go on, Maeve."

Maeve stood up.

"I'll talk to you later," Ash looked relieved to see the back of her.

The bed she was given, was on the basement floor, in a room which contained three narrow bunks. A strip of window at the top of the wall let a little daylight in.

"You'll have the room to yourself," the woman told her. "We're understaffed at the moment."

Another woman peered round the door. "We're always understaffed."

"There'll be plenty for you to do." The first woman folded her arms. "You're not too good for domestic work, are you?"

Maeve only just managed to stop an eye roll. "No. I'll do anything." She kept her voice soft and submissive.

"There's a uniform for you." The second woman handed her a stack of blue cloth.

Maeve shook it out. It was a coverall, like the one the other women wore. The quality was better than that of her most expensive skinsuit.

"Put it on, and come and find us. We're in the next room. And bring that tunic you're wearing. It belongs to Ashkir."

The uniform was too big for Maeve. She adjusted it as best she could and headed next door. Barefoot. There were no shoes, but she supposed it didn't matter indoors. The floor underfoot was warm and caressing to the soles of her feet. She hesitated in the doorway of a room that was identical to the one she'd been given. The two women were talking, sitting facing each other on opposite beds. They seemed a lot more friendly than the one who was Ash's bodyguard.

"What do you want me to do?" She'd heard that many households had completely automated cleaning systems and housekeeping functions.

"You can start by checking the family rooms. Remove any uneaten food, utensils, that sort of thing. Check the cleaning drones are working. Do you know where the utility rooms are?"

"No."

One of the women stood. "I'll show you."

~~~

The family rooms were usually deserted in the early morning. As far as Maeve could tell, they were barely used. She'd been doing the job for a week, and occasionally found empty glasses, half-full plates, discarded items of clothing in the mornings, but that was all. The cleaning drones worked perfectly. As she headed for the smaller of the reception rooms, she considered her future. She had less than three weeks left of the contract. Maybe she could stay on here, if she was lucky. It was a cushy job. She wouldn't want to do it forever, but it was a breathing space. She made up her mind to ask.

She slowed her steps as voices drifted through the open door. One of the voices was from Ash's mother, but the male voice was unfamiliar. She hesitated. She still hadn't seen Ash's father.

"This has got to stop," the man said. "He's a disgrace, an embarrassment to the family. Even I've heard gossip about his chem problem. I instructed you to deal with it."

"I spoke to him," Marm Willim said. "Marcus, I—"

"And the violence. You know what the guard said about him."

"What do you expect me to do? I had him whipped after the last time."

"A lot of good that did. This time the woman was a citizen," the man said. "For heaven's sake, Fallon, you must know there'll be repercussions. Her employer tried to blackmail me. I've shut her up for the present, but—"

"She was level one," Marm Willim hissed. "She was a sex worker. No one important. You could shut the employer up permanently if you wanted to."

"Don't be ridiculous," the man said. "It's just going to happen again. You've obviously failed to make any impression on him. His behaviour impacts on me, on the business, on my reputation. I won't allow him to ruin us all. This time I'll deal with him."

"Let me talk to him," Marm Willim said.

"Talk to him? Fallon it's too late for talking, we need—"

"He's your son."

"He didn't inherit his problems from me," the man said. "I'm shipping him off planet. I don't want to hear any more horror stories about his behaviour. He can work for one of the outer world subsidiaries. I'll organise an entry level position for him. And I'll limit his credits. That should put a leash on him. It'll be good for him."

"You can't do that. He's just a boy."

"He's twenty-six and he's a psychopath. This is his last chance. He might be my son, but if he causes more trouble, I'll report him. You know what that'll mean?"

"He'll be executed." Marm Willim drew in an audible breath. "I thought you were grooming him to follow you in the business. I thought you said you wanted him to move into a political role."

"I wanted a lot from him," the man said. "It's not going to happen though. Fallon, you must know it's impossible. Flora will be my heir now."

"The guard could be lying," Marm Willim said. "And Flora's not up to the job."

The man didn't reply.

"Have you told Serran?"

"Not yet." The man's voice got closer. "He's not here. I will though. And you're wrong about Flora. You've always been blind about the children."

Maeve pressed herself against the wall as Marm Willim and the man swept through the door.

Marm Willim stopped. "Have you been eavesdropping, girl? What did you hear?"

"No, Marm." Maeve lowered her eyes. "Nothing, Marm."

"If I hear any gossip, you'll be in big trouble." She stamped after the man, her long cloak swirling after her.

Maeve watched them go, before entering the reception room. A single coffee cup marred its neatness. She picked it up, considering what she'd heard. What had Serran done? It must be bad, if his own father was planning to disown him. That's what it had sounded like. And his mother thought he might be executed. What could have happened? She'd check his rooms next. His father had said he was still out, so she should be fine.

Serran's private reception room was empty. It looked as though he hadn't used it recently, so Maeve did a quick sweep of it, before checking the bedroom, which was also pristine, and finally, the hygiene facility. Someone had showered since it was last cleaned. Splashes of water formed puddles on the floor, but the cleaning drones would deal with that. Maeve pressed the button that called them. A leather thong hung over the edge of the bath. She picked it up, intending to return it to one of the storage cupboards. Hooking her finger through it, she frowned at the dangling pendant. It didn't look like something Serran would wear; cheap synth leather, and a roughly shaped metallic heart. A dark red smear stained the silver surface. She'd seen it before, somewhere.

The outer door hissed closed. Maeve swung round. Serran must be back. She edged out of the bathroom, hoping to get out of his quarters before he saw her, but she was too late. He was shrugging out of a fashionable jacket, a copy of the armoured ones worn by the military. One of his bodyguards waited by the door. No way could she sneak past both of them.

"Hey you? What are you doing in my room?"

"Cleaning, Sir."

"Aren't you the pleasagurl I gave to Ash?"

"Yes, Sir."

"So why are you cleaning?"

"Your mother wanted me to make myself useful," Maeve said.

Serran laughed. "She found you then? What did she say?"

"To make myself useful while I was here."

"About Ash, I mean, having a cheap pleasar in his rooms."

"She said you were a good brother, and she was pleased the two of you were on good terms again." Maeve took another step towards the door.

Serran laughed harder, his features manic. Maeve reached the door.

"What have you got there?" His eyes focussed on the pendant.

She'd forgotten it was still in her hand. "I was going to put it in your locker."

"Give it here."

Maeve handed it to him.

He swung it from his forefinger. "You know who this belonged to, don't you?"

"No, I—"

He lunged at her, fastening his hand around her throat, pushing her back to the wall. "Don't lie to me." His face was too close, the white of his eyes were stained pink, the pupils huge. The stench of R'lax drifted from his lips, followed by an acetic sourness.

Maeve gagged, her throat rippling against his fingers. She grabbed his wrist and tried to prise his hand away. It tightened, until she could barely breathe. She sank her nails into the flesh of his arm.

He laughed, using his free hand to swing the pendant against her cheek. His eyes glittered with excitement. "Whose is it?"

Maeve couldn't speak, she couldn't even cough properly."

Serran loosened his grip a fraction. "Whose is it?"

"I don't know." Maeve's voice shook. "I've seen it before, but I can't remember where."

"I think you're lying." His fingers tightened again. She squeezed her eyes closed, scrabbling at his arm. Fear loosened the muscles in her legs. She was going to die.

"Sir?" A new voice penetrated the pounding in her ears. "Sir?"

"Give me a knife."

Maeve's heart felt as though it wanted to burst out of her chest. "Sir?"

"I'll take her tongue. Then she won't be talking. That'll teach her to spy on me."

"Sir. Let go of her."

The fingers relaxed. "What?"

Maeve opened her eyes, pulling in an inadequate breath.

The bodyguard had one hand on Serran's shoulder. "You can't kill a servant in your parent's house."

"She's unlicensed."

"It doesn't matter. Your father will be furious. Let her go, Sir. She's just a servant."

Serran's fingers tightened again before he released her. Maeve took a huge breath, coughed and wiped her watering eyes with the back of her hand. Her legs wouldn't support her for much longer.

"Get out," the guard said to her. "Now. Quickly."

Maeve hurried out of the room, and along the corridor. She ran downstairs, back to her room, before her legs gave way. She sank onto the bed. Her heart still pounded in her ears. She finally remembered where she'd seen that necklace. It had belonged to Tooley, the dominatrix from the club. Why did Serran have it? What had he done? She had to find out.

Ash was in his room, when she walked in. He looked up from his desk. "Maeve. How are you getting on?"

"I'm okay." She fingered her neck. The bruises hadn't formed yet. "I wanted to ask you about Serran."

His face froze. "What?"

"Could he kill someone?"

Ash shrugged, avoiding her eyes. "Everyone could, if the situation was right."

"I'm talking about Serran." She paused, unwilling to voice her suspicions. "I heard your parents talking about him, this morning. I think they're going to send him off planet. He'd done something bad."

"Seriously? Father threatened that before, but mother stopped him. He'd smashed up a drinking club and put one of the staff in hospital. Father had to pay compensation. He's a loose cannon. He didn't kill anyone though. And Father calmed down. Eventually."

"I think your father meant it. And I found something in his room. In Serran's room. A pendant with blood on it."

"It doesn't mean—"

"And he tried to strangle me."

"Stay away from him," Ash said.

"Has he ever killed anyone, though?" Maeve persisted.

"I don't know," he said. "I've tried not to think about it. I wouldn't be surprised."

"But you don't know for sure."

He shook his head. "There are rumours from the guards. Serran's are his own though, and—"

"Tooley." Adrenaline drained from her system, leaving her weak again. Maeve sat on one of the sofas.

"What?"

"One of the staff at the place I came from." Maeve rested her head in her hands. "I found her pendant in his bathroom. It had blood on it."

"That doesn't prove anything. Are you sure it was hers?"

"I think so, and he had an appointment to see her. And your father said something about a level-one citizen."

"Oh."

"Why does he have her necklace?"

"I don't know."

"Could he have killed her? Shouldn't we tell someone?" Maeve raised her head to stare at Ash.

"It sounds like my father's dealing with him."

"But he might do it again. He could do it anywhere they send him."

Ash rubbed his eyes. "You don't know anything for definite. Let me think about it. See what happens. See if he really gets banished."

"Fine." Maeve stood up. "I think you should tell the Guard though." She stalked out of the room. No way was she going to the Guard herself. Look what had happened when she'd accused Scarlet. Although that had been a spiteful mistake on her part. Maybe her fear and anger at Serran were making her irrational. Ash was right. She didn't know anything for sure. Her throat hurt. She lay on her bed, closing her eyes for a moment.

She woke at the sound of voices from the next room. Sliding of the bed, she went to investigate. "What's going on?"

"Big excitement," one of the women told her. "Serran tried to knife his sister."

"What? You *are* joking, aren't you?"

"No. Their father named her as his heir and disowned Serran," the other woman said. "He threw a knife at her. It got her in the shoulder. He pulled it out and went for her face, said he would cut her treacherous tongue out. He's been locked in his rooms until the next shuttle leaves for the hub base."

"How do you know?"

"The whole household knows," the woman said.

"Is she okay?" Why did Serran carry a knife in his own house, Maeve wondered. Had he *planned* to attack his sister?

"Mostly, I think. I heard her bodyguards stopped him touching her face."

"He's leaving then? For definite?" Relief swamped Maeve.

"Being sent away," the woman said. "Although, I heard he's going to Eden Fields. Most of us would kill to get on a settlement ship going out there."

"He did, didn't he?" the other woman said.

"What?"

"Killed. One of the guards told me Serran's bodyguards have had to get rid of bodies before."

"No!"

The woman shrugged. "It might not be true."

"Marm Willim says her son isn't going to exile alone. She'll go with him," the other woman said. "I'm going up now, to help her get ready."

She returned five minutes later, peering round Maeve's door. "The mistress wants to see you, in her rooms. What have you done?"

"Nothing." Maeve got up. "That I know of, anyway." She had no idea why Marm Willim would want to see her.

When Maeve entered the room, Marm Willim was sitting in an upright chair, while her personal maid wove twists of colour through her blond hair. Serran paced restlessly across the room, his mouth fixed in a sullen line. He was supposed to be confined to his room, wasn't he?

"Come over here," Marm Willim beckoned her.

Maeve took a couple of steps further into the room, keeping a careful eye on Serran.

"Here." Marm Willim pointed at the floor in front of her chair.

Maeve moved closer.

"I will be taking a trip to the family holdings on Eden Fields," Marm Willim said. "I need a member of staff to accompany me, and it occurred to me that you may like the opportunity."

Maeve blinked. The maid looked up, briefly meeting her eyes.

"You have no future on Earth, isn't that right?"

"I don't know. I hope I have." Maeve touched the tip of her finger to her throat. Surely the bruises must be visible by now.

"There is no requirement for registered citizenship on the colony planets," Marm Willim said. "Your horizons wouldn't be so limited. It's a wonderful opportunity for you."

Maeve shifted her weight from one foot to the other. "I don't think—"

"I own your time for another week," Serran said. "We aren't giving you the choice. You're coming with us."

"Be quiet, Serran. You've done enough. If it wasn't for you and your appalling..." His mother glared at him. "Never mind that, now. Maeve, if you decide you aren't happy on Eden Fields, we can discuss paying your return passage. That would depend on your performance of course. Your behaviour."

"I—"

Serran folded his arms. "No choice, girlie."

"Serran, leave us." Marm Willim pointed at the door. "Go straight to your room."

Serran flicked Maeve's cheek with one finger as he left.

"There are a few things I want to say to you." Marm Willim's eyes drifted to Maeve's neck, narrowing, as though she hadn't noticed the marks before. "Where did those bruises come from?"

"Serran tried to strangle me."

Marm Willim sighed. "What did you do?"

"Nothing, Marm." Surely, she wasn't getting the blame for Serran's assault? "He asked me something and I didn't know the answer."

"The pendant? He told me you found it."

"Yes." Maeve hesitated. "Thanks for the offer, but I don't want to go with you. He scares me."

"Ridiculous," Marm Willim said. "And it's no wonder you didn't recognise the pendant. It's one I gave him years ago."

"I see." What a liar the mother was. As if anyone with her money would buy a cheap piece of jewellery like that pendant. Maeve was more than ever convinced that it had belonged to Tooley.

"You haven't mentioned it to the other servants?"

"No."

"Good. I insist on absolute discretion." Marm Willim didn't give Maeve a chance to speak. "My son will be returning to Earth, eventually, to take up a political career. I would be very displeased if any unsavoury rumours spread from my own household."

"I won't say anything. I don't know anything."

"Good girl. You'll be leaving with us anyway."

"But I don't want to leave Earth." Not with Serran, at least. "And Serran could have killed me. He might try again."

"Nonsense." Marm Willim pursed her lips. She was like a steam roller. Not that Maeve had ever seen one. She didn't even know what one was, or where the phrase had come from.

"But, Marm—"

"You have my word he won't touch you. Now, go and ready yourself to leave. You've got half an hour."

Chapter 21

Eleven days after leaving Earth, the shuttle docked into hub-station three, exactly on time. Scarlet checked each of the ten economy passenger groups, counting them out of the bunkrooms, updating their records and directing them in the direction of the exit tube. It had been an easy job, and a pity he couldn't keep it for a while longer. Once station security cleared them, the passengers disappeared into the hub-station and most of the crew signed off duty. The shuttle wasn't scheduled to return to Earth for a couple of days.

Scarlet collected his pay credits from the Second Officer's desk, posted his uniform into the laundry slot, and headed for the exit with his bag, one of the last to leave. The flexible tube between the shuttle and the station was a zero-gravity zone, and once the passengers were all off, the magnetic strip de-activated. Scarlet manoeuvred himself along, clinging to the hand grips on the edge, trying not to think about what he would do next. The Chief Security Officer followed him down the tube to the hub-station, catching him up at the point where the tube became solid ground, with near Earth gravity. Scarlet tested his balance carefully, before taking a step.

"You'll get used to it," the Chief told him.

"Yeah." Scarlet didn't think he'd have the chance.

"You did an okay job. You going back on an Earthbound shuttle?"

"I don't know what I'm doing yet. Do you know a place I can stay while I try for work?"

The Chief grimaced. "Good luck with that. The crews stay in a hostel close to the port. I'm walking over there now. We don't turn round until the day after tomorrow, so I'll be staying the night. Walk with me? It's cheap and basic, but you get a bed and fed."

Scarlet fell in step with him as they left the shuttle area. The transit hub was the weirdest place he'd ever been, a completely enclosed environment. He took a deep breath, sniffing air that had a distinctive odour, a mixture of plasmetal and damp vegetation, pervasive, but not unpleasant. He slowed his pace, wrinkling his nose.

The Chief matched his pace. "I'd forgotten how these places smell. It's maintenance. There's a huge amount of space dedicated to horticulture. They circulate their air around the entire construct. It's not a bad smell."

"No." Just different from the air Scarlet breathed on Earth. He looked back over his shoulder at the shuttle. It was still docked on the outside of the station, at a purpose-built port-pod, linked by flexible tubes to the main hub, and forming a globule of light against the darkness of space. The port-pod was a sizeable concourse, oval with docking stations around two thirds of the plasglass walls. Floor and ceiling lights bounced off all the surfaces, dazzling in their brightness. Auto-carriers buzzed between the shuttle tubes and the pod's access points, supervised by people in beige coveralls. All the passengers had passed through immigration, disappearing to their hotels, hostels and homes, leaving the vast area sparsely populated.

"Where do the starships dock?" Scarlet asked.

"The other side of the station," his companion said. "They don't dock, though, they're far too big. They wait further out, a few hundred kilometres away. There's another shuttle system for them. Another port-pod."

"Oh."

On the side of the concourse, opposite the docking tubes, the exit terminal was manned by two immigration officials and two guards with trank-guns. They checked Scarlet's id, but waved his boss through with a nod of acknowledgement. The exit took them through a broad tube, leading off the port-pod and into a wide plaza, where stacks of crates moved along conveyor belts, supervised by workers in uniform coveralls. The plaza looked as though it was a warehousing facility, or an industrial zone. A couple of small bars advertised food and drink. Groups of cargo handlers busied themselves around the four tunnels which led out from the far side.

"How big is the hub-station?" Scarlet asked.

"Big."

"How many people?"

"It's probably the size of London, but three dimensional. It's a series of habitats and work zones, connected by tubes. Any of them can be isolated if there's a vacuum breach."

"Does that happen often?" Scarlet asked.

"Never, as far as I know," the Chief said. "But no spacer takes a risk with air pressure. More than twenty thousand people live here permanently, and none of them want to breath vacuum."

Scarlet nodded. It sounded like a particularly horrible way to die.

"The population explodes when a colony ship's about to leave. The place is full of people who don't know what they're doing. Safety procedures are the most strictly enforced laws once you're off Earth."

They turned into one of the tunnels, a broad walkway, with a raised conveyer belt on each side. Freight containers drifted past, in both directions. A hundred metres further on, the tunnel opened out into another square. "This is a residential zone," the Chief said. "The people who work at the port mostly live in those." He pointed at the steely blue buildings lining two sides of the square. Each had three levels, with external open staircases leading up to rows of doors. Small, immature trees grew along all the facades. At one end, a maintenance worker was leaning out from the top of a small cherry picker. He appeared to be fixing something to the building.

"Nice," Scarlet said. The units looked clean and well-maintained.

"Basic Accommodation," the Chief said. "They're standard on all the hub stations." A hostel and a couple of restaurants filled the third side of the square, and the fourth had two bars with an exit tunnel between them.

"The place is like a maze," the Chief added. "I can't remember exactly how many pods it has now, but it's still expanding. You can pick up a pathfinder at the hostel. You'll need it."

Scarlet looked up. The top of the pod was at least fifty feet above his head and made of thick plasglass. Even the poor quality of the glass, and the low-level lighting didn't completely suppress the effect of the stars, and the milky clouds of a distant galaxy. He stared until the Chief nudged his arm.

"You need to check in. There'll be plenty of time to gape later, and better places to stargaze than this." Without waiting, he walked up to the doors of the smaller accommodation building, which opened automatically for him.

"Don't they scan id?" Scarlet hurried after him, knowing he looked like a complete doodle-dud.

"They'll ask for it when you check in. The consensus of the hub's security team is that by the time anyone manages to disembark here, they've probably been over-checked anyway."

Fortunate for people like him, Scarlet thought, but if he was in charge, the whole security thing would be a billion times tighter.

"Life's a bit more relaxed up here," the Chief said. "They don't have the same problems as Earth."

Scarlet nodded, unconvinced. People were people wherever they were, and would get away with as much as they could.

A woman manned the reception desk, dressed in a uniform that consisted of a close-fitting tunic, in the grey favoured by the port workers, and a long, loose skirt in the same colour. She smiled as she recognised the Chief. "Welcome back. I suppose you want a room?"

"And one for my colleague here." The Chief inclined his head in Scarlet's direction.

"No problem. Let me have your ids."

The Chief held up his wrist for the scanner.

"You've got room 14," she told him.

"Ben?" He looked over his shoulder as he left. "Remember to pick up your pathfinder. Most of the shuttle crew meet in the bar closest to the landing pods. The Explorer, it's called. If you want a drink, come down."

Scarlet nodded.

"Your wrist, please?" the receptionist said.

Scarlet raised his arm.

"It's your first time here?"

He nodded. "First time off Earth."

"Exciting for you. I hope you enjoy it and decide to come back." She checked her screen. "Room 27. It's on the first floor. Read the safety instructions before you do anything else. Have a good stay."

Scarlet squeezed past the desk and jogged up the stairs. At the top, a solid door stood in his way. He held up his wrist. It clicked open and he walked through into another corridor, lined with doors. They all had numbers, odd on one side, even on the other. Number 27 was halfway along.

The room was tiny, containing a narrow bunk, a tall thin cupboard and a small pull-down desk with a folding chair. When he pulled it out, he had zero standing room. It was still more space than he'd had on the shuttle. He tossed his bag onto the bunk and opened the cupboard door. Breathing apparatus was stored on the top shelf, together with a pressure suit similar to the one he'd had for the shuttle journey. The oxygen cannister was full. There were three empty shelves, so he picked his bag up and placed it on the middle one.

The desk surface turned into an info-screen when he touched it, the opening page giving a map of the hostel and links to safety information and evacuation routes. It wouldn't scroll on until he'd read them. Once he'd trawled though the safety notes and realised, that if anything happened to the station systems, they were all doomed, whatever procedures they followed, he sat on the bunk and wondered what to do next. The windowless room was giving him a queasy claustrophobic feeling in his stomach. Surely no one spent much time in these little cubicles? It was funny that he hadn't felt like that on the shuttle. He'd only been in the dormitory to sleep, though, and there had always been other people around, even if they'd been so busy, he barely saw them. He'd hardly ever been alone, before this. Mink and Koo-Suki were usually close-by, in the different roles they'd taken with each other – lovers, family, colleagues, comrades. Even that monster mutant of Mink's would be better than his own company. It might be months before he saw Koo and Mink again. *If ever*, a negative voice in his head suggested. He squashed it. The Chief had suggested a bar. He'd said the rest of the crew would be there. One of them might know of a job, or at least where to look for one.

Scarlet pushed the desk back into the wall, and returned to reception where he collected a pathfinder.

His shuttle couldn't have been the only one landing in the afternoon. People milled about the square, most of them dressed in expensive and fashionable skinsuits, suggesting they were higher-level colonists, the privileged sort who'd bought themselves a place on one of the desirable planets. Primoris or Eden Fields, as far as Scarlet could recall. He wondered how much it cost to buy passage to one of them. More than he could afford, for sure.

He crossed the square, consulted his pathfinder, and took the exit tunnel towards the bar. After a couple of minutes there were no longer hordes of people around. Ahead of him, he caught a glimpse of red hair. He squinted. It looked like Sula, the woman who'd shown him to the shuttle. He increased his pace to catch up, feeling a sense of relief at the thought of finding a familiar face. "Sula?"

She turned her head. "Ben? You going to the Explorer?"

"That's where my boss suggested."

"Yeah. I think there'll be a few people there. Most of them are shipping out again the day after tomorrow, so they'll be celebrating time off, today." She tapped the arm of the man with her. "Have you met Jon?"

"No." Scarlet hadn't noticed he was there.

"He's junior pilot on your shuttle."

"You do this trip all the time?" Scarlet asked him. He looked vaguely familiar.

"Yeah." Jon was young, his expression open and friendly. "For the last couple of years, backwards and forwards between Earth and the hub. Junior pilot's a big title. I'm more maintenance."

"You like it?"

"It's fine for now. I'm looking for promotion though. Junior to Senior. I'm a career spacer. I'd like to move to one of the interstellar ships eventually. One of the explorer class."

"Right." Scarlet glanced at Sula.

"I was thinking I might try for a job in maintenance on one of the deep spacers," she said. "Jon and I want to stay together. I've got a good track record on station, so I should be able to find something."

The tunnel opened out into a small pod, this time with a much lower, solid grey ceiling. Scattered amongst the maintenance buildings were a couple of restaurants, cafés, and a discrete bar, with 'Explorer' picked out in white plasteel above the entrance.

"This is where I'll be working for the next couple of weeks," Sula said. "We're going to green this pod. It's been a bit neglected so far. A lot of spacers come here. It's enough off the beaten track that the colonists and tourists don't find it." She grinned. "Spacers don't much like their passengers."

Scarlet raised an eyebrow. "Tourists? On a hub-station?" He couldn't believe anyone would view this dismal hunk of plasmetal as a desirable destination. Maybe he was missing something. Maybe he should explore the place, before dismissing it out of hand.

"Some people want an armchair adventure," Jon said. "Weird. Hard to get your head round."

Scarlet followed the two of them into a dimly lit space, filled with round tables and semi-circular benches.

Sula pushed her way to a table, while Jon headed to the bar, nodding to a few people on the way. Scarlet followed him.

"What do you want?" he asked.

"Some sort of beer? Anything."

Jon leaned on the bar and shouted his order. The bartender came back with three long tubes of pale amber-coloured liquid. He handed one to Scarlet, who took a tentative sip.

"Thanks."

Jon carried the two remaining drinks back to Sula. Three other people, a woman and two men were already seated. Jon waved Scarlet to the bench before sliding in opposite, next to Sula. "Nica, Tomas, Lenny – this is Ben Scarlet. He was temporary crew on the last shuttle. Junior security."

All three nodded a greeting. Scarlet had seen them during his job, but hadn't had a chance to talk to any of them.

"You coming back with us?" Nica, the woman, asked.

Scarlet shook his head. "One way trip. I think you're getting your old security officer back. I'm looking for employment."

Nica stared at him for a second. "You must be mad," she said. "Coming up here without a definite job offer? You'll end up mining uranium on Volcas 12."

"Volcas 12?"

"An asteroid in the Volcas belt," she said. "High uranium content. They can never get enough miners, and they don't last long. It's even worse than the local mining operations, and they're bad enough."

Jon reached over and jabbed a finger in her shoulder. "Don't frighten him. Volcas 12 is a penal colony. They use convict labour, and the miners are given a choice of working there."

"Yeah," Nica sneered. "Penal servitude – short and sour – or execution."

"You might find something," Tomas said. "Just be careful though. Some of those contracts are open-ended and you end up in debt and tied to the company for the rest of your life."

"Which won't be very long in some of those places." Nica leaned over the table. "It's scandalous that it's allowed to go on."

Scarlet shrugged. "It's not much different on Earth, is it really?"

"You're not worked to death there."

"What about unlicensed conscripts?"

"They aren't citizens though, are they?" Nica said. "I'm talking about citizens. People who have rights."

"Still people."

"You're even more radical than Nica," Jon said. "Is that why you wanted a change from Earth? Someone heard you talking like that?"

Scarlet shrugged. "I wanted to try something different. Somewhere different."

"I get that." Nica leaned towards him. "But you need to be careful what you say. Even up here. You don't know us. We could be anyone."

Scarlet stared at her. She sounded concerned. "Okay." He didn't have a clue what subjects were acceptable and what weren't. He took a sip of his beer while the conversation moved on to gossip about fellow spacers.

A hand fell on his shoulder and he whirled round, ready to fight.

The Chief Security Officer backed away. "Hey. Calm down."

"Sorry." Scarlet held up his hands. "Remnant from my days as a bodyguard."

"What the fuck were you guarding?" the Chief muttered. "I wanted to ask you a favour."

Scarlet waited.

"My regular junior is finishing off some work for station security," the Chief said. "Would you like to do tonight's duty at the port-pod? You'd get a bonus and I'd be willing to give you a job recommendation?"

"When do I start?" A job recommendation would be useful. The credits would come in handy as well.

"Now." The Chief handed him a bag. "Here's your uniform."

"Okay." Scarlet drained his beer. "Just let me buy drinks for this lot."

"I'll do it," the chief said. "You get yourself down to the docking bays."

No Good Deed

Chapter 22

Scarlet signed on at the duty station in the port-pod and checked out a trank-gun. He took up a position near the shuttle's exit tube. Its access was blocked, and the tube floated loose in the darkness of space. No one could get aboard without a deep vacuum suit, and the codes to release the access airlock. This was going to be a boring night. When he looked round at the other docking stations, all the ones with shuttles had guards. Most of them were dressed in the grey uniform of Space services, like the one Scarlet wore, but a couple were more colourful, and he guessed they worked for private craft. All of them carried the same tranker as his. Lethal projectile weapons were completely banned on the station. Civilians weren't allowed any weapons at all. It was very different from Earth, but the hostel's safety data had described what might happen if the station's hull got damaged. In excruciating detail. Reinforced plasteel lined the docking bays, and the plasglass on the exit side was double thickness, but even so...

Beyond the glass, misty trails blurred across the darkness, star fields distorted by the window. All the shuttles save one, were dark, difficult to make out, against the darkness of space. The active one was three berths down from Scarlet. He squinted at it, wishing he could get another job like the one he'd just done. He wouldn't mind a job on any sort of space transport, even the Explorer star ships. Especially the Explorer star ships. Imagine the excitement of being one of the first people to see a new habitat? If only Koo-Suki and Mink were here, and if only they had enough credits, they could have joined some colonisation ship, bought their way into emigrant status, become legal. Then they could have found real jobs, in one of the colonies, or even on one of the deep space explorer ships.

It was just a dream. Most habitable planets, the good ones, wanted certain levels of citizenship, as well as a sizeable payment. The less good ones wanted labour. What was he going to do? He couldn't go back to Earth, yet, even if he could afford the passenger fare. The woman in the bar had scared him with her talk of convict labour and penal colonies. Something better than that must be out there.

He wondered where Koo and Mink were now, and whether they'd managed to stay out of the law's way. How long would it be until he heard from them? He missed them. He reminded himself that he was lucky to be alive enough to feel lonely. He could have been in a cell in Security Central, back on Earth, full of drugs and possibly well on the way to being vivisected. They wouldn't believe he knew nothing about the Silencer until they'd almost killed him. He'd heard a lot of stories about the state interrogators, everyone had. The only reason they would leave him alive is so they'd have a puppet for the public execution. He stretched his arms above his head and forced his mind back to his job.

The docking bay next to him clanked into activity. Lights came on, and the embarkation tube clipped into position. Seconds later, a man emerged from a private shuttle and with a nod at his guard, he headed for the exit gate. Scarlet's gaze followed him across the square. He was dressed in the high fashion of Earth, long, layered robes, over a close-fitting skinsuit, all in shades of dark red.

Another shuttle was approaching, white lights standing out against the vast darkness. It slowed, almost to a stop, and drifted into a free dock, where the tube snaked out and connected with the airlock. No staff attended. *Strange.* Scarlet met the eyes of the guard to his right, the one from the private shuttle. "Is that normal?" It wasn't any of his business. He was paid to keep an eye on the official Earth shuttle, but he was curious.

The other guard shook his head, a puzzled frown on his face.

The barrier to the tube connector swung open. A couple of guards moved away from their stations and walked over to it, hands on their trankers. Scarlet squinted into the dim light that illuminated the barrier, just as one of the guards convulsed and fell to the ground. The other shouted at a woman, who stepped out of the tube and darted to one side.

She ignored his instruction to stand still, and reached into the bag hanging from her shoulder. When her hand reappeared, it had a gun in it. Even from a distance, Scarlet could see it was one of the weapons banned on the station. A man walked after her, carrying a shock tazer. He must be the one who'd stunned the guard. Pointing the tazer at the other guard, he dropped him as well. Like the woman, he was dressed in rough, undyed coveralls. Behind them, more people crowded down the tube, all wearing the same sort of coverall. Scarlet looked around the pod. None of the other guards moved, they all seemed stunned into silence.

"Should we do something?" he asked the guard on his right.

"Spaceport security will stop them at the gates," he replied. "They won't get out of the docks."

The cluster of men and women passed the original woman and rushed for the exit.

"She's got a high energy, high velocity gun," Scarlet said. "Didn't you see it."

"Are you sure?"

"Yeah. I'm going to see if they need help, over there. There's only two men on duty. I don't think that shuttle was expected." He didn't bother waiting for a reply. The gun bothered him a lot.

None of the group around the entrance noticed him approaching. The woman held her gun loosely at her side. What was she doing with it? He couldn't see her expression, but didn't she know the penalties for possession of a lethal weapon? That thing could do a colossal amount of damage to the hub structure.

Scarlet sprinted towards her, fear lending him speed. She finally heard him coming and spun round. The man with the tazer fired at him as he tackled the woman, knocking her to the ground. Needles skimmed past his ear, missing him by a millimetre. He pinned the woman to the floor, holding her down with the weight of his body, and grabbed her gun hand. From the corner of his eye, he saw the

208

other guard tackle the tazer man. He tightened his grip on the woman's wrist, squeezing until the bones creaked. She screamed and thrashed, pummelling at him with her free hand, but she dropped the gun. He let go of her wrist and grabbed the weapon. The woman stiffened, then went limp beneath him. He scrambled off her, seized an arm and hauled her to her feet.

She was thin and age-worn, with colourless hair cropped close to her scalp. Her coverall swamped her.

"What the hell are you doing with that gun?" he asked. "Do you know the sort of damage it could cause on a station like this?"

She pressed her lips together and stared through him. Her eyes were unnaturally wide.

One of the gate guards approached. "I'll take her."

"She's using chem," Scarlet said. Tremors shook the woman's body. He studied her eyes. "It might be DoubleD."

"DeathDreamer?" The other guard took out a set of restraints and bound her wrists behind her back.

"Maybe." Scarlet still had the gun. He held it out.

"Hang on to it." The gate guard steered the woman towards the exit. "I'll call hub security. They'll send someone down to collect it."

Scarlet walked back to his place by the Earth shuttle's docking station, to wait for hub security. The gun made him nervous. He wanted someone else to take it.

The guard who'd tackled the tazer man joined him. "How did you know she had a gun? That sort of gun?"

Scarlet shrugged, wincing as he became aware of a wrenched muscle in his shoulder. "I don't know. I just did."

"Are you all right? He nearly got you with the tazer."

"Yeah." Scarlet rotated his sore shoulder and glanced at the gate. A couple of men had arrived. They wore black uniforms, and the gate guards deferred to them. "It's just a pulled muscle. He missed me with the tazer."

One of the newcomers peeled away from the small huddle by the gate and marched over to him. He was a middle-aged man, in good shape, with dark skin and short dark hair. Two interlinked silver circles decorated the left sleeve of his uniform. "Hub Security," he said. "You've got the gun?"

"Here." Scarlet held it out.

The officer examined it. He whistled. "Use this right, and you could make a big hole on the casing. Then bang – we're all dead. I wonder what they planned. I guess we'll find out."

"What happens to her now?" Scarlet asked.

"Questions," the officer said. "The station is divided into sections, so a hole in just one would affect a small area. That could be up to a thousand people exposed to vacuum, if it was a residential sector. She's in serious trouble."

"Who was she?"

"No idea," the officer said. "We'll find that out as well. When does your shift finish?"

"In four hours."

"Okay. You'll need to come down to Hub Station Security, to give a report. What's your name?"

"Benaiah Scarlet." He wanted to ask about the small mob who'd followed the woman off the shuttle, but the officer had already turned away, hurrying back to his colleagues.

Scarlet watched him go, uneasy at the idea of visiting law enforcement.

~~~

With the help of his pathfinder, Hub Station Security was easy enough to get to, at the centre of the hub station, in the original habitat. One of the tunnels from the docks led directly to it, passing through two more sectors on the way, before spawning a series of smaller thoroughfares, leading into different parts of the station. The main tunnel opened out into a wide six-sided area, single level, with soaring walls surrounding it. Groups of young fruit trees, underplanted with grasses and small shrubs, occupied beds which aligned with the sides of the hexagon. Rampant green climbers scrambled over the buildings around the perimeter, some of them covered in pink and white flowers. Multilayer, high-visibility plasglass formed the ceiling. As Scarlet entered the plaza, the lights went out. His stomach dropped through the floor. A few seconds later they came on again, and his stomach leapt to his throat. He swallowed, wondering what had just happened.

"Isn't it amazing?" It was still very early in the work cycle, but a few visitors wandered round the hexagon. The one who spoke to him was an elderly woman, silver-haired, perfectly groomed, and dressed in a crimson body-fitting skinsuit covered by a knee-length over-tunic.

"What?" Scarlet had no idea what she was talking about.

"The star view. Is this the first time you've been here? They switch the lights off for a few seconds every hour. Once every cycle, they're off for ten minutes. It's so you get the benefit of the galaxy, and mainly for the visitors. The view's better from the viewing platforms, but this is good enough for me."

"Oh. Yes. I'm working here," Scarlet said. "First time off Earth."

"Enjoy." The woman patted his arm and walked away.

Scarlet tilted his head to stare through the roof. Despite the lights, he could still see streaks of moving whiteness, points of bright light that blurred as the station moved. *Stars.* Hundreds of light years away, each one the centre of their own system, each one with the possibility of planets that might be habitable, that might already be occupied. All that space out there made him feel very small and inconsequential. He yawned and shook his head in an attempt to detach the negativity. He was just tired. He yawned again.

The security building was a squat black edifice in the centre of the open space, its shape a miniature copy of Security Central in London. Scarlet had never been there, he shuddered at the idea, but he'd seen it from a distance. It dominated the south bank of The Thames, its solid black façade dimly lit even at night. This one had a green roof, and was covered with more climbing plants, diluting the menace factor. He presented his wrist to the automatic scanner at the entrance.

The doors slid open. A wide counter separated the main part of the room from the entrance, and behind it, two uniformed men sat at a table, drinking tubes in front of them. They looked up at Scarlet's entrance. One of them smiled. "Yes? Can I help you?"

"I was told to come and give a report. I was at the docks, last night."

"What's your name."

"Benaiah Scarlet."

"Oh yes. We've been expecting you." The man passed him a tube containing a drink. "Heard you did good, last night."

"Just my job." Scarlet sniffed at the tube before risking a taste. It smelled vaguely like coffee, so he sipped at it. "Thanks. Do you know if the rest of the group got caught?"

"Yeah," the man said. "All of them, I think. They didn't get far. They didn't have a clue where they were going."

A door opened at the back of the reception area. "Benaiah Scarlet?" A man stood in the opening. "Come through, will you?"

Scarlet got up and followed him into a small office, where a uniformed officer sat behind a desk. She could have been any age, between forty and sixty, her features angular, her medium brown hair clipped close to her head. The sleeve of her uniform displayed a lot of silver.

"Thank you for coming," she said. "I'm Comisario Leyland. I run policing and security for the hub station."

The man closed the door behind him and joined his colleague behind the desk. He waved Scarlet to a seat on the opposite side and activated a recorder. "Tell us what happened, last night, as you saw it."

Scarlet recited the story as best he could remember. "Who were they?" he asked, when he'd finished. "Terrorists? What did they want?"

"Not terrorists." The Comisario shook her head. "They were a crew from one of the mining asteroids. Protesting against conditions, they said. Can't blame them really, but we can blame them for bringing that sort of weapon on station. They're in serious trouble, but I don't think we'll ever see the woman in court. She's medically incapable. She'd taken DoubleD, almost an overdose amount. When we gave her the truth drug, she passed out. She's still in a coma."

"Where did she get the gun from?"

"Stole it off one of the supervisors. The same one she got the DoubleD from. He's been summoned back to answer a few questions. His bosses are probably tolerant of chem, but that sort of gun's banned in any off-planet habitat. They won't want trouble with the law." She put her drinking tube in a table holder. "We need your id for the report."

Scarlet held out his wrist for the scanner. He'd never undergone so much scanning in his life before. If this was what registered citizens put up with, perhaps he didn't want to be legal after all.

"We'll be checking with your employer," the Comisario said. "But you can go now. Last night was the most excitement we've had up here in years. Anyway, thank you for your help."

Chapter 23

A loud buzz from somewhere close by woke him. Scarlet rolled over and almost fell off the narrow bunk. The lights in the tiny room gradually brightened. A messenger drone hovered by his ear, informing him that Hub Station Security was trying to contact him. "Why?"

The drone didn't respond.

A pulse thudded in his temple. He swung his legs round to perch on the edge of the bed, and activated the reply option. "Yes?"

"Benaiah Scarlet? Can you come down to Hub Security?" A man's voice. "The Comisario would like to talk to you."

Scarlet suppressed his instinctive worry, telling himself that security here wasn't like the organisation on Earth. "When?"

"As soon as possible."

"Half an hour all right?" It would take him that long to dress and find the route he'd taken yesterday. The station was an absolute warren.

"Fine." The link closed and the drone returned to its docking station.

Scarlet pulled on his own skinsuit and boots. He must remember to return the borrowed uniform to the shuttle office. The last think he needed, was to be arrested for theft. He collected his pathfinder and left the hostel.

"Hey?"

He looked round.

Sula jogged to catch him up. "I heard you were at the docks yesterday when that trouble went down. What happened?"

Word obviously spread fast on the hub station. "A discontented mining crew, I think," Scarlet told her. "That's what I heard, anyway."

"Hard to blame them." She strode along next to him. "Want to go for a drink, tonight? I'm on an eight-hour shift, but when I've finished, Jon and I are meeting a few people for drinks and some food before he has to take the shuttle back."

Scarlet nodded. Any company would be good, and Sula was staying on station after Jon left. She would be someone he knew. "Yeah. Okay. Here, let me give you my contact."

The two of them swapped details. At the opposite end of the square, Sula slowed. "I'll give you a tour of the station's hydroponics if you like. We're expanding the useful growth into all the pods. It'll look great, and really add to the amount of fresh food we can provide. Would you like to see it? Maybe tomorrow? We can talk about it tonight."

"Yeah, I'd love to see it. Thanks." He'd be fascinated to see the source of the earthy scent in the air. It was obvious that Sula was passionate about her job. "I'm going this way. See you later."

When he arrived at Hub Security, the Chief Security Officer from the shuttle was talking to Comisario Leyland. Scarlet hesitated in the doorway.

"Come in." The Comisario waved him in. "We're just getting the paperwork for last night, and needed to confirm you came in on that shuttle."

"That's right." Scarlet glanced at the Chief, wondering why he'd bothered to come in person.

"And you're looking for work?"

"Yes."

"You were rash to head out into space without any definite prospect of employment." The Comisario raised an eyebrow. "Vagrants end up press-ganged into the most dangerous and unpleasant jobs. Unpaid ones."

"I wanted a change." He wasn't a vagrant. "I've saved enough to last me for a little while. Enough to get back to Earth if I have to. I thought I'd be able to find another job once I got here."

"A bit naïve. You might have found yourself hauling radioactive ore."

Scarlet grimaced. "That's not the sort of adventure I had in mind. I hope I can get something a bit better than that."

His old boss interrupted. "I've got a possibility for you. A year's contract on a supply shuttle for the local asteroid mines. Would you be interested?"

"Definitely." A year was longer than he wanted to be stuck out here, but it was still better than he'd expected. He couldn't believe he was considering a year of legitimate work. Hopefully, the modifications to his wrist chip would last that long.

"It would be on my personal recommendation, so don't screw up. You'll need to talk to the captain, and you'd be doing general duties as well as security."

"It sounds good."

"Not that good, but it's better than nothing. It would start in a couple of weeks. The present crewman is transferring to an interstellar transport after this cycle."

"Right." Scarlet wondered what that would be like, crewing on the huge intergalactic ships. His face must have shown his curiosity.

"You want to go out on the interstellar ships?"

"Maybe one day, but I can't afford to be fussy at the moment." Scarlet remembered his cover story. "And anything would be a change from bodyguarding spoiled rich kids."

The Comisario cleared her throat. "Would you consider taking a temporary post on the station, while you wait?"

Scarlet gaped. Law enforcement? Him?

"We've got two colony transports leaving in the next few days, a crowd of future colonists coming in on the shuttles, and a temporary shortage of staff. There are usually fifteen of us working in three shifts, but three are on vacation, Kier's recovering from an accident, and Richenda's just given birth. It would basically be a patrol job, with some immigration duty. Three weeks. You've dealt with high level citizens, so you know what a pain they can be."

Scarlet cleared his throat. "I could do that." It would mean he didn't have to waste his saved credits on station living expenses, and surely, he'd hear from Koo-Suki or Mink in the next couple of weeks. At least four shuttles should arrive from Earth in that time.

"And if you want to go out on something a bit more adventurous after you've done the supply job, working on station would look positive in any application."

"Great. When do I start?"

"Tomorrow. We've got your data from the investigation, so that's all right. We just need to get you a contract. You can talk to admin now."

"Right," Scarlet said.

The Comisario frowned at him. "I don't really buy into your story of needing a change, but your reasons for coming here are your own, and you proved yourself last night. We're not nosy like the dust eaters. As long as you do your job and don't cause any trouble, you'll be all right."

Scarlet made an effort to smile. "Dust eaters?"

"Earth types."

His old boss stood up. "I'm off. My mate on the supply shuttle should call you sometime today. Remember it's my reputation at stake as well as yours." He waved at the Comisario and left.

Scarlet visited admin, signed a three-week temporary contract and picked up his new uniform. It was a matt black coverall with a simple silver circle on the left arm. He dropped it back at his hostel, and wondered how to fill the rest of his day. Once he'd returned his shuttle uniform and caught up on sleep, he might as well explore as much of the hub station as he could manage. All he'd seen so far was the shuttle port, his hostel, and the central pod with the plaza. And a lot of tunnels. The promised tour of the hydroponics facility sounded interesting, if it fitted in with his new job, but there must be masses of other places he could visit. He couldn't help smiling to himself. Things had worked out a lot better than he'd feared. Was he lucky or what? He celebrated by ordering a coffee and a breakfast pastry in one of the small cafés around the square. They'd told him he could reasonably expect a year from his fake identity chip, so he didn't need to worry for a while. The real killer might be caught before then, and he could go back to Earth. He finished his meal and headed down an unfamiliar tunnel, consulting his pathfinder as he walked.

That evening he met Sula outside the hostel. "I thought we could go to the observation station before meeting the group at the Explorer," she said. "There's a restaurant there. The food's okay, it's for tourists really, but the views are amazing. Jon and I go there at least once a month."

It was a part of the hub that Scarlet hadn't seen yet. "Anywhere's fine. It's all new to me."

The observation station was a tiny pod on the outside of the hub, constructed completely from clear, high-quality plasglass.

Scarlet followed Sula out of the access tunnel and came to a sudden halt. All around them, the vastness of space stretched to infinity. The pod lights went out as they arrived, and fields of stars, white lace clouds, dense patches of light drifted past as the station slowly turned.

"Wow." Excitement curled through his nerves. He still felt small, but in a good way. "Wow," he said again. "That is so..."

"It is isn't it?" Sula smiled with satisfaction. "Doesn't it just call out to you?"

Scarlet stared at a spiral of silver white, at the intense spots of light in it. "Yeah."

"I thought you'd like it."

He looked back in the direction they'd come from. The main hub station hung in the background, a mass of dark globes, functional pods linked by long snaking tubes and dotted with lights where the exterior walls were made of plasglas. On one of the exterior pods, he thought he could make out the tiny shape of the Earth shuttle. He squinted at it.

"Come on, Ben." Sula laughed at the expression on his face. "Don't gawk like a tourist."

The restaurant was more of a café and bar, scattered with small tables and the sort of stools that didn't encourage the diners to linger. Jon waited at one, with a tall drink in front of him. There were no servers, human or otherwise, but the tabletop served as a menu and ordering station.

"Does the hub have to import all its food from the planets, at the moment?" Scarlet asked.

Sula shook her head. "We grow fruit and vegetables on the station. There are a lot of agriculture pods distributed round the place, and there's a big protein production facility as well. It has three vats. Nothing's wasted, everything's recycled. I think the station produces almost everything it needs, and like I told you, this morning, we're increasing the flora, everywhere. It's helpful with the air purity, and everyone knows plants are good for people's mental health. Of course, some luxury things are imported – coffee, some alcohol, sugared food, that sort of thing. We don't have enough growth media for protein manufacture, but we're getting there."

"Right." Scarlet perused the drinks menu and chose a beer. "How many of you work in hydroponics?"

"There's a few of us, engineers like me, and technicians. We link with the clean air crew and the whole maintenance comes together. It's pretty neat."

"What did you do today?" Jon said to him.

"I found a job." Scarlet smiled, still amazed at the way things had worked out.

"That's great. What sort of job?"

"Station security temp. Pretty junior, but it's better than I expected. I'd resigned myself to hacking asteroids into chunks."

Sula laughed. "Congratulations. How—"

"Shuttle Security recommended me. He got me a longer job on a supply shuttle as well. I met the Comisario for hub security when I was questioned about last night, and she needed extra staff while the colony ships prepare. She offered me the job. I wanted to kiss her."

"Two jobs?" Jon shook his head. "You've the luck of the devil."

The drinks appeared, delivered by an autoserver. Scarlet took a cautious sip from the tube. It tasted fine, better than fine. "It means I probably won't be able to come and see the hydroponic stuff, tomorrow," he said. "Can we do it another time?"

"Yeah, no problem," Sula said. "Let me know when you have a free day."

"Thanks."

"So now you're a resident, you should get to know people," Sula said. "The people from general maintenance go out for a drink every Friday. I join them when I'm up here. Occasionally we go dancing as well. You could come along if you like?"

"You should," Jon said. "They're a nice bunch of people."

Scarlet nodded. "I'd like that." Once he was working on a shuttle service, it would be good to get back to base and have people he could meet for a drink. He was still trying not to think about Mink and Koo-Suki. He 'd never been away from them for so long before. He must hear from them soon.

Chapter 24

Marm Willim, Ash and Serran shared a luxury stateroom in the first-class section of the shuttle. Maeve had a berth in the economy section, the sort of accommodation where there was a permanent queue for the hygiene facility. She lay on her back in a hammock, just below the ceiling, staring up at the smooth lining of the compartment. She had been the first of the sixteen berths to board. Marm Willim had been in a hurry.

Maeve's heart was beating hard enough to shake her whole body. She thought she was hyperventilating. She felt sick. By some weird and unfathomable coincidence, Koo-Suki was on the shuttle, in the same economy compartment. So were Mink and his pet, but Mink didn't worry her half as much as Koo-Suki, and the monster didn't worry her at all. How could it have happened? A shuttle left the spaceport every morning, carrying at least two hundred passengers, a hundred and sixty of whom were economy. Ten economy compartments, and Koo-Suki was in the same one as her. The universe hated her. The religious fringe might be right. There was a god, and if there was a god, then there was a devil, and the devil had her in his sights. Maybe if she kept absolutely quiet, they wouldn't realise she was here. *Ten days.* Ten days wasn't that long. She could manage ten days. She'd just pee into her hammock. Everyone was supposed to stay in the hammocks most of the time, anyway, and there was hardly any floor space. She didn't need to eat. Ten days was nothing.

She took a deep breath, trying to keep calm. It worked for a second. Until she began to wonder if their presence was a coincidence. Maybe they were looking for her. No way. They couldn't be. This journey must have taken a huge amount of credit and surely, they wouldn't waste their wealth looking for her?

Koo-Suki spoke. "Mink? Do you think it's okay to get up now?"

"I don't know," he said. "I can't move. I think my ribs are crushed."

"Acceleration wasn't that bad."

"I'm talking about Nyx. She's squashing me. You can have her later."

"She's your pet," Koo-Suki said.

Maeve drew in a desperate breath and squeezed her eyes closed.

"You've brought a pet?" A new voice, young and male, spoke. "Can I see?"

Mink grunted. "Come on Nyx, get up." He groaned. "Ow. That's my bladder."

Nyx landed on the deck with a thud.

"What the hell is it?" the youth said.

"It's a she and she's friendly," Mink said. "Mostly. I haven't a clue what she is. I found her as a pup, kitten, whatever, a couple of years ago. There were three of them in a box in the swamp. The other two were dead. I think she's some sort of mutant, maybe from a breeding programme. She must have been dumped with the others. Poor little thing."

Maeve peeped over the edge of her hammock. Poor little thing? Nyx took up most of the floor. How had Mink managed to get her on the shuttle? How was he going to feed her?

"Get her out of the way," Koo-Suki said. "I want to get down."

"It's a bit crowded," the youth said. "They've crammed as many of us in as they could. I suppose I'm paying minimum, so I can't complain."

Maeve pulled the thin cover over her head.

The compartment held two layers of hammocks, upper and lower, four of each on each side, with a narrow aisle between them. Mink and Koo-Suki were the last in, taking the hammocks nearest the entrance. Sixteen people and Nyx in a minute space. Koo-Suki was only a few feet away from her. Why did things keep happening to her? What had she ever done to deserve them?

"How much space do you think the premium passengers get?" Koo-Suki said.

"No idea. More than this," Mink answered. "And what about the crew? I'd get claustrophobia if I had to travel like this often."

"You'd get used to it. At least we've only got a few days in here," Koo-Suki said. "You should take the medication."

"I will if I need it, but I haven't got there yet."

Maeve wished they'd stop talking. Maybe she should take the medication. Everyone had been offered it, to keep them calm, and if she took enough, she might pass out for the entire journey. She'd been pleased she didn't have to share a luxury cabin with Serran and his mother, but this might be worse. She was trapped between two psychopaths.

"There's no way to stretch your legs," Koo-Suki said. "That monster of yours takes up the entire floor, Mink. Can't you get her back in the hammock?"

"No. She needs to stretch too."

Nyx's purring bounced off the walls, drowning the sound of the breathing occupants. Her claws tapped at the floor, went quiet, and the edge of Maeve's hammock sagged as the creature stood on its hind legs. The purr got louder.

"Go away," Maeve whispered, turning on her side, away from the animal. A cold nose nudged her shoulder. One paw pulled at the cover.

"What are you doing, Nyx?" Mink said. "Sorry, she won't hurt you."

Maeve curled into a ball, the cover pulled tightly over her head and held her breath. Why had she ever encouraged the animal? All she'd ever done was stroke it. Twice. Maybe three times. Nyx nudged her again, before she was pulled away.

"Sorry," Mink repeated.

Maeve sucked in a lungful of air. Ten days of this would kill her. Her life had escaped her control again. She tried to concentrate on the future, the fairly distant future. *Eden Fields.* She'd checked a data file on it, before leaving the Willim house. It was an Earth-like agricultural planet, high on the list of desirable habitats. If she could get free of the Willims, she might be able to find a job there. They didn't have citizen registration in the same way as Earth. She might stand a chance. She knew she wouldn't normally have been accepted as an emigrant, would never have been able to afford the fare out to the planet, even if she had been accepted. If she got there, if Serran didn't kill her, if Koo-Suki didn't, then things might get better. Rich people always needed servants. She just had to get a foot on the first rung of the ladder. If she did that, she could climb. She wouldn't always be a servant.

Everyone else in the room appeared to be taking it in turns to get out of their hammocks and to shake the stiffness from their limbs. Maeve would have liked to move, but she didn't dare. The hellhound of Mink's came back, sticking her nose into Maeve's hammock.

"Go away," she hissed.

The think licked her nose with a rough tongue. She sneezed.

"Sorry," Mink's voice was far too close. "She must like you. She doesn't normally behave like this." He pushed the beast's head away. "Are you all right?"

Maeve clutched the thin cover. "Fine." She dropped her voice as low as she could manage.

"You sound odd. I could call one of the crew."

"I'm fine." She found herself shouting.

Mink shut up. Seconds later, someone ripped the cover from the hammock.

"What the hell are you doing here?" Koo-Suki's voice was as blank as her expression.

Maeve sat up, wincing as her head hit the low ceiling. "Travelling to hub station 3." She flopped back into the hammock, turned onto her side and glared at Koo-Suki. "What about you? Are you following me?"

"Following you? Why would I do that?"

"You wanted to kill me."

"I still do," Koo-Suki said, "and I'm not the only one. I wouldn't come this far to do it though. You aren't that important. And I wouldn't do it here anyway. Do you think I'm as stupid as you?"

Maeve turned her back and snatched her cover from Koo-Suki. "Go away."

Koo-Suki pulled it off her. "How come you're on this shuttle? Who's paying for you?"

Maeve sat up again, taking care to keep her head down this time. "I've got a job. I'm accompanying my employer."

"Really? What employer? Where? And how?"

"They booked luxury class for themselves. They're a rich family."

"Why you? Why give you a job at all? Do they know what—"

"Mind your own business. I don't—"

"First Shift in fifteen minutes." The loud message echoed from a speaker in the ceiling. "Everyone to their berths. Fasten restraints. Spatial shift in fifteen minutes."

Koo-Suki's tilted brown eyes narrowed. "We'll talk soon." She disappeared back to her own hammock.

Five minutes later one of the shuttle crew appeared, checked each hammock and paused by Mink. "You can't keep that animal there. It's not safe."

"I paid for her."

"A bribe? I don't care. It's still not safe."

Maeve leaned over the edge of her hammock. Nyx might have led Koo-Suki to her, but she still didn't want her shoved out of an airlock.

Mink wrapped his arms around Nyx. He said nothing.

The crewman sighed heavily. He raised his arm and tapped his wrist. Mink blew out a breath of exasperation and extended his wrist to touch the attendant's.

"Okay." The attendant disappeared, returning thirty seconds later, with an extra hammock rolled up under one arm. "It's still not safe. I don't want to lose my job by getting a passenger killed." He pulled a couple of pegs from the ceiling and hung the hammock down the centre of the aisle. "Fasten it in there," he said.

Maeve peered over the edge of her own hammock. Mink had climbed out of his hammock and seemed to be fastening Nyx into his own berth. He levered himself into the temporary hammock and lay down. The staff member watched him with folded arms, checked his restraints and left again.

"Another bribe?" Koo-Suki said. "That animal's bleeding you dry."

"Bleeding us dry," Mink said. "What do you want me to do? Let them throw her to vacuum?"

"No. You should have told the attendant to piss off."

Maeve closed her eyes and waited for the shuttle to enter its Shift mode.

~~~

Scarlet turned up for his fourth day at work, to find he'd been assigned to immigration. He would be working with one of the regular security people, a man who introduced himself as Inspector Chang, and would be responsible for checking ids, handing out pathfinders and updating the records.

"We've got three shuttles coming in today," Chang told him as they walked towards the docks. "There're two colony ships in waiting off-station at the moment. One for Eden Fields, and one for Hope. They're both taking over five thousand colonists out, so we'll have five days of shuttle transfers."

"I've heard of Eden Fields," Scarlet said. Everyone had. It was a new jewel in the collection of Earth colonies.

"Yeah." Chang grimaced. "You don't get accepted there without wealth and influence. We'll have a bunch of entitled assholes on station for the next few days."

"What's the other one? Hope?"

"A terraforming project," Chang said. "There're only a couple of thousand people there at the moment, and apart from the scientists and engineers, they work in construction and labour, building secure habitats for the next influx. The first shipload were non-citizens. They were promised level one if they worked out there for ten years. Now it's plain they've survived, the colonisation department are taking low-level citizens, who can pay their own costs, but not much more. It'll still be hard labour, but I think I'd rather chance that than Eden Fields."

"Right." Scarlet opened the immigration point while Chang set up the scanning equipment. He could imagine this sort of job might get boring, but at the moment it was okay. He liked the people he worked with, he liked the uniform, the smart black coverall with soft boots. He liked the fact that none of the security staff carried lethal weapons, just stun tasers. He liked the fact that he was paid a decent amount. If he was truly and legally Benaiah Scarlet, he would be happy with his life. He pressed the transfer button and watched the tube connect with the side of the station, heard the thud as the airlocks sealed and the tube extended into vacuum. The thick plasglass didn't give him much of a view, but he could see the illuminated shape of the expected passenger shuttle drift closer. Ten minutes later, the tube caught and the system bleeped the signal that the shuttle was safely attached. The gates opened and the first passengers disembarked. The luxury class ones. Ten at a time entered the first airlock, then exited the second airlock individually. Scarlet checked their wrist chips and sent them through to the waiting area, where their accommodation contacts would collect them. Once they'd dispersed, the second group of ten came through, one at a time.

A young man strolled through first, tall, blond and familiar. Scarlet stared, not sure if he knew him. He'd seen him somewhere before. *Serran Willim.* That was his name, he'd met him at a London party. Completely different context, but it was definitely him, and if it wasn't, it was his twin.

Serran held his wrist out, gave Scarlet a disinterested glance and looked away. Blood red eyes and a crest of hair had served Scarlet well. They were all anyone had ever noticed about him. He scanned Serran's wrist and stood back to let him through, sighing with relief as he headed for the exit. The older woman, his mother, came next, and she ignored Scarlet, too. He took a deep breath and waited for the next passenger. Ashkir, the third and adopted child. He, too, glanced at Scarlet with no recognition. What were they *doing* here? They couldn't possibly be emigrating to a colony planet. Not even Eden Fields could come close to the life they lived on Earth. He frowned as he puzzled over it.

Once the luxury passengers were gone, the livestock class began to trickle through, all of them weary and travel stained. He handed everyone a small pathfinder. Most of them would be staying in basic hostels, like the one he lived in, while they waited for transfer to the colony ships.

Three groups of sixteen passed through. Scarlet worked in a rhythm now, he scanned wrists and pointed the owners towards the exit, while Inspector Chang entered all the details in the station log. He looked up as the first of the next cohort arrived from the airlock. His mouth dropped open. He squeezed his eyes closed, blinked hard, and looked again. It *was* Koo-Suki. She hadn't seen him yet, but as he stared, she raised her head.

She almost ran towards him. "Scarlet?" She reached him and skidded to a halt. "I don't believe it."

Scarlet wanted to hug her, but aware of Inspector Chang's interest, he gave her a small smile instead. "Wrist chip? As she held out her arm, he leaned towards her. "I'm in the spacer's hostel in Plaza 2. I'll be back in five hours. Come and see me there?"

"With Mink." She walked to the exit, looked back over her shoulder. "Maeve's on the shuttle, too."

Scarlet stared at her back, his mind seething with questions. Maeve? What the hell was she doing here? She could ruin everything for him. And how could she afford to join a colony ship? For that matter, how had Koo-Suki and Mink managed the costs?

When Mink arrived, Scarlet was prepared. He wasn't prepared for Nyx, who prowled at Mink's heels, her head level with his waist.

Mink looked up, smiled as though he'd expected to see Scarlet, and held out his wrist.

"I've told Koo where I'm staying," Scarlet muttered. He rubbed Nyx's ears. "I'll see you later."

"Watch out," Mink said. "Maeve's on the shuttle. She said she'd keep quiet, but I don't trust her." He strode towards the exit.

Maeve was the last of the group of sixteen to disembark. She wobbled from the tube as though she was sleepwalking and rubbed pink-rimmed eyes with her knuckles. She wore a plain blue coverall, and her hair was tightly fastened at the back of her head. She held out her wrist automatically, glanced at him and away. Her head jerked up. "Scarlet?" Her voice was a horrified whisper.

He bared his teeth in an imitation smile as he scanned her chip.

"What are you...? Why...How...?" She stuttered to a stop and took a deep breath. "I'm sorry. About what I said. I didn't mean—"

"Move along," Scarlet told her. "And keep your mouth closed." He didn't want to hear anything she said.

She passed through the gate, looking back over her shoulder. Would she keep quiet? She had enough secrets herself, and hopefully she'd learned something from the past. He wondered whether Koo-Suki was still in a killing rage. And *why* were they all up here? A tiny percentage of citizens shipped out to the colonies. It was against all logic that practically everyone he knew should be on the same shuttle.

The first airlock opened to let the next sixteen through. Scarlet's colleague stretched his arms above his head, calling to Scarlet. "Did you know those people? The one with the giant cat-thing?"

"Yeah," Scarlet said. "Acquaintances from my Earth job. What a coincidence. I've arranged to meet them for a drink later. Looks like they might be on their way to that planet you mentioned."

"Hope?"

"Yeah."

~~~

229

When Scarlet arrived back at his hostel, Koo-Suki and Mink were sitting on the deck, backs resting against the wall, waiting for him. The monster-mutant stretched out in front of them, attracting interest from every passer-by. Scarlet hadn't seen any animal life on the station, but he hadn't looked for any. There were insect pollinators everywhere, but that was all. Nyx was exotic, even on Earth. All three jumped to their feet at his approach. He slowed, overcome by emotion. Koo-Suki wrapped her arms around his waist, and Mink slapped his shoulder. Nyx stuck her nose in his crotch. He pushed her head away, smoothing a hand over her fur. He took a deep breath. "How did you get here? What are you doing?"

"Let's go somewhere and talk," Koo-Suki said. "Can we go to your room?"

Scarlet shook his head. "I barely fit in it. What about your hostel?"

"Same. It's just a couple of bunks."

"There's a caff across the square. Let's try that." Scarlet pointed.

Once they were sitting at a table, with beer in front of them, Scarlet jabbed his forefinger at Koo. "Spill. Tell me what's happening. I expected a message, not a personal visit. Where did you get the credits?"

"We sold the business," Koo-Suki said. "Remember Didi Ramonz? The one who was killed by a rival?"

"Yeah." Scarlet remembered. "West of London?"

"That's right. Her second in command was looking to start up again. I think he wanted revenge. Didi was his lover."

"How much did you get?"

"With our own stash, we had enough for a fake citizen chip each, and our costs to a frontier planet. We've got passage for you as well. Once we're out there, our citizenship won't matter. That's what the broker told us, anyway. Mink used up a lot of what was left, to get Nyx on the shuttle. She's listed as useful livestock." Koo rolled her eyes. Mink's mouth tilted in a small smile.

Scarlet didn't know what to say. They'd done this for him? What about all their employees? He took a deep breath. "Which planet?"

"Hope," Koo-Suki said.

"I thought that might be it. Tell me about it."

"It's still terraforming, so everyone lives under domes at the moment. They said the atmosphere was well on the way to human breathable, but they would say that, wouldn't they?"

"It was the best we could come up with," Mink said. "We applied for a family of three residency."

"They seemed to think I'd be having babies," Koo-Suki said, "but when I asked, they said it wasn't compulsory, but one of the reasons people emigrate, is to get away from the reproduction laws. So? What do you think?"

"About babies?"

She punched his arm. "No. About Hope. We don't have much choice now. We've burned our boats. It's there, or going as indentured labour on one of the asteroids."

Scarlet still couldn't believe they'd done this. "You could have stayed. The heat would have died down eventually. I could have come back."

Koo-Suki leaned her elbows on the table. "I thought hard about it. We talked." She looked at Mink for support.

"I asked myself how long we could survive the way we had been," he said. "We've done well, made a lot of credits, we've been lucky, but how many non-citizens do you know, who make it to old age? Or even middle age? I started thinking about the future. When we discussed it, Koo said she felt the same way."

"This way," Koo-Suki continued, "we're legal. We get planetary privileges. We're equal to everyone else. We have as much chance as the rest of the colonists. And we have an adventure. It was time to move on."

"Best of all," Mink said, "we don't have to watch our backs all the time."

"What about the fake citizenship?" It sounded a bit too good to be true.

231

"When they register us on planet, we become what they enter in the registry. No one bothers," Koo-Suki said. "That's what the broker told us, anyway."

Scarlet hoped she was right. "How long's the journey? And what about work?"

"Two days to the shift point, then a week after it. And we'll be assigned work when we arrive."

"I've just signed up for a job," Scarlet said. "I don't think I can get out of it. If I run out on a contract, I won't clear for passage on a colony ship. I might have to join you later. Can I defer the trip?"

"What do you mean? A contract?"

"A year shuttling supplies to some of the mining stations," he said. "I had to do something and I was pretty grateful for it. I didn't imagine you'd turn up."

Koo-Suki sucked her knuckles. Mink stroked Nyx's head.

"I only signed a week ago. I wish I'd waited."

"A year?" Mink said.

Scarlet nodded.

"Dangerous?"

"Not especially."

"Then we'll see you on Hope in a year. We can wait."

Scarlet wished he didn't have to. "I'll miss you." At least Mink and Koo-Suki were here in person. They were both fine. They hadn't been arrested.

"So how did you end up working for the law?" Mink asked.

"Tell us what you've been doing," Koo-Suki said.

"Amazingly good luck." Scarlet told them what had happened since he'd left them. "And what about Maeve?" he asked. "Suppose she says something about me?"

"She won't," Koo-Suki said. "We had a chat."

"You didn't kill her then?"

"If we hadn't been trapped on a shuttle, I might have. Every time I think about what she did, I get this sick fury. My legs go all weak."

"I'll deal with her," Scarlet said. "Otherwise, I'll be looking over my shoulder till she's gone. Is she going to Hope as well?"

Koo-Suki shook her head. "She's a domestic worker for a rich citizen and her sons. They're going to Eden Fields."

"Fallen on her feet?"

"Looks like it," Koo-Suki said. "Although I can't get my head round why people with money would emigrate. I never met them."

Scarlet ran a hand over his hair. "I think I'd better talk to her."

Chapter 25

Maeve was still asleep when the drone messenger arrived. The hotel had assigned her a berth in the servants' quarters. It was a long, low room, with two closely packed rows of bunks and no windows. She didn't care. The bed was well away from both Serran and Koo-Suki. Worry had kept her awake for most of the transit journey, and as soon as she crawled onto the bunk, she fell into a deep sleep. The buzzing at her ear pulled her out of it. She opened her eyes and squinted into the dimness of the dormitory. Where was she?

Her mind began to work. The drone was for her. It buzzed again. "Maeve, of the Willim household, proceed to reception." The message looped into a repeat.

The man in the next bunk groaned. "Just go. You're waking everyone."

"In a minute." Maeve listened again, catching the remainder of the message. Station security wanted to talk to her. She froze, wanting to know why, but message drones were simple things, and once this one had delivered its summons, it headed back to its docking station. Maeve climbed off the bunk, wriggled into her uniform, fastened her hair away from her face and trudged to the street entrance. The hub station was a closed environment with nowhere to run to. Not that there was much point in trying to avoid security. Why would she want to, anyway? She'd done nothing wrong. Exhaustion was making her fatalistic. Once she'd had a chance to sleep properly, things would be different. They might look better.

She emerged into the street atrium, covering a yawn with the back of her hand.

Scarlet stood outside the hotel, arms folded, mouth pressed into a thin line. She'd half expected him, but not in the uniform of security. She'd fallen asleep, convinced she'd hallucinated. Guilt and exhaustion had made her see things that weren't really there. He was real, though, dressed in a black coverall, with a silver circle on the left arm. A tool belt hung on his hips, a taser in one of the holsters. How had he got up here? And how in all the hells, had he ended up employed by law enforcement? At least he'd escaped from the Civil Guards. No one deserved to be questioned by Security Central. Horror stories emerged out of the dungeons from time to time, and they were enough to give anyone nightmares. Her guilt faded a little. He *had* killed Marius and wrecked her life. She rubbed her eyes. She'd wrecked her own life, even if she didn't want to dwell on it. Did Scarlet want vengeance, though? A Security officer could make a lot of trouble for her, even up here. She wished her mind was sharper, that she wasn't still half-asleep.

She halted, five feet from him. The silence extended.

"What are you doing here?" Scarlet finally spoke. Something was different about him, but she couldn't be bothered to work out what it was.

"You summoned me." She rubbed her eyes again. "The drone said—"

"I mean here. On the hub station."

"Working."

"Working?"

"Yes. My employer brought me with her."

"Who are you working for? Do they know you're unlicensed?"

Maeve's head jerked up. "Of course, they do. I'm practically indentured. Marm Willim is my employer. She's a wealthy elite and—"

Scarlet's eyes widened. He let out a snort of laughter. "I don't believe it."

"What? I'm not lying." She'd worked out what was different about him. His eyes were a normal brown, and they had whites.

"I've met her. How did you end up working for her?" His expression had relaxed.

"Her son bought me out of a club," Maeve muttered.

"Why did she bring you up here, though. She must have loads of highly trained servants."

Maeve blinked the tiredness away. Maybe she should tell Scarlet about her suspicions. She was desperate to tell someone. "She wanted to keep me quiet."

"Quiet about what?"

"Her son's a psychopath."

"Serran or Ash?" Scarlet raised his eyebrows in exaggerated disbelief. "And why should she care. The world's full of psychopaths."

"Serran. I think he killed someone from the club I worked in." She hesitated. "I think he might be the Silencer."

Scarlet frowned, serious again. "What's *he* done to upset you? You can't go around making accusations like that. Haven't you learned anything?"

Maybe Scarlet wasn't the best person to share her suspicions with, but she'd started now. "Just check him out. There's something not quite right about him. And why would his mother be so keen to get him away if he hadn't done something bad?"

Scarlet's frown deepened. "All I want to know, is whether you're going to keep quiet about me. You mustn't keep making wild accusations. If you do, someone will kill you. Me, if I get a chance, because you're annoying me a lot, but your employer might not like what you're saying, either."

Maeve caught a glimpse of a couple of people on the other side of the square. She narrowed her eyes. It was Koo-Suki and Mink, with that animal of Mink's. "I said I was sorry, and I won't make trouble. I'm not going to say anything about you. But couldn't you just check up on Serran? Please? There's something really wrong with him."

Scarlet rolled his eyes. "On your say-so? No way, and even if I wanted to, I'm bottom level station security. I mostly work patrol. I

redirect lost visitors and fill in immigration forms. Grow up, Maeve."
He stalked away, joining his friends.

Anger washed over Maeve. Someone had to believe her. The
problem was, she knew no one up here, she had no friends and no
way of knowing who she could talk to. She yawned again. Maybe
Serran would change his ways on a new world. Make a new start.
She wished she believed it. Maybe he wasn't the Silencer, but she
was pretty sure he was a murderer. She wished she wasn't so tired,
but what was the point of wishing for anything? Her mind was a fog.
She returned to her bunk, deeply depressed. Before she fell asleep,
she realised what else was different about Scarlet. His crest of
ebony hair had gone, along with the ornate beading.

Much later, another summons from the drone woke her. This time,
Marm Willim wanted to see her. She pulled her uniform on again. It
still looked good, proving quality counted. She dragged her hair into
a high ponytail, feeling refreshed and a bit more positive. She'd slept
for ten hours.

Marm Willim and Serran waited in the reception area of their
luxury hotel suite, both dressed to go out, in simple skinsuits, and
thin cloaks. Serran lounged on a cushion, legs stretched out in front
of him, and mouth drooping in his normal expression of discontent.
His eyes looked weird. Maeve couldn't work out exactly what was
wrong with them. The pupils were enlarged, but that wasn't it.
Maybe it was the flecks of pink snaking through the whites.

"What took you so long?" He jumped to his feet. "Come on Ma, I'm
bored with this place."

Marm Willim ignored him. "Maeve. Serran and I are having lunch
in the core restaurant. We'll be out for a couple of hours. While
we're gone, I want you to check our luggage has arrived safely. I've
given you access to our rooms. You've got a list of everything that
should be here. You can store our things in the cupboards as you
tick them off. When you've finished that, go down to the docks and
make sure they're transporting our crates out to the colony ship."

"Yes, Marm. Please? Where's Ashkir?"

"He went exploring," Serran said. "I think he wanted to get away from us."

"Don't be ridiculous." Marm Willim strode towards the door. "Come along."

Serran gave his mother a death stare. He tapped Maeve's cheek with the palm of his hand.

She flinched and backed away.

He smiled. "See you later."

Maeve gritted her teeth. He wouldn't see her at all, if she could help it. Her throat still had bruises. Fading, but she could just about see them if she squinted into the mirror, and the light was bright enough. Maybe she should have shown them to Scarlet. She moved her fingers lightly over the skin of her throat. When it didn't hurt, she rubbed harder. He probably wouldn't have believed her, whatever she said.

She'd assumed the hub station was a frontier habitat with the bare minimum its residents needed to survive, but the Willims had a luxury suite, with three bedrooms, a shared hygiene facility and a lounge area. It was small, but Maeve wandered from room to room, marvelling at the ostentatious comfort. Eventually, she took out her list of permissible luggage and opened Marm Willim's bag, comparing the contents with the packing details. Everything was as it should be. She took out the carefully folded skinsuits, tunics, kimonos and cloaks, piling them neatly in the generous cupboard space, wondering why one woman needed so much for such a short stay. She did the same for Ash's more limited possessions, before moving onto Serran. At the bottom of his luggage, in a side-pocket, she found a small drawstring bag. There was no record of it on her list. She dropped it on the couch and knelt on the soft floor to examine it. Before she could change her mind, she loosened the drawstring and shook the contents onto the couch. A tangle of synth leather and metal spilled out. Recognising Tooley's necklace, she pressed a hand against her mouth. Smears of dried blood still stained the metal heart. More small pieces of jewellery rattled in the bottom of the bag, bracelets and anklets. She untangled two linked earcuffs, made from cheap, gaudy plasteel, silver in colour, with a crimson-black stain on one of them. Her heartbeat pounded in her ears. What was she supposed to do about this? Report it to Serran and Marm Willim? Instinct told her 'no way'. She scooped everything up, stuffing it back into the bag, and forcing it deep into the side-pocket she'd found it in. Did Marm Willim know about the bag and the jewellery? Serran must have known she'd find it. *Tooley's necklace.* She had to tell someone. And what if Marm Willim did know about her son? She leaned against the couch, resting her head on her arms. Five minutes passed before she forced herself to move.

The hotel was in the core zone of the hub station, and on the way to the port-pod, she passed through the central atrium. It was a wide, single level area, hexagonal in shape, with a rigid tube tunnel leading away from each edge. Lush plant life relieved the expanse of plasmetal and glass. Maeve consulted her pathfinder. The hub-station had been built in stages, the core zone constructed first, and a mish-mash of residential, maintenance and business zones added as pods later. The port-pods were furthest away, but a transport service ran along one of the tunnels from the centre. Maeve set off towards it, but slowed and stopped, turning to survey the atrium. Station Security sat in the middle of it, a squat black building, among a cluster of embassies and station management offices, all covered in green climbing plants. She halted, wondering if Scarlet might be there. Stiffening her spine, she marched towards the doors, determined to try again. She'd been half asleep last time she'd talked to him, and incoherent. If he wouldn't listen to her, she'd demand to speak to someone else.

"I'd like to see Scarlet."

The man on reception raised his eyebrows. "The temp? Benaiah?"

"Scarlet."

"He's not in at the moment. He comes on duty in a couple of hours. You can wait, if you like."

Maeve shook her head. "I'll come back. Two hours?"

"Two and a half, then he'll be out on patrol."

Maeve made her way to the shuttle port, checked that the Willim's crates were labelled and ready to be loaded on the transport to the colony ship, and collected a receipt from an impatient official. She caught the transport back to the atrium and, not sure if she was an idiot, walked slowly to Station Security. The same man was on reception.

"You're early. He'll be here in a minute. Come through. Take a seat. Can I get you a drink?"

Maeve shook her head, eyeing him nervously. Law enforcement didn't offer people drinks. Not on Earth, anyway. She perched on the edge of a bench in the reception area.

Scarlet arrived ten minutes later, dressed in his black security uniform. Without the expanse of red which had covered his eyes, he didn't look half as menacing, and now that his mane of elaborately arranged ebony hair was gone, clipped to lie close to his skull, he could pass as ordinary. Good-looking, but ordinary. His new image suited him, the short hair revealing sharply defined cheekbones, and wide-set eyes. She studied him while he talked to the man on reception, wondering how he had got this job, how he had turned from illegal non-citizen, to law enforcement in such a brief time.

The receptionist pointed at her.

Scarlet turned, raising his eyebrows. "What do you want?" His tone wasn't encouraging.

"To talk to you about Serran."

He gave an exaggerated sigh. "I told you—"

"Please? You're law enforcement now. It's your job. Just listen. You don't have to do anything. I've got to tell someone."

~~~

Scarlet narrowed his eyes at her. He didn't trust her one little bit. She had a lot of nerve, bothering him like this. Why didn't she just go away and leave him alone. She was right though. It was his job. Sort of. Although he was patrol and immigration, not crime. There wasn't much crime on the hub station, and from what his new colleagues had told him, it mostly involved drunk and disorderly spacer crews, looking for a good time, after months on a dry star ship. Sometimes it was drunk and disorderly colonists trying for a last fling before heading out to places where alcohol wasn't freely available. He blew out another sigh. "Go on, then. Tell me."

She clasped her hands tightly together. "Serran's father disinherited him. I'm not sure why, but the gossip was that one of the guards told him Serran killed someone. I think it was Tooley."

"Tooley told him? Tooley was the guard?" It sounded unlikely to Scarlet. That sort of thing didn't happen in the elite Earth families. He thought about his initial impression of Serran. Thought about the fact that he hadn't liked him much.

"No. She was one of the fems in the club I worked in, the one I think he killed."

"What evidence do you have?"

Maeve wouldn't meet his eyes. She perched on the very edge of the bench, winding her hands together, while she stared at the floor. "I found her necklace in his rooms. He's brought it with him. He's got other jewellery too, cheap stuff, stuff he wouldn't wear."

"That's not evidence."

"And when his father disinherited him, he tried to kill his sister."

"Seriously?" How was he supposed to believe this? It sounded like a tall tale to him. Entertaining, but completely unbelievable. "Maeve, I've already warned you about—"

She jumped up, interrupting him. "Yes. I'm absolutely serious. After his father told him that Flora would be his heir, he attacked her. He tried to stab her."

"And then fled Earth?" He couldn't keep the incredulity out of his voice. "With his mother and brother? And you?"

"It's true. I swear it's true." She took a step towards him, spreading her hands in a plea, her blue eyes wide and guileless. "Seriously Scarlet, his father told him to go. They have a stake in Eden Fields, and businesses up there, so he didn't really flee, just withdrew for a while. I'm not lying. I'm not."

Scarlet backed away.

"His father said he'd call the Civilian Guard, if he didn't go. He said Serran was no longer his son."

"I suppose you were there while all this happened?"

"Not exactly." Her face flushed. "I heard some of it, but—"

"So how do you know?"

"One of the house security guards told the housekeeper. Then everyone knew."

"Everyone?" It sounded like one of the holo-soaps to Scarlet.

"The whole household was talking about it. That's why Marm Willim got them both on the first colony ship to Eden Fields."

Scarlet considered what she had said. "And you? Why would she bring you with them?"

"Serran went for me when I found Tooley's necklace, tried to strangle me." Her voice faltered. Her breathing filled the reception area. She tugged at the neckline of her coverall, pulling it down. "Look. You can still see the marks. I thought I was going to die. One of the guards stopped him, but his mother heard about it. She thought I was a threat. She dragged Ash along as well, as a sort of hostage, so his father wouldn't set the Guard on them. Eden Fields has a treaty with Earth for exchange of criminals."

It should be easy enough to check. The whole tale sounded too melodramatic to be true. And Maeve was a liar. She had looked scared, though, when she'd mentioned Serran attacking her. He didn't want to build too much on that, because she might be an actress as well as a liar. He peered at her throat. The marks looked like dirt smudges, a yellowing of her biscuit-coloured skin, but they could be old bruising.

Maeve resettled the neck of her coverall. "Couldn't you just check with Earth? That I've told the truth about Serran being disinherited, at least? It must be widely known by now."

All he could see was the top of her head, her pale hair neatly groomed. She looked different, less feral. And she hadn't bothered to use her sweetly submissive, little girl act on him. "It'll take at least four days to get a message to Earth and back. We'd have to send it with the shuttle, and wait for a reply."

"That's too long." Maeve raised her head. "We'll be on our way to Eden Fields by then."

Scarlet shrugged.

"Couldn't you look at the news the next shuttle brings? There might be something. Please? I don't want to go with them."

"I don't think—"

She jerked her head up. "If you won't do anything, I want to talk to someone else. Someone who'll listen to me."

Scarlet snorted. He didn't care what she wanted, but he was curious. There was a very small chance she might not be lying, and if he managed to help apprehend a murderer, particularly a high profile one, it would look good for his career prospects in this new life. If his chip failed and he was arrested, it might work in his favour. He could check the news from Earth, at least, and talk to Koo-Suki and Mink. "I'll see what I can do. You'd better not be lying to me again. I'll have you arrested if you are." He wasn't sure if that was within his power, but Maeve wouldn't know either.

"I'm not." Maeve's eyes fixed on his, wide, innocent, and as far as he was concerned, full of shit. "I'm so sorry for what I did. You have to believe me. I was sorry as soon as I'd done it."

"Tell it to someone who cares. Clear off, now. I'll be in touch." He watched her leave the building and trudge across the square. The lights flashed out and when they came on again, she stood at the entrance to one of the tunnels, staring up at the transparent ceiling. He tapped a fingernail against his teeth, considering. If Serran was the Silencer, which was very unlikely, then he had a personal interest in catching him.

"Trouble?" The receptionist's voice broke into his introspection.

"I don't know. Can I get an appointment with the Comisario?"

"She's free," the receptionist said. "Just go straight through. We aren't formal here."

"Do you believe this woman?" Comisario Leyland asked, after he'd repeated Maeve's story. "Her story sounds a bit far-fetched."

"I don't know. It's a preposterous accusation." Scarlet shook his head. "She's not the most trustworthy person in the world. She's unlicensed, so her word counts for nothing on Earth, but if she's telling even half of the truth, there'll be other witnesses."

"It's not the same up here," Comisario Leyland said. "Anyone can give evidence in a criminal case."

"They can?" Scarlet was surprised. "I'd disregard everything she said, if I hadn't met this man myself. He's not quite right. Probably she's making it up, or imagining it, but I'd like to check."

The Comisario nodded. "Can't do any harm. Why don't you go down to the port and get the latest Earth news data from the shuttle? It's due in half an hour. Let's see if there's any reference to this family. Bring it back. We'll check it together."

"I'm supposed to be working immigration."

"Ask the man on duty if he'll do a couple of hours overtime."

Scarlet reached the port-pod five minutes before the shuttle docked, and sent a message asking for the rapid release of the news capsule.

The junior security officer disembarked before the passengers, handing a data chip to Scarlet. "What's the rush?"

"Just checking some information we've been given."

"Big case?" The security officer grinned, joking.

"Huge." Scarlet rolled his eyes. "Or not."

Back at Hub-Station Security, he and Comisario Leyland scanned through the data, concentrating on any mentions of Willim.

Marcus Willim was a regular in both the business reports and the social diaries. Scarlet skimmed over them.

"Here." Comisario Leyland pointed at an article. It was a recent publicity release from Marcus Willim, designating Flora Willim as his only heir.

"Well, she wasn't lying about that," the Comisario said. "The family rep says that Flora Willim is unavailable for interview, while she recovers from an accident."

"Interesting." Scarlet continued scanning until he hit a social page, showing images of Fallon and Serran Willim in the reception area for the hub-shuttle. Dressed in high fashion skinsuits, they had champagne glasses in their hands, and appeared completely carefree. Ashkir wasn't in the image. Neither was Fallon's husband or daughter.

The Comisario moved onto the crime listings, a fairly short section, as serious reportable crime was rare in London. "Here." He pointed at an entry, reading it aloud. "'Base level citizen murdered. Tooley Van, a sexscort in a river zone club was found dead outside the walls after an anonymous tip.'"

"I wonder who reported it," Scarlet muttered. So, she'd told the truth about that, at least. "Tooley. That's the name Maeve gave me."

"One of your suspect's guards?" the Comisario suggested. "Going by what your source said, at least."

Scarlet continued reading. "'It is suspected that Tooley Van is the latest victim of the serial killer known as The Silencer, although law enforcement remains close-mouthed on the case. If this is true, the killer's zone has shifted from outside the walls, where murder is not a crime, to low level citizens within the city. Murder of a citizen is punishable by execution. His modus operandi is expanding.'" He rubbed his eyes. "I don't believe it."

"Looks like we've got a case," the Comisario said.

"What a bizarre coincidence," Scarlet muttered.

"What?"

"I'm surprised, that's all. What are you going to do?"

"Make some enquiries with Law Enforcement on Earth," the Comisario said.

"But the Willims leave in a couple of days."

"Their transport can go without them. There'll be another ship in three months, if we're wrong. We won't say anything until they try to board. Best not look for trouble."

Chapter 26

Marm Willim had returned to the hotel by the time Maeve got back. Neither Serran nor Ash were with her. "Where have you been?"

"At the port-pod, Marm. Checking the luggage, like you said."

"It's all there? All organised?"

"Yes." Maeve kept her eyes down, sure that anyone who looked closely, would see her duplicity.

"And our personal luggage? Was that correct." She hesitated. "Did you look in Serran's bags? Was there anything there that wasn't on the list?"

"Just some cheap jewellery." Had Marm Willim meant her to search Serran's luggage? Was that why she'd dragged him out to lunch?

"Any chem?"

"Only what was in his hygiene pack. Headache pills, I think." Maeve hadn't thought of looking for chem. Finding the jewellery had been traumatic enough. Anyway, it wasn't her business.

"Show me." Marm Willim pushed open the door to Serran's bedroom.

Maeve followed. She took the hygiene pack from the shelf by the bed and handed it to the other woman.

Marm Willim took the pack, emptying the contents onto the bed. Expensive shampoo bars, dental products and some cosmetics spilled out. "Headache pills?" She picked up one of three silver boxes. The silhouette of a howling wolf was inset into the lid. "Did you look inside these?"

"No, Marm. I wouldn't do that." It hadn't occurred to her.

Marm Willim unscrewed the lid, tipping a heap of small silver tablets into the palm of her hand. She held them out to show Maeve. "Do you know what these are?"

Maeve took it. It was a flat disc, with a wolf's head stamped onto it. She turned it over. The other side was identical. "No."

"They aren't headache pills." Marm Willim took the tablet back and closed the box. "They're Wildwolf. You've heard of that, haven't you?"

Maeve frowned. She'd heard it discussed when she'd worked for Scarlet's crew, but it hadn't been something they'd manufactured. There was no market outside the city. It was too expensive. "The name, maybe." Marm Willim didn't look like a chem-head, so why would she know of it?

"It's new chem that's been poisoning elite citizens for the last year. It's nasty stuff, linked to some violent crimes, and some drug-related deaths. I don't want my son contaminated with it. I can't imagine why it's in his luggage."

"No, Marm." Maeve mentally raised her eyebrows into her hairline.

"He might have more. He probably won't, but just in case, I want you to keep an eye on him, to tell me if he's using it."

Maeve had no idea how she would know, especially as she intended to give Serran a wide berth, but she nodded obediently.

Marm Willim took the other two boxes from the pack and gave them to Maeve. "Ring for coffee. When it arrives, you can go to your room. Keep those with your things. I'll let you know what I want to do with them, but I want them out of his way for now."

"Will you need me in the next couple of hours, Marm? Can I go for a walk?" She didn't want to go back to the cramped servants' dormitory.

Marm Willim waved her away. "Fine."

Maeve left, wondering where she was meant to store the small boxes. Suppose she was stopped by law enforcement, and searched? Suppose she was caught with illegal chem? Did Marm

Willim have any idea of the miniscule space she shared with all the other servants? Did she have any idea what sort of person her precious son was? She must do. Why had she left Earth so quickly if she didn't? Although it looked to Maeve as if Serran had been getting away with outrageous behaviour for years.

Slipping the boxes into her hip bag, she left the hotel and set out to explore the hub-station. A vague idea had taken form in the depths of her sub-conscious and was struggling to the surface. What would happen if she missed the shuttle to the colony ship? Could she do that? Would it be possible for her to lose herself in the maze of tunnels and habitats? At least until the shuttle had gone. She wouldn't know until she tried. Eden Fields or the hub-station? Which would give her the best chance of survival? She didn't trust Marm Willim, not at all. Serran was out of control, and his mother was in denial. Maeve slowed her pace, her mind racing. What would the consequences be, of staying on the hub station with no job, no income and no way of getting back to Earth?

Her stomach gave a loud groan, reminding her she hadn't eaten for the last twenty-four hours. She was starving, and the hunger pangs made her wonder if Earth credits would buy her food and drink on the station. The hotel must feed the servants, but if so, she hadn't worked out where or when. She'd ask someone when she got back, but she didn't want to wait until then. She walked through the central atrium, looking round for cheap-looking caffs, but the central space screamed of high prices. She kept her gaze turned away from Hub Station Security. Scarlet had been useless. Anyway, she didn't want to be caught carrying illegal and dangerous chem. It was tempting to drop them in a recycling unit, but if Marm Willim wanted them back, she'd be in big trouble.

Choosing a tunnel randomly, she walked down it. It emerged in another plaza, surrounded by residential pods, but no caffs. An area of grass and small shrubs filled the centre, deep rich compost visible between the plants. Two women, wearing maintenance uniforms, were planting a slender sapling. Maeve halted in front of them and tilted her head back. Overhead, the ceiling was opaque, pale plasteel, probably with another level built above it, but she had no idea how to get up there, not without consulting her pathfinder. The station was a three-dimensional maze. Without a pathfinder, you *could* lose yourself for days.

She hurried towards a tunnel directly opposite the one she'd arrived through and walked down it. A few other people hurried past her, but not many. She emerged into an area that looked as though it was used as a warehouse. Stacks of containers lined one side, and a small automatic carrier was disappearing into another corridor. Maeve stopped to watch. Two men and a woman supervised a series of automatic loaders. Another woman approached her. "Can I help you?"

"Thanks. I'm just exploring. I was looking for somewhere to eat."

"This isn't very exciting," the woman said, "and it's unsafe for tourists. If you take that tunnel, you'll get to a commercial area. Shops and caffs."

"Right." Caffs sounded good. Maeve hurried in the direction indicated. The warehouse might be a good place to hide out. If she could avoid the staff. It was on an almost direct path from her hotel as well.

The new tunnel opened into a small atrium on the outer rim of the station. It had one clear plasglass wall, designed to show the vastness of space. Maeve chose a caff and asked if her credits were valid.

"We take any currency," the waiter said. "Earth credits?"

Maeve nodded.

"Fine. What can I get you?"

Maeve ordered chai with a small protein bowl. She was the only customer in the place. She picked a seat facing into the small open space of the square and leaned her head back to look at the view, trying not to think beyond the next day or two. In the centre of the open space, a thicket of large-leafed trees reached up to the ceiling. A ring of lights surrounded them, buried amongst a thicket of ferns and spiky grasses at the base. Maeve barely noticed them. The presence of the Wildwolf in her bag preyed on her mind.

"Nice, aren't they?" A woman's voice interrupted her thoughts.

Maeve slowly focussed on the elderly woman in front of her. "Sorry?"

"The planting," the woman said. "Maintenance are trying to green the station. I talked to someone in horticulture yesterday. They do tours. They're working on environment improvement, they told us."

"Oh." Maeve glanced at the trees.

"May I join you?"

Maeve pulled herself together. She could use some distraction. "Of course." She forced her shy, charming smile onto her face.

The woman sat down. She was older than most people Maeve had met since she left Earth, silver-haired, expensively dressed in a simple coverall, embellished around the neck with flat opalescent gemstones. "Do you work on the station?" she asked.

Maeve shook her head. "I'm heading for Eden Fields, with my employer."

"Very nice."

"Is that where you're going?"

"No." The woman shook her head. "I've been there, though. Pleasant, but a little over-organised for my liking."

"So where are you going?"

"Hope. It's newer, more primitive than Eden Fields. It's in the last stages of terraforming."

Maeve studied her. She looked far too high-level to be a colonist on a barely liveable planet. And possibly too old for the frontier life.

"You don't think I'm suited?"

"I don't know. I'm sure you could do anything you wanted to."

"I'm visiting as Earth's ambassador," the woman said. "I've done stints on places like Eden Fields. I started out as a representative on stations like this. That was a few years ago. Now? I think I annoyed someone important, but actually I like the idea of a frontier planet."

"Domes?" Maeve wondered why such a high-level citizen was bothering to talk to her. Her uniform marked her as a servant.

"The atmosphere is almost breathable," the woman said. "Domes at present, but a few years from now, life will be much better there. I hope it happens during my tenure."

Maeve's order arrived with the waiter, who insisted on telling her that all the green stuff on the side-plate was grown on station. Her bowl was full of spiced nuts, mixed beans, and rice. Steam rose from it, along with a mixture of fragrant scents. She sniffed, her stomach growling loudly, and picked up a chunk of nut encrusted bread, nibbling on it while he rambled on. When he'd finished, her new companion ordered coffee.

"Are you alone?" Maeve put the bread down. She wanted to cram the entire piece into her mouth at once, but took a deep breath instead. "Surely you shouldn't be wandering around by yourself?" Important people always had companions or bodyguards.

"It's perfectly safe on the hub stations. There's nowhere for criminals to run." The woman waved to the other side of the square where a tall, broad man stood. "Anyway, my personal guard's over there. He won't sit down with me. Says it's unprofessional." She returned her attention to Maeve. "What's your name?"

"Maeve."

"Just Maeve?"

Maeve nodded. "I was an abandoned baby." Abandoned children were registered with the name of their institute and their year of birth. "Everyone in my year had names beginning with M."

"How old are you? You don't look old enough to be in service."

"Eighteen."

"Really?" The woman held out one hand. "I'm Alicia Lao."

Maeve shook it, wondering again, why the woman was so friendly. Her expression must have radiated suspicion, because Alicia Lao smiled. "Everyone tells me I'm too nosy. I call it benevolent curiosity. People's stories interest me. Are you sure you're eighteen? You look much younger."

"I'm at least eighteen." Maeve wasn't telling her story to anyone, let alone an entitled, privileged woman who didn't know what it was like to live on the edge of survival, but she merely smiled. "And I'm not very interesting."

"Everyone is interesting. What sort of job do you do?"

Maeve's mind went blank. She had no clue what her job title might be. "I'm an assistant. I do anything my employers want. Whatever they tell me." She played with her beaker, thinking of the pillboxes in her bag. "I'm unlicensed, so this was an opportunity." The words sounded hollow. "It's almost impossible to get citizenship on Earth, so I suppose this is my best chance."

"Yes. Those things aren't as important once you leave Earth, although Eden Fields isn't the best place for ambitious young people. There isn't much social mobility, there."

Maeve shrugged. "I didn't have a choice." She finished her chai as the woman's coffee arrived.

"Stay while I drink this?"

Maeve nodded and the woman told the waiter to bring her another beaker of chai. "It's not really fair, is it," she said. "Unless you're born into citizenship, your opportunities are always going to be limited. Things have to change."

Maeve gaped at her. Saying things like that came close to sedition. "It is what it is."

"Maybe. I wish you luck on Eden Fields. Who do you work for? What sort of people?"

"They're called Willim. Fallon Willim and her sons."

Alicia frowned. "Related to Marcus Willim?"

Maeve nodded. "Fallon's husband. You know him?"

"He's not here, is he? I've met him a couple of times, at the sort of functions where politics meets business."

"No. He's back on Earth." All these high-level citizens probably knew each other, Maeve thought.

"Strange." Alicia seemed to be talking to herself. She finished her coffee.

Maeve stood up. "I must go. I don't want them to miss me."

Alicia nodded. "Nice to talk to you, Maeve. Maybe we'll run into each other again."

Maeve doubted it, but she nodded politely. "Maybe. Thank you for the chai."

On the way back, she passed the Station Security building again, giving it a resentful stare. What was the point of law enforcement if they didn't pay attention to people's concerns? She bet Scarlet had told his boss not to listen to her.

The next day Marm Willim sent her out to the main shopping square to buy a few luxuries. "They'll have all this, or better, on Eden Fields," she said. "We should have things for the journey though." Her list included cosmetics, real chocolate and Earth-produced coffee. She slipped Maeve some extra credits. "Buy yourself something."

"Thank you, Marm." Maeve kept her eyes down. She'd save the credits. Who knew when she might need them?

Ash was in the main shopping square. It was the first time she'd seen him since leaving Earth. She'd begun to wonder if his mother, or Serran, had disappeared him. He sat outside an upmarket caff, a beaker on the table in front of him. He didn't look up as she approached.

"Hello."

He flinched. "It's you."

"Where have you been?"

"Keeping my distance. I don't want to be around Serran or Ma. They're at each other's throats all the time, anyway. They barely notice I'm there." He pointed to another chair. "Have a seat."

Maeve pulled it up to the table and sat opposite Ash. He looked tired, and a millimetre of black showed at the roots of his golden hair. "Do you know what chem Serran uses?"

He shrugged. "R'lax. Alcohol. That orange stuff he gave you. Something else that makes him moody. Euphoric or aggressive. Why?"

Maeve dug one of the pillboxes from her bag. "This?" She shielded it with her hand.

Ash frowned. "I haven't seen it before. What is it?"

"Wildwolf. Or so your mother says."

Ash frowned. "I've heard of it. It's only been around for the last year, but I've heard there've been a few incidents with it. I wouldn't have thought even Serran would be stupid enough…" His frown deepened. "It might explain why he's been even nastier than usual."

"Your mother asked me to keep it with me. What happens if I get caught?"

Ash shrugged again. "How would I know?"

He was a lot of help. Maeve slid the box back into her bag. "I'd better go."

She returned to the sound of raised voices, which stopped when she opened the door. Marm Willim and Serran were both on their feet, faces thrust at each other, bodies bristling with aggression. Serran shifted from one foot to the other, his hands curling into fists.

Marm Willim spoke in a low, forceful voice. "I won't have this sort of behaviour, Serran. It's unacceptable, and at the moment, risky for you. Are you stupid? You have to stop."

Serran's jaw clenched as tightly as his fists.

"Do you have any more of that substance? The Wildwolf?"

"Do you think I'd tell you?" Serran paced across the room and back. "You've taken my chem. It was mine. You've no right to steal my stuff."

Marm Willim ignored his words. "Anything else I need to know about?"

Serran gestured towards Maeve. "She's checked the contents of my luggage. Ask her."

Marm Fallon raised an eyebrow at Maeve. "Well?"

"Only the things on the list, Marm." Maeve wasn't sure what Marm Willim wanted her to say. She still had the silver boxes in her bag. She darted a look at Serran. "And some jewellery."

"Jewellery?" Marm Willim asked Serran.

"It must have been left off the list." Serran backed away from his mother. His focus swung to Maeve. "An accident. Incompetent staff, maybe."

"Hmm." Marm Willim took a deep breath. Maeve could tell she was still furious. "Maeve? Did you manage to get everything I asked for?"

"Yes Marm."

"Let me see."

Maeve handed the packages to her.

"You'll need to find space in our bags for this. Do it now."

Serran followed her into his mother's bedroom. "What did Ma do with my stuff?"

"I don't know." She opened Fallon's bag.

"Give me that." Serran grabbed at the bag with the chocolate. She snatched it away from him.

"Serran!" Marm Willim appeared in the doorway. "What do you think you're doing?"

"She's a thief." He seized her wrist. "I'm going to search her."

His mother stalked into the room and slapped him across the face. He let go of Maeve. "Get a hold of yourself."

"You old bitch." Serran rubbed his cheek. "One day—"

"Get out, Maeve." Marm Willim jerked her head at the door.

Maeve slipped past Serran. He was getting worse, like some moody toddler, crossed with narco-freak, but from what Ash had said, he'd always had a vicious streak. She let the door slam closed on her employer's raised voice.

The crowded bunkroom held no appeal, and she didn't want to trudge round the hub station again. It might be worth another attempt at convincing Security to listen to her. She had the chem now, as evidence. Serran wasn't going to give up on it. He might even come looking for her in the servant's dorm, so it was best if she didn't go back, just yet. She marched to the centre of the hub, wondering who to ask for. She didn't want to talk to Scarlet again, but of course, he was the first person she saw as she approached.

He emerged from one of the tunnels and crossed the atrium, towards the Security building. She halted, but he'd already seen her.

He scowled. "Back again? What now?"

"I want to know what you're doing about Serran Willim."

"I told you we'd make some checks."

"I want to talk to someone else. A real Security Officer." She glared at his back, half running to keep up with him. She followed him into Station Security.

"Fine." Scarlet asked the receptionist to let the Comisario know he was bringing someone in to see her.

"Go straight through," the receptionist said.

Maeve followed Scarlet into an inner office, where a woman in a black uniform sat behind a desk. Her left sleeve was covered in silver insignia. Her face was stern.

"This is Maeve, Comisario," Scarlet said.

"You're the one who reported her employers?" the Comisario said.

"Yes, Marm." Maeve softened her voice to respectful. It sounded like Scarlet had done something after all.

"We've sent a request to Earth for more information," she said, "but haven't had any feedback yet. Didn't Ben tell you it would take four days to get a reply." Her voice was patient as though she was explaining something to a child.

"Ben?"

"Benaiah Scarlet." The Comisario glanced at Scarlet. "I thought you knew her?"

"Not well." Scarlet scowled at Maeve. "My first name is Benaiah."

"Right, Ben." Maeve took a deep breath, squashing her temper. "I've something else. He has illegal chem." She darted a glance at Scarlet.

"What? R'lax?" the Comisario said. "It's banned up here, but that'll only get him a reprimand."

"No." Maeve stamped her foot, took another breath and swallowed her temper. "It's Wildwolf, I think."

"Wildwolf?"

"It's new," Maeve said. "And it's addictive."

The Comisario raised an eyebrow at Scarlet.

"I've heard of it," Scarlet said. "It's supposed to be nasty."

"I've never encountered it," the Comisario said. "It was listed on the banned substances document this year. Highest level, so a prison sentence if you're caught with it. That means hard labour on one of the mining colonies."

Maeve folded her arms. "Apparently it's a big problem amongst the elite. I'm sure Serran—"

"Can you prove it?" the Comisario said.

Maeve rummaged in her bag. "His mother told me to keep it. Here." She slid one of the silver pillboxes across the desk.

"Pretty. Expensive." The Comisario opened the lid and took out a tablet. "We'll have to get these analysed. Is that all of them?"

"No, I've another couple of boxes."

Scarlet leaned a hip against his boss's desk. "How do we know it's not yours? How do we know you aren't trying to frame your employer?"

"I'm not." Maeve's temper flared up again. She drew in a breath, counted backwards from ten. "I can't afford the chem, let alone those boxes. They belong to someone rich."

"You could have stolen them," Scarlet said.

"I didn't." Maeve wanted to scream with frustration. She remembered how angry she'd been with Scarlet before. "You know I didn't."

"All right." The Comisario dropped the tablet back into the box. "We'll take care of these. You'd better give us the others."

"I can't do that," Maeve said. "What do I say if Marm Willim asks for them back?" She didn't like to think what Serran would do if he came looking for his stuff and she couldn't give it him.

The Comisario fingered her chin. "Mmm. We don't want to put them on guard. Not yet. Not if there's anything in your other accusations." Her eyes bored into Maeve. "I'll take a couple of the tablets for analysis. If it's what you say it is, we'll take the rest and have a word with your employers."

"So, you aren't going to do anything?"

"In due time."

"And suppose that's too late?" Maeve snatched the box from her, spun round and stalked out, her hands trembling. She hated feeling powerless.

Chapter 27

The transfer shuttle leaves for the Eden Fields colony ship today. Maeve was barely awake when she remembered. In twelve hours, unless she did something drastic, she'd be on her way to Eden Fields. She curled into a small ball and growled under her breath. No way was she going with the Willims. She'd hide in a cupboard if she had to. Her messenger pinged her and she sat up.

"Maeve?" It was Marm Willim. "I want you in our suite, immediately."

"Uhh?"

"Now. That's an order."

Maeve blinked the sleep from her eyes. Marm Willim had sounded tense. Something must have upset her. Maybe she'd found out Maeve had talked to Security. It was too early to go into hiding. They'd have time to find her. Rolling off the bunk, Maeve grabbed her uniform, slipped into it, slid her bag onto her shoulder, and headed for the resident's part of the hotel, heart thumping. She would really like to have a knife. Just in case.

The door to the Willim suite was locked when she arrived. Her palm print failed to open it, so she spoke into the microphone. "It's Maeve."

After a moment, the door slid open. Serran stood in the gap, a hand on each side of the frame. He stared down at Maeve as though he didn't recognise her. Red streaks of broken veins marred the whites of his eyes.

"Your mother called me." Maeve slowly stepped backwards, away from the door, wariness making the back of her neck tingle. No way was she going in there. Not with Serran looking like that.

"Oh yes," he said. "That's right. I remember. I told her to. You've got some of my stuff."

"What?" Maeve hadn't expected that. She took another step away. "No. I haven't. What do you mean?"

"My chem."

She scrabbled in her bag, her fingers closing round one of the boxes. Serran was giving her the creeps. "Here. She gave me these to look after. You can have them back." She held the box at arm's length.

Serran grabbed her wrist and dragged her into the room, letting the door swing closed behind them. He jerked her wrist, bending her hand backwards.

"Ow." She dropped the box. Her eyes watered from the sudden pain.

"Pick it up."

She crouched down, rubbing her wrist, before picking the box up. He'd almost broken her wrist bones. When she got up again, she blinked the moisture away, unsure she believed what she was seeing.

Fallon Willim sat on the upright chair at the small writing desk, facing into the room. A ball-shaped gag stretched her mouth. Her eyes were furious. She was tied to the chair with a rainbow of cloth. Maeve recognised some of the fine silks she'd packed away, the day before, but where had the gag come from? She gaped and blinked again, her fingers clenching around the pillbox.

"She gave my stuff to you." Serran shoved Maeve onto the sofa and loomed over her. "I want it back. All of it. Now." He slammed the heel of his palm into her chest, pushing her into the depths of the sofa and knocking the breath out of her. "There should be three boxes. It's valuable. Give it to me or I'll call security."

She sucked in a lungful of air and slid her eyes back to Fallon. What was Serran planning to do with her? And why was he talking about security? Security would just arrest him. Maybe arrest them all. "I don't—"

He grabbed her arm, hauled her back to her feet and slapped her hard across her face. "Now. Hand it over. I know you've got it." When he released her arm, she fell back onto the sofa, dropping the box into the cushions. Her chest hurt, her ribs, her lungs, everything hurt when she tried to inhale. Her face stung, and the taste of blood filled her mouth. She swallowed and huddled into the corner, thinking hard. She had to do something. She had to get out.

Serran snatched her bag from her shoulder and emptied it onto the cushions. The two remaining silver boxes lay in the folds of her skinsuits. He snatched them up. A wide smile spread across his face. "There. I knew you had them. You should have just handed them over."

Across the room, Marm Willim closed her eyes, but not before Maeve caught a flash of fear in them.

"Get me a drink." Serran dropped one of the boxes onto the sofa and opened the other. He took a pill out and swallowed it.

Maeve couldn't move. She shrank further into the cushions of the sofa.

"Now," Serran snapped. "Unless you want me to hit you again." He dragged her up and raised his hand in threat.

Maeve hurried to the drink dispenser. "What do you want?"

"The whiskey. Get one for yourself as well."

"I don't—"

"Are you arguing with me?"

"No Sir." Maeve pressed the button on the dispenser and waited. Her cheek throbbed, and she could still taste blood. She touched one finger to her mouth. It came away with a stain of red. She needed to get out of here now. Serran was a maniac. Why was his mother tied up? And where was Ash? Unless they'd spaced him, he must be somewhere. Or was he wandering uselessly round the hubstation again? A growing anger mixed with her fear.

She took the two drinks back to Serran, watching him carefully through lowered lashes. He drank one, and appearing to forget what he'd said, took the other, holding it high in the air, walked to his mother and poured it over her head. "A drink for you, Ma. Cheers."

Fallon's eyes opened, stretching wide.

He sauntered back, pleased with himself and shoved Maeve's shoulder. "Two more, girlie. Quickly."

Maeve rushed to the dispenser again. Maybe the chem and the whiskey would quieten him down a bit.

"Do you want to know what I'm going to do?"

Maeve concentrated on the dispenser.

"Well?"

"Yes Sir." She *really* didn't want to know.

"I'm going to rid myself of a burden."

"What?" The first drink appeared, pale amber and aromatic.

"My dear mother."

Maeve turned her head, eyes darting to the furiously struggling woman.

"I've practised," Serran said. "The others, they've all been a preparation for the chief bitch. That sharp tongue must come out. It's easy to make them quiet. They want to scream. They want to tell me what to do." He smiled, moving to stand behind her. Feverish heat from his body seeped into hers. "But they can't. Not after I've stopped them."

Maeve stared into the whiskey glass, every nerve in her back aware of him. Her earlier anger was drowned by growing fear. All four limbs felt as though they'd turned to cotton. That dismembered pleasagurl, she'd seen with Temmy, it had been Serran. He'd done it. He was sick. She leaned against the dispenser, legs shaking, as she waited for the second glass to fill.

"I'll bleed the badness out of her. It works, you know."

Maeve turned round, a glass in each hand. She stiffened, ready to throw them in his face, but thought better of it. The glasses were heavy crystal, they might be effective weapons, but she had no way of getting out of the suite before he recovered.

He grabbed both glasses from her. "And it makes me feel so good. Or it did. None of the others were the right one. But after this, everything will be fine. I'll feel right, again."

Maeve checked round the room. The only available doors led to the sleeping quarters and the bathroom, and neither would protect her for long. "She's your mother. You can't do that."

Serran set the glasses down on a side table and snatched at Maeve's ponytail, jerking her head up to stare into her eyes. "Why not?" He sounded mildly curious. "She's *my* mother. I can do what I like with her."

"You'll mess up the room. Station doesn't like mess." Maeve dropped her eyes, barely knowing what she said. Surely Serran wouldn't kill his mother in front of her. She darted another quick look at him. His eyes were drowned by the darkness of the pupils, and the burst blood vessels had turned the whites to pink. She clenched her fists. His mother obviously hadn't found all his chem. He hadn't just smoked R'lax. R'lax wouldn't have such a drastic effect.

"I'm rich." He released her hair. "I'm a second-tier citizen. I'm important. I can do anything I like. I can pay for the damage. The hotel won't mind. You'll see." His voice rose in triumph. "People like me? We're in charge of the world."

Maeve closed her eyes. He was completely mad, but it sounded like he didn't mean to kill *her*. When she opened them, a movement behind one of the bedroom doors caught her attention. Ash? Wasn't he going to do something? *Useless.*

Serran took one of the silver boxes and tipped two of the tablets into the palm of his hand. He dropped one into each whisky glass. "There. It should only take a minute and we can drink it."

We? Who was he talking about?

He reached beneath the long kimono jacket covering his skinsuit and pulled a slender knife from his belt. He held it under his mother's nose, wove it in a pattern over her face. Her cheeks turned scarlet as she strained to free herself. Her mouth moved around the gag, but no sound came out. Serran laughed and drew the knife down her cheek, leaving a long shallow cut, which oozed a trail of dark red blood. "Pretty." He wiped the blade on her sleeve, repeated his action on her other cheek, and put the knife back in his belt.

Maeve clapped a hand over her mouth. He'd completely lost it. He was really going to kill his mother. He had to be bugfuck crazy.

"Drink this." He picked up one of the whisky glasses. The liquid had turned from amber, to a sparkling golden colour, a denser version of the drink he'd given her that first night.

"No, I—"

He slapped her on the same cheek, knocking her sideways. "Drink it."

Maeve's vision blurred.

"Well?"

She accepted the glass, her hand shaking so much, the liquid slopped over the edge.

"Go on."

She took a tiny sip. It fizzed down her throat, burning its way to her stomach.

"All of it."

She took another tiny sip.

Serran held the knife up again, aiming the point at Maeve's eye. "Quickly."

Closing her eyes, she swallowed the rest.

Serran put the knife away and lifted his own glass. "Cheers." He drained it, grinning at Maeve. "In a couple of minutes, you'll start to feel the effect. You'll like it. It's warm and wild. It makes you feel you can rule the world. You'll be indestructible. You'll want to fight all your enemies. Your friends as well. Then you'll want to fuck them. You won't feel guilt anymore. You won't feel inadequate. It's an amazing feeling."

She wiped her mouth with the back of her hand. The alcohol stung, where her lip had split. The sweet aftertaste lingered on her tongue.

"Would you like to kill my mother?"

"No." Maeve's voice rose to a high-pitched squeak as she focussed on Fallon, whose blood-soaked face was almost purple as she struggled to escape. It must be awful for her not to be able to give orders anymore, but she was a horrible woman. Maybe she didn't deserve to live. Maybe Serran was right. If she was dead, she couldn't take Maeve to Eden Fields. Someone should kill her. Excitement churned her gut. She could do it. "I don't have a weapon. Give me your knife. Give me it now."

"Do you want to kill me?"

Maeve felt her mouth curve into a smile. Serran was even more horrible than his mother. He was more horrible than anyone she'd ever met, but he didn't scare her. Not anymore. If she killed him, she would be doing a just thing. She would be like an angel of death. "Yes. Oh yes. Please." She could almost feel a set of black feathery wings springing from her shoulder blades. She wriggled her shoulders to get rid of the itch. She *was* an angel of death. Out of the corner of her eye, she saw Ash sidling along the wall towards the door. Maybe she hated Ash as well. She wasn't sure why, but she pretended not to see him.

She shuffled towards Serran, her fingers curving into claws. Her heart thudded in her chest, almost painful in its pounding. She rubbed her breastbone.

"I'm going to let you try." He smiled. "No weapon though. You won't be able to do it, I'm a foot taller than you. I'm strong. I'm a finely honed fighter, and I've got a knife, but it'll be fun for me, having someone who fights back. It'll be fun for you too. I'll kill you in the end, of course. Maybe we'll fuck first. Or after."

He talked too much. She could shut him up. Maeve took another small step towards him, her calf muscles feeling like coiled springs. She was like a forest cat, she thought. With wings.

"And if you do kill me, you can do my mother next."

Maeve growled. She was alert enough to realise that it wasn't a normal sound. Alarm mixed with euphoria. What was happening to her? She swung her gaze from Serran to Marm Willim. The air rippled around them, turning them into rainbow monsters. A door slammed, but no one else was in the room. She sprang forward, towards Serran.

~~~

Scarlet was signing off work when the receptionist's messenger pinged. As he got up to leave, the receptionist held up one hand. He leaned against the desk and waited.

A second later, the Comisario slammed out of his office. "Come with me. Hurry."

Scarlet obeyed, wondering what was going on. He followed his boss out of the building. On the street Ashkir Willim paced backwards and forwards, wild-eyed. "What are you waiting for. Come on. We might be too late."

"That young man, the one your friend said was a murderer, he's going to kill his mother." Comisario Leyland shouted over her shoulder as she ran across the atrium. After a brief second of shock, Scarlet sprinted after her. Ash pushed past them both, running back to the hotel. He was desperately pressing his palm against the lock when they caught up. It wouldn't open for him. The Comisario elbowed him aside and used a station override key. The door slid open.

Inside, a scene of chaos reigned. A chair lay on its side, cushions scattered around the room, and several glass tumblers rolled across the floor. A woman sat upright on a chair by the desk, tied so tightly in place that she looked like a bloodstained doll. Two more people writhed on the soft rug, locked together, snarling and growling. Mink's pet couldn't have sounded more bestial. Red smears marred the pale floor of the room.

Scarlet stared at them, realising only one person was making the growling sounds. It was Maeve. What the hell had happened to her? She was a lying manipulator, but she'd never been as out of control as this. The other person was Serran, and he laughed, a discordant high-pitched giggle. Maeve's teeth were fastened in his upper arm.

His pale skinsuit was stained with blood. Neither of the two seemed aware of anyone else in the room. Frenzi was the only thing Scarlet had seen which could make people behave like this, and the effect only lasted for seconds. This looked like a Frenzi on steroids situation.

"What the hell?" Comisario Leyland strode forward. "Get in here, Ben. We need to separate them."

"I'll get the woman," Ash said. "It'll take both of you to hold Serran." He grabbed Maeve by one arm, trying to drag her away from Serran. She still gripped his arm with her teeth. Ash hauled on her fraying ponytail, until her hold loosened.

She turned her head, blood staining her lips, legs locked around Serran's waist. Twisting her torso, her fingers reached for Ash's face.

Serran jabbed at her with a knife, missed and sliced through Ash's sleeve. There was no sign he even noticed the newcomers.

Scarlet grabbed a set of shackles from his belt and snapped one onto Serran's wrist. He twisted it until Serran dropped the knife. The Comisario snatched it up, while Scarlet shackled the other wrist, tied his ankles and, as an extra precaution, fastened his ankles to his wrists. He hadn't stopped giggling.

Ash unravelled a struggling Maeve from Serran, dragged her away and dumped her on the sofa. High-pitched growling emerged from her open mouth. Pale blond hair stuck to her face, her ponytail was half undone and hanging over one ear. Blood dripped from her lip, but it looked, to Scarlet, like it was her own. Ash kept a tight grip on her while the Comisario shackled her. She continued to thrash against the restraints. When Ash let go of her, she rolled to the floor, still snarling.

Scarlet glanced at the bound woman in the chair. Her face dripped blood and her mouth stretched round a spherical gag. Her eyes were the only part of her moving. At least she was alive. He assumed it was Fallon Willim, but she looked nothing like the fashionable woman who'd walked off the shuttle. "Shall I untie her?"

"Yes," Comisario Leyland said. "I'd better have a look at these two. We don't want them dying on us."

Serran lay on his side on the floor, watching Ash through half-closed eyes. "I was winning, Ash. You are such a killjoy. I had a knife. She just had her nails. I had first blood." He raised his head. His eyes were almost as red as Scarlet's had been. "Are you going to try and stop me killing Ma?"

Ash said nothing.

"I think we've already stopped you." Scarlet didn't look round.

"You hate her, don't you, Ash?" Serran continued. "She's a bully. I'm doing this for you as well."

"I don't want to kill her." Ash said. "Comisario? He's taken Wildwolf. It's a chem that—"

"I know."

Scarlet unfastened the woman's gag.

She spat it out, dragged in a huge breath and coughed. As soon as she could speak, she croaked at him. "Untie me. Now." She stuttered over the last word.

"Ben. You'd better untie her."

Scarlet struggled to unfasten the bonds on the woman. The knots were impossible. "I'll have to use a knife."

"Just get on with it." The gag had left purple marks radiating from the sides of her mouth.

He cut her loose. She surged to her feet, wobbled, and sprawled on the floor.

"Take it easy." Scarlet helped her up. "Your face has a couple of nasty cuts. Right down your cheeks. Let me try and clean it up."

"There's a first aid kit in the bathroom," Ash said.

"I'll get it," Scarlet said.

She pulled her arm away from him, hanging onto the desk for support. The look she directed at him was full of venom. "Later. I want to check on my son. If you've harmed him, there'll be repercussions."

Scarlett glanced over his shoulder at his boss, who raised her eyes to the ceiling. "There will definitely be repercussions. You knew your son was dependent on Wildwolf?"

"Of course, he isn't. I knew nothing of the sort."

"You asked this young woman to conceal his supply."

Maeve still thrashed on the floor, teeth bared and a low growl-hiss-groan coming from her mouth. Her ripped skinsuit revealed an expanse of pale flesh, marred by a long bloody gash. Scarlet frowned.

"I did not. She stole it for herself. Look at the state of her. You can't believe someone like that." Fallon coughed again.

"She came to report it to us," the Comisario said. "As was correct. I'm afraid I'm going to have to take you all into custody. Your son's likely to be charged with assault at the very least. I'll make sure you see a medic, once you're in custody."

Ash interrupted. "Maeve didn't want to take the chem. Serran forced her."

Comisario Leyland crouched next to Serran, unfastening his kimono and checking him over. "It's not his blood, anyway. He doesn't seem to be hurt."

Maeve continued to writhe and growl.

"Hold her still for a minute, Ash," Scarlet said. Maeve was covered in blood too, it had to be coming from somewhere. Ash held her on her back, on the floor while Scarlet bent over her. The front of her uniform coverall was dark and damp. She arched her back and snarled, snapping bared teeth at him. He pulled the material away from her stomach. It split all the way from beneath her breasts to just above her groin. "He must have slashed her with the knife. It's a shallow cut, bloody but not life-threatening. The chem might be, though."

Ash released her and stood up. "He gave her the same amount as he took. She's not used to it and she's half his size."

Comisario Leyland pursed her lips. "You." She pointed at Ash. "Call the station medical facility. The number's on the messenger. Tell him we've got a chem problem as well as the knife wounds and a human bite."

Chapter 28

Scarlet drained his beer and placed the empty beaker on the table. He was in a caff-bar on the outer port-pod, the one which ran the shuttles out to the big people-carrying star ships. Koo-Suki and Mink had berths on the next ride to the Hope colony ship. Every table in the place was full, and small groups of travellers clustered at the entrance, beakers in their hands. In the next couple of hours, three shuttles were due to leave for the Hope transport.

"So Serran Willim really was the Silencer?" Koo-Suki said. "And you actually met him that last time you went into London?"

"Yeah. Maeve was telling the truth. Who'd have thought it?" He leaned back in his chair. "Sorry I couldn't tell you earlier, but my boss told me to keep quiet."

"I'm sure he didn't mean not to tell us," she said.

"Maybe not, but I thought I'd better be cautious." He hesitated. "I thought the arrest might look good for my career prospects."

"Career?" Koo-Suki grinned. "Just listen to yourself."

Scarlet laughed.

"Did Serran look like a crazed killer, when you saw him the first time?"

"He looked like a chem head. So yes. Definitely." Hindsight was always clear. "He was seriously crazed a few days ago. He was like something out of a horror movie."

"Is Maeve okay?" Mink asked.

"She will be. I haven't seen her, but apparently, she's up and walking. She must have a constitution like stone. You should have seen her when we peeled her off Serran, covered in blood, and snarling like a killer zombie. It was all shallow cuts, though. He wanted to draw things out, take his time and use her as a warm-up for his mother. The chem was worse. That could have killed her. She was rabid. She went into a coma on the way to the clinic, and then had a fit. They had to give her something to stop her heart bursting. The station medic was pretty good. He said she'd be okay as long as she stayed away from the chem. Serran's an addict, though. He'll never give it up, even if he wasn't facing a trial for multiple murder. They're shipping him back to Earth. His mother and Ash are supposed to go with him, but I think Ash would rather carry on with the journey by himself. Obviously, they won't let him, he'll have to be a witness. Serran got him with the knife as well. No one noticed until they'd taken the others away. The Comisario sent a message to his father. She's just waiting for the reply."

"And Maeve? What's going to happen to her?"

"Fallon Willim wants her arrested, but they've no grounds. She's refused to pay her fare back to Earth, and she can't go to Eden Fields without a sponsor, so she's a problem the station will have to deal with. Fallon Willim refuses to talk to the law at all. I'm staying out of it, but the Comisario might have to give evidence. I think she can send a recording, though."

Koo-Suki waved at one of the bartenders. "More beer?"

"Your shuttle goes in a couple of hours," Scarlet said.

"We're ready," she said. "Our stuff's been loaded. We've just got to walk down to the shuttle gate. You are going to see us off, aren't you?"

"Yeah," Scarlet said. "I wish I was coming with you."

"I wish you were, too. You start your new contract next week, don't you? Your new career?"

Scarlet nodded. "I suppose it'll be something new. And it was you who said we needed to go legal, if we could. I hope my chip lasts."

"Yeah," Koo-Suki said. "Good luck."

Nyx rubbed her head against Scarlet's thigh. "You didn't have any problem getting her on the shuttle?" he asked Mink.

Mink grimaced. "I've an official certificate that says she's a working animal. I got it from the Embassy. For a few credits to the right official. I'm almost broke now."

After finishing the beers, they walked slowly down to the departure gate. A line of people snaked out from the exit point for the economy transit. Fewer than ten people waited in the queue for the luxury passengers. Hope wasn't a planet that attracted the wealthy. Not yet, anyway.

Mink nudged Scarlet. "What the hell? Is that who I think it is?"

Scarlet looked in the direction Mink indicated. "Maeve? I thought she was still in Medicare. What on Earth is—?"

"She's getting on our shuttle. To Hope. I don't believe it." Koo-Suki stared.

"I'm going to find out," Scarlet said. "Wait a second. I'll be back."

He jumped over the low barrier separating economy from luxury and strode towards Maeve. "Where do you think you're going?"

Maeve was more subdued than he'd ever seen her. Multi-coloured bruising surrounded one of her eyes, and a deep cut bisected her lower lip, but she gave him a small smile that had some of her old bravado. "I've got another job." She carried two small bags, one in each hand. She raised one, winced and lowered her arm, dropping the bag to the ground. "That cut still stings. It's all the way down my torso."

"I saw it," Scarlet said. "It won't even leave a scar. You were telling me where you're going."

"With them." She pointed towards a silver-haired woman, a few metres in front of her, who was talking to a man. Both were dressed in loose, layered robes, muted grey and blue. Both looked tall, confident, entitled. "She's the Earth ambassador to Hope. She's booked me a berth in luxury. I don't have to travel economy." Her voice vibrated with excitement. "I can barely believe it."

"How did you manage that? And what sort of a job?" After all Scarlet had been told about the scarcity of jobs on the station, both he and Maeve, the lowest of the low, had jobs.

"I'm her assistant, for the journey, and afterwards if she thinks I can do it. She'll make sure I'm legit. If I ever go back to Earth, I'll be a citizen."

Scarlet was lost for words. "But how?"

"Her last assistant had to return to Earth for a family emergency. I met her in a caff near the inward-bound shuttle port. She knew the Willims, and when she heard about Serran getting arrested, she asked about me. She came to see me in the clinic. I looked awful, and I think she felt sorry for me. She said she thought I was interesting. And I hadn't even tried to impress her." Maeve's eyes moved back to her new employer. "When she heard I was out of a job, she offered me this. She said I might be useful."

Scarlet shook his head, dumb with surprise.

"Well? Aren't you going to say anything?"

"Same planet as Koo-Suki and Mink?"

"Yeah." She scratched at the flooring with the toe of her boot. "I really am sorry, Scarlet. I keep saying it, but I truly am. I shouldn't have lied about you. I used to have a terrible temper. Koo-Suki had better leave me alone though. Ambassador Lao says she's protective of her people. She argued with some Earth lawyer, who wanted me back as a witness. It was wonderful. And she made me see a medic before we left, to check that I was fit for the shuttle trip." Her voice dropped. "And she offered to support me here, until the next ship left, if the medic wouldn't let me travel. Can you believe it?"

"Not really." Scarlet shook his head again. It sounded dodgy to him. "I'm lost for words."

Maeve glanced up, her eyes narrowing in thought. "I don't understand why she's so nice. She barely knows me. I don't like to be too happy about things, in case it all goes wrong again. It won't will it? She is for real?"

"How would I know?" He jumped back over the barrier and repeated everything he'd heard to Koo-Suki and Mink.

"No shit?" Mink grinned.

"She apologised again. Said she used to have a terrible temper."

"Used to?"

"Yeah." Scarlet didn't think anyone could change that quickly. "I'd keep an eye on her, if I were you."

"Do you think her employer's on the level?" Mink said. "It seems a bit strange, to me."

"She's an ambassador," Scarlet said. "She must be. The strange thing is her giving Maeve a job. She's not exactly servant material."

"She's unbelievable." Koo-Suki glared across the barrier.

Maeve waved at her.

Koo-Suki turned away. "She's a monster." Her lips quivered and she started to laugh, turning away and covering her mouth.

"Yeah." Scarlet supposed it was a bit funny. "Let's hope you don't bump into her much."

"She's like a cat," Mink said.

"Nine lives?" Koo-Suki managed to stop laughing.

"And always lands on her feet."

Author Biography

Anne Cleasby lives in the UK, on the edge of the Lake District. She shares her home with two cats, and a dog.

Also, by Anne Cleasby

Almost Human (Degrees of Freedom, Book 1)
Power Games (Degrees of Freedom, Book 2)

Writing as Annalisa Carr

Exile in Darkness (The British Coven, Book 1)
Displaced Demon (The British Covens, Book 2)
Family Magic
Children of Poseidon: Lykos
Children of Poseidon: Rann
Children of Poseidon: Damnamenos
Better Together

Printed in Great Britain
by Amazon